Safe in Death

An Esther Hardy Victorian Mystery

S.K. Rizzolo

Cover design by Rolf Busch
Interior design by Sue Trowbridge, Interbridge.com

Print ISBN 979-8-9914785-0-2
Digital ISBN 979-8-9914785-1-9
Library of Congress Control Number: 2024915476

Published in the United States of America

Also By S.K. Rizzolo

Regency Mysteries
The Rose in the Wheel
Blood for Blood
Die I Will Not
On a Desert Shore

". . . Say nothing to any one of what we have heard and seen."
"Why not?"
"Because silence is safe—and we have need of safety in this house."
from *The Woman in White* by Wilkie Collins

Chapter 1

I was sitting alone by the fire when the front bell rang. The little hairs on the back of my neck did not prickle. No wind howled at the window. No icy draft made me shiver with dread. I merely told myself it was the wrong time for a caller. Four o'clock on a winter's day when making any sort of effort seemed intolerable. Yawning, I got to my feet.

It had been a perfectly ordinary, perfectly dull day. As it happened, everyone else in the household was occupied that afternoon. My father, a surgeon, volunteered at a local dispensary. Granny-Cook had returned to the market after discovering a blotch on her cabbage. Our housemaid Phoebe and Bert, Granny-Cook's great-nephew, were in the kitchen telling ghost stories. My mother had gone upstairs for a rest or, more likely, a peek into our translation of *Les Trois Mousquetaires*. Mama often stuffed it under a pillow whenever anyone called. This after our neighbor Miss Meadows caught sight of the volume and recommended throwing that filth onto the fire.

This same Miss Meadows—a pink-cheeked spinster whose conversation was about as agreeable as the shrill of a tea-kettle— had asked me to tea. An invitation I refused. According to dear

Mama, my unsociability dated from the end of my engagement to the clergyman Benedict Caxton two years before. Another story. But I suspected I'd always been this way. Too solitary. Too prickly. Too observant of the gap between word and deed.

"But if people refuse to like each other," Papa had argued over the breakfast table that morning, "it would break up the whole show."

"Perhaps that curtain better come down," I replied through a mouthful of toast. "Wouldn't that be entertaining?"

Though Papa had laughed, I fell silent, contemplating the trailing vines and flowers on the wallpaper. At the ripe old age of twenty-six, I wasn't waiting for marriage, though I sometimes thought I might be brave enough to attempt what the world was pleased to call wedded bliss. *If* I could be sure of striking a fair bargain. Which no woman ever could. But now, as I shuffled down the passage in my shabby slippers to answer the bell, I had no idea my life was about to change. I was wondering if Miss Meadows was back again and swearing under my breath.

It wasn't Miss Meadows.

I threw open the door to confront a man in a black greatcoat and stout boots cracked with age. He stood in an aggressive stance, gray-brown hair wafting in the breeze, mouth set in an unfriendly line. Startled, I gazed into owlish eyes that looked back at me, unimpressed. A hansom cab waited at the curb behind him, its lamps lit in the gathering darkness, its wheels splattered with mud. The horse, a balding beast of an uncertain color, stood with its head drooping.

"Trouble, miss," the man said.

"My father's out, I'm afraid."

He jerked a thumb at his cab. "Brought a lady from the Surrey side. Church of St. George on the High Street."

"I'm sorry," I said, though I wasn't. "Surgery hours are over."

"Surgery?" Confusion creased his face; then he nodded, as if something had become clear to him. "So that's why. A doctor is just what's needed, miss."

"I told you. My father is not expected for at least an hour. If the lady is ill, she must seek treatment elsewhere."

"Tell her yourself." With that, the cabman strode to his horse, bending to whisper in its ear. The horse butted its head against his hand, and he attached a nosebag of feed.

The rain that had kept me company all afternoon was over, but the air oozed moisture. As I approached the cab, my slippers were soaked at once, which did not improve my temper. London on a December evening was not a pleasant place. Even if you weren't floundering in a fog or trudging through pellets of foul-smelling sleet, you could be sure to end up with horse manure on your person and possibly an infection of the lung. Respectable women who had no carriage to ride in did better to remain at home, doing very little good to anyone.

The hansom's passenger was visible through the open door—a woman slumped against the cushions. She had extended an arm to brace herself, the fingers of one hand clutching the seat, her other arm curled around her body. From this angle, a bonnet obscured her features, its feather almost touching the coach's roof.

I tapped her on the shoulder. "The driver says you're ill, ma'am?"

The woman turned, and with a jolt, I recognized her—Alice Denton, who sometimes called on us to eat Granny-Cook's biscuits or consult my father. Alice had been at our door a few days ago when Papa had again been out. Hadn't I noticed a strange, furtive gleam in the gray eyes behind Alice's spectacles? Observed and almost as quickly dismissed when one of the surgery patients interrupted us.

Now, those eyes, their enormous pupils like black pools, stared back at me. A faint sound escaped Alice's throat, too low to be called a groan, more like a jagged breath. Her mouth moved as she struggled to speak. She had lost her spectacles, and their absence made her look like a frightened child.

I touched her arm, feeling the coldness of the woman's flesh through the cloak. "I need you, driver," I called. As I climbed into the vehicle, my nose twitched at the odor of damp mixed with something metallic.

The cabman was at the door. "*Women*," he said.

"Stand close and be ready." As gently as I could, I pushed Alice across the seat into the cabbie's arms. I looped Alice's umbrella over my arm and joined him on the pavement.

After leading the way into the house, I opened the door to my father's consulting room on the ground floor. The cabman seemed to take in the clean tile floor, the walls lined with books, and the framed anatomical drawings, as if he'd never seen such a place before. I motioned him through a pair of pocket doors that opened into an alcove. This was a rectangular space with room for a tray to hold medical instruments, as well as supplies of bandages and vials of various solutions. By the table sat a leather chair-bed, which I lowered so the cabbie could lay the woman across its surface. It was then I noticed the red smears on Alice's collar. *Blood?* A perfectly ordinary, perfectly dull day . . .

"She's hurt," I said.

"Not my lookout." He took a step toward the door.

At that point, I almost railed at him like a fishwife, but I caught myself. As my eyes met his, I read his worry. No doubt he feared being blamed for his passenger's condition. A person of his class would be wary, especially of the educated and well dressed. At the very least, he would have to deal with the authorities, and questions would be asked about his own conduct. He would regret ever having encountered Alice Denton. Why, after all, was he here? I understood him.

"What happened?" My words came out harsher than I intended.

"Nothing to do with me. She bid me wait by the church. When she didn't come back, I poked my head in the gate and let out a bellow. No answer. Then I goes in and sees her on the ground. Muddled, she was. But she gave me your direction, miss."

"Never mind. I need you to fetch my father from the medical dispensary where he's working. His name is Theodore Hardy. Tell him his daughter needs him."

"The horse is spent. Send one of your servants."

"It's not far, and our boy will accompany you." When the driver looked mutinous, I added, "We'll pay for your time. What's your name, cabbie?"

"Billings, miss. William Billings."

"Please, Mr. Billings." I recited the address of the dispensary to forestall further argument. "Wait in the hall while I make the arrangements."

Reluctantly, Billings turned to obey, colliding with our maid Phoebe, who had appeared in the doorway. She was a young woman in a white cap and starched apron whose demure prettiness made her seem less original than she was.

Phoebe gasped as the cabman shoved past her and shot me an indignant glare. "What's this?"

"We need help," I said. "Please inform my mother. Also, go down to the kitchen and ask Bert to ride along with the driver."

Questions trembled on Phoebe's lips, but for once, she didn't utter them. "Yes, miss. Back in a tick, miss."

Bending over Alice Denton, I removed her cloak. Alice wore frayed gloves, a gray serge gown, and black boots crusted with mud. Her light brown hair tumbled about her face. She was the kind of woman no one looked at twice until you noticed the beauty of her bone structure. Even with her skin leached of color.

My eyes sharpened. There was a crumpled bit of fabric in her fist. Extracting it, I unfolded a fine cambric handkerchief. It had a hem-stitched border and a cleverly designed monogram in one corner: an "N," a central larger "F," and another "N." All rendered in white satin embroidery in antique-style letters, ivy leaves woven among them. I winced at the scarlet marks marring the material and set the handkerchief aside on the tray with the umbrella.

Inside Alice's cloak, I found a reticule, which I slipped into my pocket for safekeeping. Next, I removed her dark green bonnet with its dashing ebony feather and matching pink roses on either side. The fabric was wet on the back. Swallowing nausea, I hung it on the wall peg and cupped my hand around the woman's skull to prod the spongy, broken area near the crown. How had she hit her head? It was a miracle she'd survived the trip across the city.

Phoebe returned to catch her first full look at the patient. "Why, it's Miss Denton," she said in a shocked voice.

"Build up the fire, Phoebe. Is my mother coming?"

The maid gulped an assent and moved to the hearth to replenish the coals. I tucked a blanket around Alice and laid some dressings on her wound. Finally, I gave her two drops of brandy, one of which rolled down her chin.

My mother swept in. "I hear we have an emergency. A sick woman?"

"Not ill, Mama," I said. "Oh God, how long until Papa comes? I've sent Bert with the driver to the dispensary."

Mama approached the chair-bed. "Is that Alice Denton?"

"I'm afraid so. She has a head injury."

An odd expression tightened my mother's face, and her attention turned inward, as if unwelcome thoughts rushed upon her. "Why did you send Bert? You shouldn't have let him leave the house."

I was puzzled. It wasn't like my mother to fuss about the boy riding a short distance with an adult. "He's fine, Mama. He's with the cab driver and will return in a few minutes. I've tended to Miss Denton's wound as best I can."

"Poor thing. What more can we do for her, dear?"

We looked at each other, helpless.

The wait seemed to drag on for hours, but according to the mantel clock, only twenty minutes had passed when we heard the front door opening. The tension in my chest eased—my father would know what to do. Mama went to meet him, skirts rustling in her haste, Phoebe right behind her. Alice and I were left alone.

"Can you hear me, Alice?" I said, taking the limp hand in mine.

With one last effort, she shifted her head. Her eyes slitted; she seemed too tired to force them up. A spasm contorted her mouth. "Where's—" she said.

Then she died. I felt the moment when her soul slipped free.

Chapter 2

It didn't take long for Papa to complete his examination. Sighing, he drew up the blanket to cover the dead woman's face. Before he could say anything, I glanced up to see Bert, a sturdy, fair-haired boy of eleven, hovering in the doorway. He craned his neck to get a better look at the muffled figure on the bed.

"You're not needed here, Bert," my father said. When Bert didn't budge, Papa added more gently, "You may go sit with Granny-Cook and the cabman."

The boy made a face and obeyed. At least he remembered not to bang the door as he left.

After using the washbasin to cleanse his hands, Papa turned to me. My father was a neat, well-barbered man in his fifties. He had a keen-eyed expression and decisive movements that often bordered on impatience. "Why the deuce are you standing there, Esther? Sit down at once." But he held out his arms to hug me, patting my back with vigor. "My dear, I'm sorry. You've had a shock. A mouthful of that brandy wouldn't come amiss."

"Such an awful thing, Papa. Did the blow to her head kill her, do you think?"

"With an injury of this type—"

I pulled back to study his somber face. "An accident?"

"I don't think so. Someone bashed her skull in two places. I can't tell you what the weapon was, perhaps a cudgel or a club with a rounded end."

Alice was struck deliberately? But that meant . . . *murder*. I went rigid. Alice's death felt like an insistent tap on my shoulder. No, what it really felt like was a bucketful of icy water, terrifying and invigorating, rousing me from a dead sleep. What villain had she met in that churchyard? And why did she tell the cabman to bring her to us?

"Aren't there hospitals in Southwark?" I said as I started to shiver.

"Southwark? What are you talking about, Esther?"

"Didn't the cab driver tell you, Papa? He'd taken Alice to St. George's church on Borough High Street. She went into the churchyard. When she didn't come out again, he went inside and found her."

"I didn't get that far with the man."

"Would she have survived with prompt medical attention?"

"Probably not," my father said. "The blows were fierce. Her bonnet provided some protection but not enough. The blood from the surface lacerations is not the main problem. The skull is depressed, the bones crushed inward. The postmortem will no doubt reveal substantial hemorrhage. Bleeding in the brain."

"She was able to speak to the driver."

He shook his head. "Sometimes, the full effects of a blow are not apparent at once, my dear. Patients are alert; however, as the brain swells and the bleeding spreads, their condition deteriorates."

I approached the shrouded form, fighting an impulse to fold back the sheet and look on her face once more. The truth was I had no reason to care about Alice Denton, even though she'd expired in my presence. Was that why I had this perplexing feeling that something more was required of me? I looked at my father. "Why would anyone attack a poor creature like her?"

He rolled down his sleeves and refastened his cuffs. "Who knows? She was an unusual woman. Eccentric, some would say." His gaze softened. "Go upstairs and wash while I inform the authorities. Let's hope Granny-Cook's soup has sweetened the cab driver's temper. He must remain long enough to tell his story to the police."

~

Upstairs, I found my gray tabby Fosco asleep on my bed. I lit the lamp and moved to the washstand. Next, I removed my gown and winter vest to scrub my face, neck, and arms. When I felt clean, I donned a fresh gown and fixed my hair. Much better. Fosco, observing these exertions through narrowed eyes, rolled onto his back so I could rub his belly. I leaned over him, sinking my fingers into his fur until he snapped his jaws perilously close to my fingers, batted me with one large paw, and rolled the other way.

"Ungrateful animal," I murmured.

Before I left the room, I remembered the victim's reticule and pulled it from my pocket, laying out the items on the dressing table. The small knitted bag held a purse with some coins, a bottle of smelling salts, and a packet of pins. Nothing unusual, though the fact that the money had not been stolen seemed significant. I restored Alice's possessions and took the reticule downstairs.

Papa returned with news that word had been sent to Scotland Yard. Ordinarily, the incident would fall under the jurisdiction of the Southwark division, but, since this was deemed a case of murder, the local authorities had referred the matter to the detective branch. Granny-Cook sent up a tray of food, and I waited with my parents in the dining room. After the morgue attendants collected the body, Inspector Sydney Jessup descended to the basement kitchen to question the cab driver and the servants.

Half an hour later, our maid Phoebe ushered the inspector into the dining room and left again, closing the door behind her. From my seat at the table, I took stock of the man. Tall and heavyset, Jessup had poppy-red cheeks and a bulbous nose. He wore a friendly expression belied by a pair of watchful black eyes.

My father rose to greet him. "Coffee's still hot, Inspector. We've even managed to save you a few sandwiches. Have you finished with the cabbie?"

Jessup looked startled. Few people considered the police respectable enough to warrant this consideration. "Yes, sir," he said. "My sergeant has gone with the van, and your maid has shown the cab driver out."

Papa motioned him to a seat and sat down himself. My mother poured the detective a cup of coffee and offered him the plate of sandwiches. A poor substitute for our missed dinner, though Inspector Jessup seemed grateful for them. He took a sandwich, eating it in precise bites.

"Any useful information?" Papa said.

Jessup stirred sugar and cream into his cup. "Not much, sir. Billings picked up Miss Denton at a cab stand on Percy Street, Tottenham Court Road. He drove her to the Surrey side and waited for her at St. George's church on Borough High Street."

Papa tapped the table with his finger. "Cabs are expensive. She was none too plump in the pocket, Inspector. Was she meeting someone?"

"Unclear. The cab driver parked on a street south of the church. No reason to disbelieve the man, Mr. Hardy. And no motive to harm her as far as I can see."

"Seems a decent fellow," Papa agreed. "He'd hardly bring her to us if he'd done something wrong. But I'm far from satisfied with any innocent explanation for Miss Denton's injury."

"Tell me why you say so, sir," Jessup said.

My father's tone was dry. "The small matter of the depression at the back of her skull, as well as the fracture radiating from the impact. Consistent with several blows given by an object with a small surface area. Rather than, say, falling over a tombstone. A rock, perhaps?"

The police detective nodded, as if this confirmed what he himself thought. "Why did she come to you?"

"I suppose she sought my aid. She was a lonely woman, Inspector. She called on us occasionally to . . . consult me about her health and chat with my servants."

"I don't quite follow you, Mr. Hardy. Could Miss Denton afford your fees?"

"Oh, our connection goes back some years," Papa said. "She paid me a few shillings on account now and then. My dear wife will tell you I'm a poor businessman."

Mama laid a hand on his arm. "Undoubtedly—but a decent human being, and I suppose that's what counts. At least until the butcher's bill arrives."

They exchanged forced smiles.

The talk of money reminded me of the dead woman's reticule. I fished it out of my pocket. "I found this when I was tending to her."

"Thank you, miss." The inspector extended a large hand to pick it up, then dumped out the contents.

"Her belongings seem intact," I said. "However, her spectacles are missing. Perhaps she lost them in the churchyard? A shame there's no engagement diary."

Jessup's brows shot up. "You examined the reticule yourself, Miss Hardy?" he asked with an avuncular smile. "I regret that you were troubled."

"I did examine it to see if I could learn anything." I didn't like his metaphorical pat on the head, but I rose to retrieve Alice's umbrella, cloak, and handkerchief from the surgery. Soon I was back with them.

Taking my place at the table, I held out the handkerchief. "She had this in her hand, Inspector. Notice the monogram in one corner."

Jessup examined the bloodied cloth. "Looks like she used it on her wound. And the monogram—"

"Someone's initials? The central 'F' would be the surname, I suppose," I said. "What murderer is foolish enough to leave something so incriminating behind?"

"You'd be surprised, miss." Stowing the handkerchief in the reticule, Jessup addressed my father. "What more can you tell me about the woman's history, sir?"

"She was the daughter of a lawyer's clerk. Her mother died when she was small. Her father was later killed in an accident. She worked for her bread."

"No one to keep her out of trouble."

A shadow crossed Papa's face. "Sadly, that's true, Inspector."

By this time, my alarm bells were clanging. My papa was always sparing with his words, especially since his struggles to get ahead in the cutthroat medical profession had taught him their power to wound. But I sensed an unusual reticence in him and thought Jessup had observed it too.

"Something dubious in her history?" the inspector murmured. He shifted in his chair, glanced over his shoulder at the door behind him, and jotted a note in his pocketbook. After another pause, he said, "You'll pardon my saying, sir, that if the police are to discover the guilty party, we need information. The victim came to you after she'd been mortally injured."

"You are correct." My father continued with evident reluctance. "I have long suspected that Alice Denton was connected to a murder in the year '50. You'll understand that I didn't have any proof one way or the other. Anything I did surmise was protected by professional confidentiality."

The policeman leaned forward. "Murder?"

"No doubt you recall the case? A young man, a baronet's son, was struck down in the library of his home in Portman Square. His mistress, an orphan girl taken in by the family, was believed to be responsible. The young gentleman had abandoned her to marry into his own class, and she sought revenge."

"Ancient history, eh? I believe you refer to Perry Beldenfield. Gentleman murdered by his light-skirt?"

"She was no light-skirt, Inspector," Papa said.

Jessup disregarded the reproof. "Yes, I remember. A witness saw the girl jump off Southwark Bridge a few hours after Beldenfield's death. I believe her corpse was never recovered."

I tried and failed to catch my mother's eye, my sense of mystery deepening. "You never told me about this."

Mama gave a tiny shake of her head. "It wasn't our story to tell, Esther. Besides, you were in school at the time. According to the papers, Muriel had been turned out of doors by the Beldenfields and fled to the Mint. A rookery where lodging was cheap and she could hide her shame."

"Muriel?" The inspector frowned.

"That was her name," Mama said. "Muriel Dane."

"Papa, what happened to the child?" I demanded.

My father stared into his coffee cup. "A witness swore he saw a baby in her arms as she jumped into the Thames."

"Excuse me, sir," Jessup said. "What connection does Alice Denton have to this accused murderess and female suicide?"

Papa looked up. "They are one and the same, Inspector. Or so I have always suspected."

I remained still in my chair after my father spoke. Then I looked around the table without allowing any reaction to show on my face. Jessup had put down his second sandwich to await developments. Papa regarded the inspector with a bleak expression. He reached for my mother's hand.

My thoughts were in turmoil. It seemed that Alice Denton had been two women in one skin—one a colorless spinster, the other a passionate woman who murdered for revenge. The idea of loving a man enough to kill him and murdering one's child made my skin crawl. Still, I thought I understood something of what Alice might have felt. I was the dutiful daughter who busied herself with the dusting and the mending basket, even as my heart rebelled and resentment simmered. But I had a family to love and support me. Alice's rage and desperation would have been a thousand times stronger.

"Her death can have nothing to do with that old crime," Papa said into the silence.

"Hard to say, sir," Jessup said. "A murder might have a bit of juice left in it yet. Tell me, why do you believe this Alice Denton was, in truth, Muriel Dane?"

Sitting up straighter, my father released Mama's hand. "At the time, I'd been working among the poor of St. George's parish. One day, when I was dining at a chop-house, a man approached me. He asked me to accompany him to the bedside of a woman birthing a child. Said she was likely to die."

"Wait a minute. This was Muriel Dane?"

"I neither knew nor cared who she was, Inspector. Too busy trying to save her life. She labored for a full day and night, but mother and child both came through."

"Who was the man who summoned you?"

"Never gave his name. He said someone had pointed me out to him. What could I know of either of them? The woman I met in the Mint—and whom you removed from my home as a corpse —was always Alice Denton to me. She made me promise never to reveal what I might surmise about her to any living soul."

"You did wrong if you let a murderess escape justice," Jessup said.

"She was always the mildest of women," Mama burst out. "We never saw any madness in her constitution. It was just . . . she let slip a few details, and the papers were so full of Muriel Dane's story."

"Nan," Papa said.

"I won't have you accused after all you did for her, Theo."

The inspector frowned. "If Muriel Dane didn't make a hole in the river, what became of her child?"

"Possibly you'll find an answer to that question in Alice's effects." Papa looked away.

Jessup's frown deepened, but he let the matter drop. "It's

intriguing that Alice Denton was struck down near the spot where Muriel Dane once lived. Did Miss Denton have connections in Southwark, sir?"

My father shrugged. "I believe she lodged not far from here in Burton Street these days."

I turned to the policeman. "The monogram of the handkerchief must be significant, don't you agree, Inspector? The style is somewhat masculine, but I wouldn't swear to that. Perhaps you can find out?"

Merely grunting in reply, Jessup pocketed the victim's reticule and picked up the umbrella. He pushed back his chair and stood. "The news about the victim's connection to the Beldenfield case will soon leak out. Be prepared to see your name in the papers."

"Something to look forward to," Papa said.

"Hah!" Jessup looked down his nose at us. "None of you know of any particular reason why Miss Denton instructed the cabman to convey her to your door?"

My father swiped his brow. "I was her doctor. She must have expected to find me at home. My God, medical attention was available nearby. She was a fool to come so far."

I spoke without thinking. "She knew she was dying."

"Did she say anything when you were alone with her, miss?" Jessup waited as I groped for words.

"No . . . nothing."

"Esther?" Mama said.

I gathered my wits. "Alice tried to ask for someone." My mind was racing, and the shaky feeling was back. "Also, I forgot to mention that she called to see Papa the other day when he was out. What if she wanted to tell us something? Or warn us."

"Not much to go on, miss," Jessup said.

Before I could deliver what would undoubtedly have been a rude response, the policeman glanced over his shoulder for the second or third time. He strode to the door. Opening it, he reached down to pluck up a fistful of jacket in his ham-sized hands—Bert's jacket, attached to a writhing mass of boy.

The boy struggled in Jessup's grip, round blue eyes bulging. He cried out in a high-pitched voice, "Lemme go. You've no call to touch me, rozzer or no!"

"I thought I heard a noise. Suspected you had mice behind the wainscotting," Jessup said. "This is a big one, isn't it?"

My parents were too surprised to react. Like them, I hadn't heard a thing. Jessup, on the other hand, must have had the ears of a cat.

"No mouse but a curious child, Inspector," I said lightly. "Do put Bert down. He meant no harm."

"I don't hold with little boys interfering in police affairs." With this show of virtue, Jessup deposited Bert on the carpet and took his leave.

Chapter 3

When I broke my betrothal to the clergyman Benedict Caxton, plenty of people informed me I was throwing away my one chance in life. Part of me had feared they could be right. When word leaked out, I'd been known as the neighborhood jilt for the better part of a year until Benedict obliged me by installing someone else in the role of adoring helpmeet.

I couldn't be that woman.

The truth was that he bored me into screaming fits and also bored my parents, who both had impeccable taste in human beings. Which was why my engagement had ended in an explosion of anger on his side and withering sarcasm on mine. My father remarked that I'd shown remarkable good sense in ridding myself of a pompous windbag. My mother had been more subdued, though I could tell she didn't disagree.

All of which is to explain how I had joined the ranks of Britain's hundreds of thousands of "redundant" women. We surplus females, according to a recent census—women who hadn't caught a husband and couldn't relieve their families of the burden of feeding them. Limpets who really ought to be shipped off to the colonies instead of sticking to the nation's back . . .

Redundant or not, one of my chief delights in life was to read the London papers with my mother. We would pore over the accounts of scandalous divorces and brutal crimes, as if these events had happened to people we knew. Nor were any listings of births, marriages, and deaths—"hatched, matched, and dispatched" columns, as we called them—safe from the Hardy women. "Ghoulish curiosity," my father would say.

But in the aftermath of Alice Denton's murder, this routine took on a more businesslike air. We subscribed to two newspapers, and Mama sent out for three more. On Sunday, the reports of the incident were scattered and somewhat inaccurate, with no mention of Muriel Dane. By Monday morning, that had changed.

We retired to the small table by the fire in the parlor, where we sometimes enjoyed a cozy breakfast. Mama pushed the jam-pot toward me and attended to the tea. We tackled our plates of eggs and bacon, but after a few bites, we put down our forks and turned to the precious stack of newspapers. Mama handed me the first one. It was my job to read aloud since she was beginning to find the small type a chore. As was our habit, we first checked for bulletins about Queen Victoria's husband, Prince Albert, who was ill with a fever at Windsor. No one seemed to know how sick the Prince Consort really was. We shook our heads over the recent report. Then I came upon these paragraphs in the first paper:

Woman Mortally Injured in Churchyard

A woman, identified as Miss Alice Denton of No. 29 Burton Street, was fatally injured in the churchyard of St. George the Martyr, Southwark, on Saturday afternoon. The cab driver, who had driven Miss Denton across the Thames, discovered her in a pitiable state with a blow to the head. Not being at that point completely insensible, she required him to convey her to the home of her surgeon, Mr. Theodore Hardy of No. 3 Charlotte Street, Bedford Square. However, the victim expired before medical assistance could be rendered. According to Inspector Jessup of Scotland Yard, Miss Denton was a spinster employed as a seamstress and occasional law copier.

Or was she? Patience, dear readers, while we inquire further into an intriguing possibility whispered into our ears from a source close to the police. It seems that Alice Denton may yet prove to be the alias of a certain female said to have drowned herself over a decade ago after foully slaying her lover. Readers will recall that the gentleman was the scion of one of our illustrious families. Indeed, the son and heir of a baronet.

"That was fast. Someone's already opened his mouth to the press." Without waiting for a response, I picked up the second newspaper, which covered only the barest details of the police inquiry. This article again included my father's name.

Mama fanned her cheeks with a napkin. "Our neighbors must have seen the authorities carrying poor Alice's remains to the mortuary cart. Mark my words, Miss Meadows will be with us this very day to find out what's what. Your father won't like the publicity."

She was right. A surgeon's reputation was a precarious thing. Papa might not be a fashionable physician, but he was well known in medical circles, part of the new breed of general practitioners—scientific men with the appropriate diplomas who used the stethoscope and rarely bled their patients. And yet it seemed to me that we could not ignore this murder.

"Miss Meadows and the rest of them should mind their own affairs." I dipped my napkin in the water jug and handed the cloth across to Mama so she could wipe her face. In the grip of one of her hot spells, she accepted gratefully.

As my mother's color receded, I noticed the dark circles beneath her eyes. Clearly, she hadn't been sleeping well either. Nevertheless, I sat back in my chair, judging it time to initiate the plan I'd hatched while tossing in my bed the last two nights, the murdered woman's face ever present in my mind.

"Mama," I went on in an offhand way, "Alice—or was it Muriel?—came here twice in the last week of her life. What did she want?"

Mama swallowed a bite of her eggs, coughing a little as it caught in her throat. "Heavens, I can't imagine. As Papa says, she was an odd duck."

"Isn't it possible she needed our help?" I drew a breath. "What if whoever clapped her over the head comes after us next? She died in this house. Someone might think she revealed her killer to us."

"Esther, stop creating problems out of thin air."

"Papa looked worried as he spoke to Inspector Jessup. Is there more to the story?"

"He was upset. We all were."

"But why didn't you tell me about Muriel Dane before? The pair of you are too ridiculous sometimes. You treat me like a child." I couldn't keep my bitterness from showing. It didn't matter. Mama knew every inflection of my voice.

"It was such a long time ago. No reason to speak of it." She sounded apologetic.

"No reason when a suspected murderess shows up at the door to expire in my arms? You can't be serious. It's not like Papa to lend himself to something clandestine."

I was behaving badly, but I felt in my bones that Alice's death was connected to the Beldenfield case. The police would not be eager to resurrect their inquiry, particularly if it turned out they'd allowed Muriel Dane to escape justice. I waited. Usually, at this point in an argument, Mama would give in and tell me what I wanted to know. Not this time.

"Well, Esther, if you don't wish us to treat you as a child, don't act like one."

My mouth dropped open. I was speechless.

Mama buttered a piece of toast from the rack. She took one bite and let the rest sit. "I didn't mean to scold, dear. Your father was kind to Miss Denton because she was a fellow human being in need. Do you imagine he would let any woman suffer when he could help her?"

"But, Mama—"

"I won't have you pestering him. As it is, you and Papa will have to testify at the coroner's inquest." She looked at me steadily. "I saw a library book on the hall table this morning. Were you planning to exchange it today?"

I offered her a nod and a bland smile. I had intended to reveal the rest of my plan. But hurt feelings, as well as the fear Mama might try to stop me, stilled my tongue. I got up from my seat to drop a kiss on her cheek. "I thought I'd choose another novel since we're through with *Three Times Dead*."

Skepticism flashed in Mama's eyes. "Good idea. And do you have other errands?"

~

The Hardy women weren't the only ones interested in the newspaper reports about Muriel Dane's murder that Monday morning. After breakfast, Samuel Godwin—nephew to Sir Percival Beldenfield and cousin to the late Perry Beldenfield—entered a lady's boudoir at Beldenfield House. The boudoir belonged to Perry's widow, Lydia, but she wasn't there.

Instead, the under-housemaid was at the hearth, a lit match between her fingers, her thin shoulders shaking with sobs. Godwin stopped short. The fires should have been laid hours ago. Was the maid crying because she feared a scolding? The child, no more than sixteen, was small-boned like a bird. When he cleared his throat, she jumped and raised tear-drenched eyes to his face.

"What's wrong?" He fumbled for her name. "It's Dulcie, isn't it?"

The paper under the coals caught fire, and flames shot up. She scooted backward. "Yes, sir. Sorry, sir. I . . . I am late at my work this morning."

He smiled at her. "I didn't mean to startle you. I was looking for Mrs. Beldenfield. Are you in trouble today, young Dulcie?"

Color flooded her cheeks. "Not that I know of, sir. Will you excuse me? I've got the other rooms to do."

Getting to her feet, Dulcie bobbed a curtsy, hoisted her cinder pail, and whisked herself out the door.

A sensitive creature, he thought. Was he so terrifying? Or perhaps it was just that, like many of the servants at Beldenfield House, Dulcie couldn't fathom Sir Percival's "foreign" nephew despite the fact he'd lived in England for twenty-five years. To the servants, Godwin was the member of the family who ruined pair after pair of excellent boots walking the streets at night and brought filth into the house for them to clean. They saw a man with overlong black hair that never looked quite civilized. A man who brought home friends who weren't quite the right kind and worried the rich uncle who had saved him from poverty and obscurity. The servants didn't understand him, and why should they? His uncle didn't either. Godwin was the flaw in the pattern.

As he paced the hearthrug, he decided it didn't matter. He'd heard something disturbing, something that demanded an explanation. Whether or not his inquiries cracked the pretty facade his family had constructed over the years, Godwin just as much as the rest of them. Why? Because the facade made his life easier. It gave him a measure of freedom as long as he kept his doubts to himself . . .

A few minutes later, Perry's widow came in. Lydia Beldenfield was garbed in her usual mourning dress, though lately, Godwin had noticed the inclusion of glossier fabrics and more ornamentation. A jet brooch glimmered at her breast. She wore white lace on her sleeves and at her neck.

"Samuel," she said, "were you waiting for me? Cook was being difficult about the profiteroles. I thought you and Papa-in-law would enjoy them for tea." She peered at him. "You look tired. Another night walk?"

"I need to talk to you, Lydia."

She nodded toward the pair of gilded armchairs pulled up in front of the fire. "That sounds serious. Do sit down and tell me about it."

He waited until she settled herself, then took his seat. His nerves itched so that remaining still was almost painful to him. "John mentioned some gossip among the servants. About a low fellow who called here Thursday last."

"Gossiping with the footman, Samuel? I can imagine what your uncle would say."

"Evidence of my undesirable tendencies?" When Lydia looked embarrassed, he drew a breath to calm himself. He shouldn't upset her. She'd been married only a few months before her bridegroom had been murdered, plunging her into a decade of joyless mourning. Godwin was glad she seemed more interested in rejoining society lately. These days, she paid a few calls and collected *carte-de-visite* photographs of prominent people and fashionable hostesses to exchange with her friends. He'd even noticed her smiling at *him* more often, this woman his uncle had chosen to be his wife. Not that he'd asked her . . . yet.

"Your uncle doesn't think that," she said.

She was wrong. Sir Percival Beldenfield had fixed ideas about the conduct of an English gentleman. It was bad enough that Godwin's mother—Sir Percival's younger sister—had run away to marry her music teacher and died abroad. Sir Percival had rescued his nephew from what he always called "that squalid Italian village," carrying him off to England. At the age of six, Godwin had done his best to fit in, though he'd been sunk in misery and bewildered by the change in his life. Sir Percival had decreed that his relation would henceforth be known as Samuel Godwin, dropping the Italian surname Vincenti—his true name.

What would he have done without his cousin Perry? Sir Percival was a widower of long standing. In this household of three males, it was Perry who taught Godwin everything from table manners to how to dress, stand, and speak. It took time for Godwin to learn fluent English, more time to lose the accent that made his uncle cringe every time he opened his mouth. No letters ever arrived from Italy, though Godwin had written to his father for years. At his loneliest, he would walk up and down the back-stairs of the mansion in Portman Square, trying to conjure the spirit of his mother, wondering why she'd left England and whether she'd be pleased her son had become an Englishman.

He'd let the silence go on for too long. Noticing Lydia's gaze upon his fingers, clenching and unclenching on the arm of the chair, he relaxed them. "I wanted to ask you about this caller," he said. "According to John, Thompkins admitted him to the house. Who was it?"

"You and Sir Percival were out, so Thompkins brought him to me. And before you ask, he didn't identify himself." She spoke with simple dignity, but a tremor passed over her face.

Godwin plunged on. "John overheard the man mention a name I never expected to hear again. A name from the past—Muriel Dane. Was that the reason Thompkins let him in?"

"You'd think that after all this time, it wouldn't hurt me to hear her spoken of."

"I'm sorry, Lydia. But there's more. I've just seen a report in the paper about a woman who was attacked in a Southwark churchyard on Saturday. The author of the piece insinuates that the victim was once linked to the murder of a baronet's son."

"Attacked?" she echoed, turning pale.

"The article must be referring to Perry." He steeled himself to ignore her distress. "Tell me, what exactly did this caller say to you? The news report can't be a coincidence."

"He was an odious little insect out to extort money for his information. I got rid of him as soon as I could."

"Did you inform my uncle?"

"Of course I did." Now she was beseeching. "Sir Percival has been waiting for the right moment to speak to you about the matter, Samuel. I didn't believe a word of what the man said. But if the papers have picked up the story, perhaps it's true."

"*What* story?"

She covered his hand with hers. "Oh, Samuel, he told me that Perry's murderess is still alive. Alive all these years and living under a false name. Sir Percival and I weren't sure what to think— or do."

"If the newspaper story is correct," Godwin said, "someone has handled the problem for us."

CHAPTER 4

With my mind on murder, I forgot the library book at home. Under gray clouds and threatening skies, I walked the short distance to the address the newspapers had given for Alice's lodgings. Even if the accused murderess didn't jump into the Thames, that didn't mean her baby had survived. Infanticide had increased in recent years, becoming a source of public agitation. The perpetrators were usually domestic servants or sometimes poor women who killed for the insurance payout from burial clubs. Regardless, most of the females convicted of this crime were not executed. If a woman cried an ocean of tears and confessed her wickedness, the jury often recommended mercy.

My thoughts bumped to a halt. Did Alice-Muriel deserve such mercy? I didn't know. Still, I was conscious of a desire to avenge her death—a feeling I didn't choose to look at too closely. And now I had an even more powerful reason to investigate, for it was clear Mama was keeping something from me.

I soon reached my destination, a rundown part of Bloomsbury with boarding houses and coffee shops. Customers thronged the chandler and fruiterer, and children played marbles on the pavement. At a first-floor window along the terrace, a man in his shirtsleeves leaned on the sill, blowing smoke into the morning air.

A limp mourning wreath and a knocker tied up in black crape announced that a death had occurred among the inhabitants at Alice's lodgings. A sign affixed to the peeling wood also informed me about rooms to let. I knocked.

A freckle-faced, diminutive maid of about fifteen answered my summons. "Yes, miss?" she said in a pleasing Irish brogue.

I gestured to the mourning wreath. "I wonder if your mistress could spare me a few minutes. On a personal matter relating to Alice Denton, who was a tenant here."

Taking my card, the maid looked me over with a bright gaze. "Come in, miss. I'll inquire if Mrs. Carver is free to receive you."

"That would be most kind."

I waited in an entryway that smelled of onions and fried fish. Coats of various shapes and sizes dangled from a rack, and someone had left a pair of muddy boots next to the boot scraper. Three umbrellas and a walking stick leaned against the wall. A cheap gilt frame mirror shed bits of glitter onto the table underneath. Affixed to this mirror was a notice written in the same wobbly copperplate that appeared on the sign outside: *Wipe your boots before going upstairs. Kindly remember: YOU are observed.*

The maid returned. "Mrs. Carver will see you, miss."

I followed her into a room at the front of the house.

A woman rose from an armchair by the fire, her improbably golden ringlets bouncing as she pranced forward. At least fifty years old, she wore a pink gown that was too thin for winter, but she'd compensated by wrapping her fleshy form in a thick brown shawl. She stretched her lips in a parody of welcome that I immediately found repellent. A gaunt, dirty-white dog asleep on the rug did not move. It looked as if it hadn't eaten in days.

A spasm contorted the landlady's face. "The upstairs corridor won't get itself mopped, Rose," she said to the maid. "As the Good Book says, we must work while we live."

"*All* of us, mum?" Rose put one hand on her hip, her gray

stuff dress swimming on her slight figure. She, too, seemed in need of a few good meals.

Mrs. Carver glanced at me as if to say: *do you see what I must put up with?* "None of your cheek, girl. Stay out of the way until I call you. I know your tricks. No listening at the keyhole, mind."

"Here's me wondering who's to answer the knocker." Rose flounced out of the room.

When she was gone, Mrs. Carver picked up my calling card from the table. "Hardy. Now, where have I heard that name before?"

An awkward silence fell as the landlady's gimlet gaze absorbed every detail of my appearance. The inspection complete—neither to her satisfaction nor my own—Mrs. Carver indicated a cane-backed chair set at a right angle to her armchair. I sat down, feeling much as I used to when the headmistress of my school called me in for a "chat." Perhaps in an effort to preserve the furniture or disguise its dilapidation, the landlady kept the calico curtains at the window drawn so that we regarded each other in a half-light.

"My terms are fair, miss," she said. "You won't find better, not on this street. I can offer you two rooms, properly fit up. No thieves. No filching of coals. Front entrance locked at ten o'clock sharp, no latchkeys allowed. I keep watch, miss. I promise you that." She darted a look at me as if we shared a private joke. "Though it wouldn't be the thing to give you the rooms just yet, would it? On account of the belongings the prior occupant left behind. Not in a hurry, I trust?"

"You misunderstand me, ma'am. I don't need lodgings. I'd like to ask you some questions about Alice Denton."

"Ah." Mrs. Carver took this in stride. "Read the story in the papers, did you? Well, I'm sure you saw our mourning wreath on the door. A token of respect for the dead never did no harm, I always say, and may even do some good. There's a deal more I *could* say on the subject if I saw any use or profit in it."

I stared at her. The landlady's mode of conversation reminded me of an unrideable horse with a jerky gait I'd once rented. Suddenly, I realized that she expected remuneration. What was the appropriate sum? Feeling foolish, I fumbled in my purse and placed a few coins on the table.

"Quite right, my dear." Mrs. Carver, ringlets bouncing again, leaned forward to scoop up the money. As she inspected her palm, she shook her head. Apparently, the paltry contribution was no more than she expected from a young person of no particular breeding. She settled back in her chair, accidentally jostling the sleeping dog. The dog snuffled, sent its mistress a baleful glare, and closed its eyes again. Mrs. Carver extended one slippered foot to give it a poke in the ribs. The clock on the mantelpiece ticked. The dog resumed its snoring. Nothing stirred in the stale air until, from upstairs, came the girlish tones of the maid Rose talking to one of the boarders.

"Miss Denton knew my father, ma'am," I said. "She came to us before she died."

"So that's it. *Hardy*. The surgeon. I read the story in *The Times*. I can't say I expected to see the man's daughter in my sitting room. You'd better watch yourself, Miss Hardy, or you'll be mixed up in a nasty affair. That Alice Denton was no better than she should be, from what I hear. Paid up regular and all. But we'd come to a parting of the ways. I'd have chucked her out if she hadn't got herself killed first." She wagged a plump finger.

How to respond? My annoyance had already chilled to dislike. "I did want to learn about Miss Denton's last hours."

"Yes, I understand you perfectly, miss. I can tell you she barely touched her breakfast on Saturday. Something must have put her off her feed, or she'd got a pain in the stomach. Afterward, she went out, and I knew nothing more about her till the police arrived the next morning to make a fuss among my lodgers. Not what I like to see in a respectable house, boots tramping on the carpets."

"Did she tell you where she was going?"

"Not her. She sauntered out with her nose in the air." The

landlady paused, then suggested with a delicate leer, "By chance, have you come to return her reticule? The authorities have assured me they'll try to locate any family. I would be most happy to pass it on—"

"The police took Miss Denton's reticule," I cut in. "You didn't get on with her, ma'am? May I ask why?"

"Why, I know a thing or two about her that'd make your ears burn." She clamped her lips shut. "Never you mind, miss. Why should I talk to you when others have a far better claim to my notice?"

In other words, if the landlady had something more than innuendo for sale, she had no intention of wasting her information on me.

"Alice Denton has been murdered," I said. "Undoubtedly, the police will have further questions for you, ma'am."

Mrs. Carver bristled. "Let them come and ask. Until then, I have nothing to say to some chit of a girl with more hair than wit. Good day to you, Miss Hardy."

Routed in the skirmish, I emerged from the landlady's sitting room. I was about to take my leave when the maid Rose, who must have been on the watch, set her bucket on the landing and ran down the stairs to join me.

"Anything I can help you with, miss?" said Rose in an eager voice.

"You can, actually. I was hoping to see Miss Denton's rooms."

The girl's expression was grave. "You knew her, did you?"

"Yes, my family was acquainted with her for some years."

I reached for my reticule, but Rose stopped me. "Lord bless you, miss. I'd never take your money for that. I'll show you her rooms."

"What about Mrs. Carver?"

"Time for her nip of gin and a snooze. Besides, if you were Miss Denton's friend, that's enough for me."

"She was kind to you, Rose?"

A sheen of tears showed in the girl's clear blue eyes. "A polite-spoken lady, she was. Always took the time of day, if you know what I mean."

So far, Rose was the only one who seemed to mourn the dead woman, though I suspected my parents were more shaken than they admitted. I smiled at her, touched by this tribute. "I won't get you into trouble, will I? I don't think your mistress approves of me."

"Not to worry, miss. I muck out her grates and scrub her floors. She won't find another maid to put up with that creature."

The sudden venom surprised me. "You mean the dog?"

Rose sniffed. "Filthy thing, shedding hairs on the carpet and slobbering on the cushions. Still, she has no right to starve the poor beast."

"Why does she keep it if she dislikes it so much?"

"Why, it won't be lost, miss. Belonged to an old gent who died in his room. Mrs. Carver paid a boy to take the mongrel to some waste ground and leave it, but it kept coming back. She thinks it would be bad luck to poison it."

With this, Rose marched to the staircase, and together we ascended to the floor above. As we moved down the passage, a head popped out of one of the rooms. "Bring me a piece of lint and a plaster, Rose." The speaker was a young man in his shirt-sleeves. Dark and handsome, he had a cloth pressed against the side of his chin. A strong smell of eau de cologne wafted into the corridor with him.

"Nicked yourself shaving again, have you, Mr. Tibbs?" Rose sang out.

"None of your sauce, girl." Tibbs eyed me with interest. "Who's this then?"

"Miss Hardy. Friend of the late departed."

"Ah, yes." Mr. Tibbs inclined his head. "May I offer my

condolences, ma'am? A tragedy indeed." He retreated. "Don't be too long with the plaster," he shot at Rose as his door closed.

"What cheek," she muttered, "as if I didn't have a thousand-and-one things to do this morning."

She threw open the next door and stepped back for me to enter. Apparently in no hurry to tackle her thousand-and-one chores, Rose observed, arms folded, while I looked around. What had once been a single room was partitioned into a cramped sitting room and bedchamber. The sitting room held a faded armchair placed next to the mantel. A miniature red kettle on the hob shelf inside the fireplace added a cheerful note, and a dresser displayed a collection of mismatched glass and dishware. I also noted a drop-leaf table where Alice would have consumed any meals not shared with her fellow lodgers and attended to her correspondence. The table held a stack of books, an inkstand, and a pen.

A picture of the murder victim as an educated woman living in reduced circumstances formed in my mind, difficult to reconcile with the wild-eyed murderess the police had sought. I glanced toward those tantalizing dresser drawers, wondering whether they held personal documents. But under Rose's scrutiny, I left them alone.

The bedchamber, hardly bigger than a penny stamp, consisted of a bed, a washstand, and a trunk for clothing jammed in one corner. As my gaze traveled over the cramped space, a lump formed in my throat. I could see Alice waking in the morning, listening to the noises of the house that came through the thin walls and twitching the equally thin counterpane back over her cold feet. Alice would have leaped from the covers to wash before putting on one of the dresses that hung in the wardrobe, all of darker colors that would be less likely to show wear. She would stand at the strip of mirror where I now stood, using the pins in the tray on the washstand shelf to fix her hair. I stroked a finger across the hairbrush and comb in which one long hair was tangled.

I turned to Rose. "Had you noticed anything out of the ordinary in Miss Denton's behavior? Mrs. Carver thinks she was involved in something suspicious."

"Mrs. Carver would say that, peeping and prying as she does. She'd count every breath you take and charge you for it, wouldn't she?"

"Nothing particular then?"

Rose shrugged. "I wouldn't know, miss."

My hand hovered over the shelf. "Where was Miss Denton going on Saturday?"

"That was her business, wasn't it? Though some in this house don't respect that, *I* do. Mrs. C. keeps back the letters if the rent isn't paid, or even when it is. She once held back a note from Mr. Tibbs' lady friend for more 'n a week. The lady had nothing to say to him after that."

"Did Miss Denton receive much correspondence?"

"Once or twice a letter on fine stationery," Rose said. "Ladies who wanted to employ her for some stitchery. Or legal gentlemen with law copying work."

"Do you recall any names?"

"No, miss."

"It's just that I wondered if something was wrong." I studied the girl's downcast face. "If Miss Denton said anything to you—"

"She didn't! My mam would say I'm no better than Mrs. Carver, letting my tongue run away like this. Honor her memory, I say. If that's possible in this house."

I pulled out a sketch I'd made of the handkerchief's monogram after the police removed Alice's belongings. "Look, Rose. Have you ever seen Miss Denton carry linen embroidered with these initials?"

She took her time inspecting the drawing. "Miss Denton used to sew quality linen for ladies," she said at last. "Not that they paid her more than a pittance for it. Can't say more than that." The tiny maid stepped closer to look up into my eyes. Her freckles stood out sharply in the sunshine trickling through the dusty window.

"You look like you want to tell me something. What is it, Rose?"

"Yes, miss. Just a man who rang the bell late the night Miss Denton didn't come home. Mrs. Carver took him upstairs. Mrs. Sawyer—that's our cook, miss. Well, she was snoring loud enough to bring the house down. I would have heard nothing, only after a while, it got real quiet. Our chamber is in the attic above this one." She pointed at the ceiling. "That's how I heard the voices and the drawers banging in Miss Denton's rooms. They were in here ever so long, pawing through her things. Not much to be got, though."

No, there wasn't. But what had the mysterious man and Mrs. Carver been looking for? He could've taken whatever it was, bribing the landlady to keep silent. The thought of Mrs. Carver's greed made my blood boil, and I had to bite back an acid comment. "Everything is neat as a pin," I said instead. "Is that your doing?"

She nodded. "I slipped in the next day and set all to rights."

"What manner of person was this man, Rose?"

"Tell you this, miss. I crept out on the landing and heard him talking as he was going down the stairs. He weren't no gentleman to my ears. Saw his shabby coat and big black boots, I did. Didn't see his face, but Mrs. Carver made two of him."

"Did she tell the police about him when they came?"

"No, miss. Told me he was a friend of Miss Denton's from way back and said to mind my own business."

We were back in Alice's sitting room, and I'd better depart before the gorgon in the downstairs parlor set eyes on me again. I put the sketch of the monogram back in my reticule, then held out my hand. "Thank you very much, Rose. I'm glad you told me, but I mustn't keep you any longer." I thought about asking the girl whether Alice had ever mentioned the Beldenfields but decided against it.

Without encountering Mrs. Carver, I made my way back outside and was walking away when I heard my name called. Rose had followed me into the street.

"One moment, Miss Hardy." She came up, a little out of breath in her haste. "I . . . I forgot something. Truth is, I wasn't sure if I ought to tell or not."

I smiled at her. "You can trust me."

"Yes, I'm sure I can, miss. At any rate, I got no one else. It's been bothering me since we heard the news. Miss Denton—" Rose stopped, embarrassed. "She was always that nice to me, no matter what Mrs. Carver says."

"Go on, Rose."

"Miss Denton was expecting an important letter," Rose said in a rush. "She asked me to watch for the postman and slip aught for her into my apron pocket on the quiet. Didn't want the old witch to snoop, I expect. Made me swear I'd never breathe a word."

I was thrilled by this development. *A clue, a genuine clue!*

"Did she tell you what it was about?" I asked.

"No, miss. But she had the blue devils when she never got any reply. That's when she dug that old bonnet out of her trunk. Cheer herself up, like. Don't think it worked, though."

"The green one with pink roses?" My elation faded as a feeling of foreboding struck me. In all the upheaval after Alice's death, I'd neglected to return that same bonnet to Inspector Jessup with the rest of her things. It felt like . . . fate.

"Why, yes. The one with a black plume," Rose said. "She wore it on the day she died."

"Nothing more specific, Rose?"

After a brief hesitation, she reached into her pocket and pulled out a piece of paper. "There is one thing, though I can't see how it's of any use."

"What's this?" I took the charred and crumbling paper between my fingers.

Rose gazed at me anxiously. "Just a bit of paper I found at the back of the grate when I cleaned Miss Denton's room. Likely nothing, miss."

I smoothed the fragment. It consisted of portions of words written in an elegant script. The paper read: *lent Wom*. And below that: *cage Alley*. I frowned down at it. An address? How could I find out why someone had found it worthwhile to burn it?

"May I keep this?"

"Yes, miss."

"Rose, did Miss Denton ever talk about her life before she came to this house?"

"Not a word, miss."

"Please let me know if you think of anything else." I opened my reticule, slipped the fragment of paper inside, and removed one of my cards. I picked up the maid's work-roughened hand and folded the card into it. "Keep that safe, will you?"

Chapter 5

Three cabmen had gathered in a circle to pass the time of day. Another man sat atop his box, newspaper in hand. A fifth driver leaned against his cab, a pint of porter at his mouth, while another brushed his cushions. This was the cab rank off Tottenham Court Road where I had come to seek the driver William Billings. I tried not to be too obvious as I moved down the line, wishing I'd taken note of Billings' badge number. I could only hope this was his regular stand.

I was about to address a driver who'd just emerged from the adjacent pub when I realized my luck. At the head of the rank stood Billings himself, identifiable by the truculent set of his shoulders and the flyaway hair around his hat. Or perhaps I wasn't so lucky. A red-faced gentleman in a top hat and greatcoat stood at the open door of the hansom, his booted foot on the step. I hurried over, worried that if the cabman drove off now, it could be hours before he returned.

"I beg your pardon, sir," I said to the gentleman. "I need a word with this driver. May I trouble you to take a different hansom?"

"A positive wealth of vehicles awaits your convenience,

madam," he snapped. "I've already made my arrangements with this fellow."

I kept my smile intact. "I have private business with him, sir. Surely you can grant me this small favor with little loss of time or inconvenience to yourself."

"Private business with the cabbie?" the gentleman said.

At this, the cabman behind Billings perked up, scenting a fare, and the rickety waterman with his heavy pails staggered toward us.

Billings regarded me with an unfathomable look. "Changed my mind. I'll take her."

As the customer began to fume in earnest, the second cabman intervened. "This way, sir." With a huff the gentleman condescended to board the other vehicle.

Thunder rumbled, and the first drops of rain plunked on the paving stones. The cabbies broke off their socializing and manned their boxes, no doubt anticipating an onslaught of customers.

Billings' gaze shifted toward the sky. "Well, miss?"

How were we to have this conversation? I could not accompany the cabbie into the pub to be gawked at, and he would be anxious to get his share of the fares brought by the rain. A little voice whispered an idea to me, so breathtaking that I wondered where it had come from. The strange thing was that it had been at the back of my mind since I awakened that morning. Mentally, I reviewed the remaining funds in my purse, telling myself that my mother would not be seriously alarmed as long as I was back before dark, though the same little voice hinted at the weakness of this reasoning. I silenced it and told Billings what I had in mind.

The cab driver bared his brown teeth in a grin. "Got a taste for murder, do you, miss?"

The rain poured harder. The damp seeped through my bonnet and soaked my hair. "I suppose I do, Mr. Billings. Will you take me or not?"

He put his head to one side. "You've cost me one fare today, miss. And I don't care overmuch for driving unprotected females, especially when they get themselves clouted on the head and bleed all over on the cushions."

I reached up to dash away the water dripping from my chin. "Look, what harm can it do?"

For some reason, this struck him as funny. He gave an odd humphing laugh, twitched his lips a few times, and nodded.

The old waterman, who had watched this exchange, put down his pails and tottered to the coach door. He threw it open with a flourish. "Madam?"

A tremor of mingled excitement and fear gave me pause.

Misinterpreting, Billings said, "You won't soil your dress, miss. Sponged and brushed this morning, it was."

I handed the waterman his penny and boarded the cab. The hansom lurched away, and we were off before I could question my decision.

~

"Through there." Billings pointed at the churchyard gate.

It had taken some time in heavy traffic for us to make our way across London Bridge into Southwark. The cabbie had pulled off Borough High Street and now sat atop his box, reins draped across his lap. I stood on the footway. Around me, people went in and out of lodging-houses, and a hard-faced woman peered at me from behind a half-open door. The air smelled of bad drains. Piles of horse muck decorated the street, and I'd spotted several broken windows. My father had never said much about his employment in this parish, though I knew that the poverty and disease had enraged him.

Billings said, "Queers me why you wanted to come, miss. What if a villain coshes you over the head too? Want me to go along with you?" He cast a doubtful look at his horse.

"A murderer lurking in the bushes twice in the same week?" But I looked around uncertainly. No one other than the hard-faced woman seemed to be paying me any attention.

"I'll be as quick as I can," I said. When Billings merely sniffed, I added, "Did you notice anyone while you waited for Miss Denton that day?"

"The rozzers asked me that. Lots of people passed by. Minding their own business as far as I could see."

"Did anyone besides you go into the churchyard?"

"Not that I saw. Not on this end, at any rate."

I was cold, and I had forgotten my umbrella at home. The rain had tapered off, but a persistent mist dampened my cloak. And why was that rude woman still staring at me? As I returned the hostile stare with one of my own, the woman opened the door wider and stepped onto her stoop.

"Are you sure, Mr. Billings?" I said. "You'd inform the police, wouldn't you?"

"Would I risk losing my license? You think I want my wife and younglings to starve?"

"What about when you went to fetch Miss Denton?"

"It were only for a minute or two. I weren't having no fool make off with my horse. I goes in the churchyard and calls out. And I sees her on the ground. So I picks her up, along with her umbrella and wipe—"

"Her handkerchief?"

"That's right. She'd dropped it."

"What makes you so sure the handkerchief was hers? It could have belonged to the person she met, couldn't it?"

"How in blazes would I know that, miss?"

I nodded. Fair point. "Where was she exactly?"

"Next to the big tomb against the wall by the old prison. In a swoon. Roused herself to give me your papa's address, and I helped her back to the cab. Weren't my fault, none of it."

"No, it wasn't, Mr. Billings."

By any standard, the cabman had acted honorably. Alice-Muriel had asked him to wait, and he did. He drove her back across the city and gave his report to the police. Now he'd carried me to the same spot, even though he claimed to dislike taking fares from single ladies. Suddenly, this conduct seemed inexplicable.

"Why did you do it, Mr. Billings? Why didn't you leave her?"

"Dunno, miss. There's the fact . . . well, it don't matter, anyway. She's dead."

"The fact of what?"

"She were a nice-spoken lady." He stared fiercely over my head.

Rose had said something similar about Alice Denton. I smiled up at him. "You mean that you liked her?"

He made a disgusted noise. "You talk pretty, don't you, miss? She paid me for my time, that's all. And I expect you'll do likewise. Get on with you. I don't have all day. Catch your death in this weather."

"I won't be long." I took a few steps toward the gate but halted when he spoke again.

"She didn't go thataway. I let her off on the High Street, so I expect she went down the passage by the old prison."

I thanked him and walked away. It was a short distance to Borough High Street, where I got a view of the front of the church with its red brick facade, stone tower, and white clock face. Following Billings' instructions, I turned into a narrow alley lined by the churchyard on one side and a tall brick wall on the other. When I reached a pair of iron gates, I peeked into a paved courtyard. In front of me sprawled a vast structure. Someone had put up a hand-lettered sign advertising a makeshift shop, and I could hear hammering. I saw people lounging on the exterior staircases that provided access to the upper floors of the terrace. The building seemed to be sinking in on itself.

These had to be the remains of the Marshalsea Prison. I recalled Mr. Dickens' story about the angelic Amy Dorrit reared within these precincts after her father was imprisoned for debt. Fortunate Amy eventually achieved a happy new life with a man who loved her. Unlike Alice Denton.

I entered the churchyard on the opposite side and wandered

down the path. Not much to see. Gravestones, a few bare trees, a sickly shrub or two. I paused to study the inscription on the old tomb under the high wall, which matched Billings' description. Removing one of my gloves, I scraped at the moss on the stone, first with my fingernail, then with a stick. I could not decipher the name on the tomb but managed to uncover the rest of the inscription:

How lov'd, how valu'd once avails thee not
To whom related or by whom begot;
A heap of Dust alone remains of thee
'Tis all thou art and all the Proud shall be.

Pointless claptrap. Of what solace was it to the dead that the proud and prosperous perished too? No one escaped in the end. I tossed the stick aside. My finger tapped the stone as my confidence ebbed. Had I believed I could play detective like a character in a novel? Even if I wanted to, how did one go about it? I stepped away from the tomb to walk a few paces toward the exit. Then I saw them, half obscured in a mound of dirt next to a bush. A pair of spectacles. I dropped to my knees to pick them up. They looked exactly like the ones that had belonged to the victim.

My father had said that Alice was struck from behind. Which suggested she'd felt safe enough with her attacker to turn her back —or perhaps was running away? The spectacles were not broken, which also meant they could have flown off when she was attacked to land in this soft mud at the side of the path. And what about the murder weapon? I peered under the bush, looking for a stone or something of that nature.

Alice could have met someone under the trees with no one the wiser. I pictured her waiting in the rain, perhaps never suspecting that someone was about to steal her life until it was too late to get away. Had she been taken by surprise? Or had time to feel terror?

I was halfway under the bush, the scene vivid in my imagination, when a voice spoke above my head.

"What are you doing down there?"

I froze as fear ballooned in my chest. For an instant, I thought that the murderer might have returned. Or a random thief who would see me as an easy mark with my face in the mud and my hind quarters protruding from the shrub. But when I yanked my head free to look up at the person who'd addressed me, I realized it was only the vicar, an Anglo-Indian gentleman in a black suit, carrying an umbrella. He was gazing down at me with obvious concern. My apprehension giving way to embarrassment, I scrambled to my feet.

"Good day, sir," I said. "I . . . I found something on the ground."

"Come to visit the Marshalsea and Little Dorrit's church?" he asked with a smile that illuminated his face. He either didn't notice the spectacles in my hand or chose not to mention them. "Little Dorrit was married here," he went on, "in fiction, at any rate. The prison has been closed since '42. Some of the buildings have been rented for factories and shops, the rest turned into low lodgings. It'll all be swept away one day. The sooner, the better."

"I suppose you get the occasional literary pilgrim?"

"We do. Mind you, the neighborhood can profit from some positive associations. Most people know us for the debtors' prison and the Mint. The rookery across the way."

"My father was once a medical man in this parish."

The tired brown eyes studied me. The clergyman appeared to be in his mid-fifties. Lines bracketed his mouth, and I noticed that the hand gripping the umbrella bore a scar across the knuckles. "Indeed?" he said. "I'm sure he will have mentioned the typhus and dysentery. The Mint is a place where the poorest of the poor reside. Wretched poverty and vicious crime, always a bad marriage. I witnessed a great deal of suffering in my missionary work in Bangalore and Madras, but we match it, pound for pound. You shouldn't be on your own, ma'am. It's not safe."

"You are right to caution me. A woman known as Alice Denton was set upon in this churchyard. She has since died."

His face dropped. "Terrible business. Yes, the police came

yesterday. I believe they went into the Mint to see what they could discover."

"Why is it called that, sir?" I asked, more to cheer him than because I was actually interested.

"Ah, at one time, we were quite grand in these parts," he said, brightening. "Back when Henry VIII's brother-in-law, the Duke of Suffolk, built his palace in Southwark. He later gave it to the king, who authorized a royal mint. The district became a liberty. Debtors could not be arrested once they took refuge there, and the king's officers had no rights. The name has lingered on, though the mint and liberty are no more."

"Was Alice Denton's attacker from this rookery, do you suppose?"

"I couldn't say. At all events, this is hardly a fitting topic for a young lady." The vicar frowned as if he suspected me of being a curiosity seeker in quest of a titillating, murderous tale. I wondered if that was, in fact, what I was.

We were silent as the rain increased. My companion offered to share his umbrella, and I accepted with gratitude. Encouraged, I said, "You must wonder why I inquired about Miss Denton, sir. I was with her when she died. My name is Esther Hardy."

The umbrella dipped as he bowed. "Is that so? Cornelius Walsh at your service, Miss Hardy."

"An honor to meet you, sir." I hesitated. "You were once employed abroad? The work must've been interesting and valuable."

"I was born in India. We did our best to bring the Christian faith to the people, Miss Hardy. Founding schools and providing pastoral care, that sort of thing. My father had been a British offi-cer, and my mother—" He stopped to flick a glance at me as though checking for my reaction. When I nodded gravely, he continued. "I never knew her. My father thought it best to sepa-rate us for my own good. Who can say whether he was right?"

I knew my opinion but had the tact to keep my reflections to myself. When I thought of my relationship with my own mama, the love, the companionship, the *fun* we had together . . .

Walsh sighed. "No matter. All in the past, as they say. I'm afraid I can't tell you much more about the woman who died. As I informed the police, our sexton had gone home for the day, and my curate was otherwise engaged. I myself was occupied at the time of the . . . incident."

"Had you ever met Alice Denton, sir?"

His expression changed. "Not that I am aware of, no."

I held up the spectacles. "I've just found these beside the path, and I'm certain they belonged to the victim. The attack must have happened close to this spot." I held his gaze. "Is it possible, Mr. Walsh, that you *do* know her? Perhaps by another name?"

"Poor forsaken creature," he said.

CHAPTER 6

Reverend Cornelius Walsh had encountered the woman on three occasions. Twice she came at twilight to walk alone in the churchyard, a hooded figure swathed in a cloak. The first time, he left her to herself, even though it disturbed him to see her walking in the dusk, moving with an awkward gait down the path.

"When I saw her the second time, I made up my mind to speak to her," Mr. Walsh said to me on that rainy day in the churchyard eleven years later.

"Did she tell you her name?" Ever since the Benedict Caxton fiasco, I tended to be wary of clergymen, particularly those of the fire-and-brimstone type, like my former fiancé. But this one I'd liked from the first.

"Not then. As soon as I got close to her, I understood her trouble. Far gone with child, Miss Hardy. I told her she should be at home, resting. But she said the peace of the churchyard gave her ease. Who was I to deny God's peace to anyone? I tried to convey I would withhold judgment if she wished to speak to me, for I could see she wore no wedding ring."

"Did she seem distressed, sir?"

"She suffered from morbid thoughts. I found her examining the church stones, and she told me it was because she would soon require one of her own. She wanted to get accustomed, as it were. To her, it seemed plausible she would not survive childbed."

I could not repress a shudder. It wasn't just the pain that some women nowadays were alleviating with the use of chloroform, but also the risk of excessive bleeding and fever. It was not lost on me that at the bottom of my rejection of Benedict had lurked a primal fear of childbirth.

"She feared her confinement that much?" I said.

"She asked me whether a woman of her . . . sort could be buried here. She was worried about what would happen to her baby, whether it would be damned eternally if it was not baptized in time." His gaze traveled over the skeletal trees and dripping bushes. To me, this churchyard was a gloomy place, but Walsh said, "She appreciated this quiet corner and hoped that if she and her child were tucked away in a forgotten spot, among the departed prisoners of the Marshalsea, no one would mind. You see, she'd been warned she might end up in the paupers' burying ground, where immoral women and their unfortunate infants are tossed willy-nilly into anonymous graves."

"Oh, poor girl." My voice choked. "Did she have no one to turn to, Mr. Walsh?"

"I gave her what I could, and she had one other friend. A woman she'd met while living in a village near Slough for a short time. She'd written to request financial assistance."

"Do you recall the friend's name, sir?"

"She didn't mention it. But I believe the woman worked as a nursemaid at the manor house in Stoke Poges. Or so I seem to recall."

Sheltering together under the umbrella had created an intimacy between us that loosened the vicar's tongue. But a crackle of lightning recalled him, and he sent a worried look at the sky. "I mustn't keep you standing any longer, Miss Hardy. The hem of your gown is sopping. Besides, Inspector Jessup requested my discretion."

"We are quite snug under your umbrella, sir. Did the inspector ask you the same questions?"

"He did, and I'm afraid it's brought the whole wretched business back. He had information linking the victim of this murder to an old crime. Though it might not have been the same woman who killed the baronet's son."

"But you think it was?"

"Something tells me so. If she'd gone astray again—lost her child or embroiled herself in further sin—perhaps she returned here for nostalgia's sake. Or . . . to punish herself with thoughts of the past? Or could it be she remembered me and sought my counsel?" He halted, confused. "No, this will not do. I'm guessing."

"I watched Alice Denton die," I said. "And I'm very much afraid my family could be at risk until her killer is caught. Please tell me the rest, Mr. Walsh."

He gave a sad smile. "As far as I know, I've never laid eyes on Miss Denton in my life. The woman I met was called Muriel. Muriel Dane."

The back of my neck tingled. I was convinced Cornelius Walsh was correct. Muriel had returned to a place that was significant in her past, only to receive her death wound. "You said you met her on three occasions, sir. When was the last time?"

"She returned one day soon after the baby was born. I recall it was a warm afternoon, and I was cutting some flowers for the church. I saw at once that her fortunes had improved. You can imagine my relief."

"The friend had helped her?"

"Must have. How happy I was to see Muriel with her baby in her arms. Truly, God's mercy is infinite. I saw how she clutched her infant, warm and dry and well wrapped up. She came to thank me and bid me goodbye. She told me she wouldn't be occupying space in my churchyard, after all. And she swore her son would be christened when she reached her new home."

"She planned to take the child away?"

He nodded. "She said something else I've never forgotten."

Walsh's black-clad shoulders slumped as he quoted softly, "*Muriel Dane may be a miserable sinner, but she will always be grateful for the compassion you have shown her.* Those were her very words, Miss Hardy."

We listened to the plinking of the rain for a minute or two. Then it was my turn to thank Mr. Walsh as Muriel Dane had done before me.

~

When I got home, Bert was in the hall, broom in hand. He grinned at me as I coughed dramatically into his cloud of dust. I removed my hat and gloves, hung up my cloak, and glanced in the coat stand mirror. There was fresh color in my cheeks as well as a glow in my eyes. Not bad for a first attempt at detective work. Rose's story about the man who rifled through Alice's belongings had to be connected to the murder, and the burned fragment of paper found in the grate also seemed significant. Even more important, Reverend Walsh's account of his dealings with Muriel Dane had convinced me that Alice and Muriel were indeed the same person.

"Where've you been, miss?" Bert demanded. "Mrs. Hardy's been popping out every minute to see if you were back."

"I've had a long ride in a cab and a walk around a churchyard." I frowned down at my muddy feet, but the boy didn't seem bothered about the new dirt being tracked across his floor.

Bert paused in his sweeping. "Something to do with the dead lady?"

I tweaked his nose. "Little children should be seen and not heard. Or so they say, brat."

"I'm not so little, miss. Nor a girl either. No one says that to boys."

"Do you think that's fair?"

He thought about that, then shook his head. "I don't make

the rules, Miss Esther. Besides, no one's ever asked me. I've got plenty of rules of my own."

"Don't we all?" I said. We nodded at each other wisely.

Bert and I were old allies. Having lived with us since he was a few weeks old, Bert had always been much more than a servant's orphaned great-nephew. It was Bert, when he was small, who'd dubbed his great-aunt Edith Kipling with the nickname Granny-Cook, which had stuck. We treated the boy almost as a member of the family, though Granny-Cook insisted on a semblance of the formalities. "You mind yourself, child," she'd say whenever Bert got in trouble at school. "You'll have your own way to make in this world, and I won't always be able to watch over you."

I sympathized with Bert's struggles. He wasn't a strong student and found it excruciating to sit for hours at a time. His small stature and chubbiness upset him, and I thought he needed more freedom to play with his friends. Nor did I think that the penny blood stories the boys traded amongst themselves were so very hazardous. Granny-Cook, on the other hand, seemed half convinced Bert would follow their example and either descend into a life of crime or become a pirate.

As I smiled down at him, I recalled the incident with Inspector Jessup. "What were you doing lurking outside the door that day? You deserved the scolding you got, Bert."

His smile evaporated. "No one tells me anything. There's Phoebe acting like a scared rabbit. Granny banging the pots and pans. Your mama looking distracted. And your papa forbidding me to put so much as a toe over the threshold."

Bert's candid blue eyes didn't waver. He was right. He was too old to be treated like a baby, and he worried about those he loved.

I patted his cheek. "Everyone's just upset about the woman who died. Granny-Cook and Phoebe knew her better than I did. What about you? Did you like her? I'm sure you must be sorry too."

"Why should I be?"

"Bert?" His stricken look gave me a pang.

"I want everyone to act normal, that's all. I gotta go, miss. Granny bade me come straight back when I was finished." He swept some of his pile into his dustpan, dispersed the remainder with his boot, and shouldered the broom. "That's done," he said with satisfaction and stepped through the door that led down to the basement kitchen. "I warrant you're in hot water with your mama, miss," he called back over his shoulder. I heard his feet clomping down the stairs.

But Bert was wrong on that score. When I proceeded up the stairs to the parlor, Mama rose from her seat by the fire and came forward. I could see she had no intention of making a fuss, for she was too experienced a tactician.

"You've been an age, dear," she said. "You missed lunch, and your feet must be horridly damp. Why don't you go upstairs and change your clothes while I ring for tea? Granny-Cook made apple spice muffins."

This speech, delivered in a hearty tone, did not fool me. Mama's face was tense with repressed curiosity. Her green eyes sparkled.

"Where's Papa? His hat and coat aren't in the hall."

"Gone out. He'll be back soon."

"Oh? You haven't told me where he went."

"An errand, dear," she said. "I'm sure he'll explain. Do hurry."

A quarter hour later, having changed my skirt and shoes, I joined my mother at the tea-table in the parlor. I launched into an account of my visit to Alice-Muriel's lodgings, telling Mama about the letter Muriel had been expecting and the "friend" who had shown up at Mrs. Carver's lodgings to search the victim's rooms.

Suitably impressed by this wealth of information, Mama agreed that Mrs. Carver was a harridan but looked dubious about involving Rose. "Was that prudent?"

"I think it was."

"But . . . what if her mistress finds out, and the girl loses her situation?"

I waved a hand. "Who would tell Mrs. Carver? I certainly won't."

"Papa won't like you getting involved, Esther."

"A woman has been murdered, Mama," I shot back.

I knew I sounded defensive, but I was tired of the endless restrictions that so often stood in the way of what any rational person could see was necessary. Mama's look of astonishment when I went on to relate my visit to the murder site might have been comical under other circumstances. But, soon recovering, she wanted to hear every detail of the meeting with the vicar Cornelius Walsh.

"Oh, what a sad story," she said afterward.

"Don't you see, Mama? This means Muriel would never have harmed her child. Mr. Walsh said she intended to have her baby baptized. Her luck had changed."

"I suppose things must've gone wrong after that."

"It's astounding how vividly Mr. Walsh remembers their few encounters, and it must be because there was something about Muriel that made people take notice. I wonder why I failed to observe it."

Mama swallowed the last bite of her muffin. "You've decided to refer to her as Muriel? We were never quite sure. It would be another matter if she'd admitted it."

"What made you suspect she *was* Muriel Dane?"

"I told you. We saw the stories in the paper and put two and two together. Not many educated women give birth in the Mint. The details fit."

"Well, if she did kill Perry Beldenfield, someone may have sought revenge." I munched my muffin—as moist and delicious as any Granny-Cook had ever created, though today I barely tasted it. "Or, if Muriel's innocent, perhaps Beldenfield's killer came for her too."

"After so many years? You're jumping to conclusions."

I groaned in exasperation. "I'm merely speculating. How else do you suggest we get to the bottom of this, Mama? No one seems to have any inkling of what occurred, except that a mysterious assailant came along at the precise time Alice Denton chose to visit the churchyard where Muriel once walked. Isn't it possible she was killed because of her past? It's a theory, at any rate."

"Perhaps." Mama's tone was noncommittal.

We had finished the muffins and most of the tea when my father came in. "Did you accomplish your business, Theo?" Mama asked.

He crossed the room to warm his hands at the fire. "Yes. I don't suppose you've left me a cup in that pot? I've a few minutes to spare until my next patient arrives."

My mother rose. "I'll ring for fresh, and there's a muffin for you too."

I was suddenly alert, observing the look my parents exchanged and the way my father folded his lips lest any unwary words escape. After Phoebe replenished the tea, I said, "What was the business, Papa?"

"I went to see that inspector at Scotland Yard."

"About the inquest?"

Papa took his place at the tea-table, sweeping up his coat-tails so they wouldn't crease. "Not that exactly. By the way, I've received a summons from the coroner's court. For you too, Esther."

"Esther visited Alice Denton's lodgings and went to the churchyard where she was attacked," Mama blurted.

Papa's cup clattered in the saucer. "Why in heaven's name would you do such a thing? You went alone to that pestilent haunt of thieves?"

"The cab driver Billings was with me, Papa," I said. "The only other person I encountered was the parish priest."

"I can't imagine what possessed you," he said.

"Esther thinks Alice's—or rather Muriel's—death is related to the murder of Perry Beldenfield." Mama spoke fast as if nervous. "Which she supposes is unsolved. Go on, dear. Tell your father the story."

I obligingly repeated my news, finishing with, "So, you see, there's more to learn about this case, Papa."

"What rot. You don't understand what you meddle with, Esther. And I can ill afford to have this matter talked about any more than it already will be." He took a sip of his tea, wincing when it scorched him. "I thought it would have cooled. Stupid, ridiculous stuff."

"You could have blown on the tea, dear," Mama said. "Now, you'd better tell Esther why you visited Inspector Jessup today."

Chapter 7

I studied my father as he glowered at the crumbs on his plate. Dear Papa—an obstinate individual who believed that the world *should* be better. More honest, just, and compassionate. As if it personally offended him that people so often didn't get what they deserved and things didn't always work out for the best. As if, despite the pious certainties of this Victorian age, the world were not an unholy mess full of turmoil and sorrow.

Was it any wonder that worries about our financial security had soured him a little? That he'd taken refuge in protecting his family and let the rest of humanity go hang? With the exception of his patients, for whom he would do almost anything. I looked across the table at his careworn face and felt my annoyance at his bad temper drain away.

Then I noticed my mother. What could be wrong? Mama sat hugging her arms and staring off into vacancy, rocking a little in her chair. I felt uneasy. Something about her tugged at my memory, but I couldn't pinpoint it. Nor had I any notion what my parents' behavior might have to do with the murder.

It was my mother who broke the silence. Her gaze snapped back into focus, and she turned to my father. "It's time, Theo. We can't keep the secret anymore. Not from our daughter, our only child."

Papa threw himself back in his chair. "If we tell her, she'll keep poking around like a dog digging up a bone. Mark my words, Nan."

I had been watching this byplay with growing dismay. "I'm sitting right here, and you're right. I do want to understand what happened to Muriel. Admit it, Papa. You feel the same."

"I'll be dashed if I do."

"Papa!"

He sighed. "Well, if you must have the sordid tale, I suppose you must, daughter. The truth is that your Muriel Dane was an exceedingly pretty girl, more than a cut above her circumstances. To her everlasting misfortune, she caught the eye of a gentleman who never had any intention of marrying someone of her class. He debauched her, probably without an instant's thought. Still, reprobate though he was, the young man didn't deserve to be murdered."

"Of course not," I said.

"Beldenfield's wife testified at the inquest," Papa added. "She witnessed Muriel escaping through the garden."

I shook my head. "Why didn't you turn her in if you and Mama were so convinced of her guilt?"

A muscle quivered next to my father's mouth. "Would *you* send a young woman to the gallows, Esther? 'Alice' told us she was the daughter of a legal clerk who'd been killed in an accident. Which matched the newspaper reports about Muriel. 'Alice' had been orphaned and taken in by a well-connected family as a kind of librarian-secretary. Again, like Muriel. But I suppose we deluded ourselves we might be mistaken about her."

"We didn't want to know," Mama said.

"She was young," my father continued. "The birth of her child had been an ordeal that nearly killed her. And sometimes new mothers sink into melancholy or even a temporary . . . insanity. She and Perry Beldenfield could have argued, and she struck out without considering her actions. From all accounts, Belden-field had behaved unforgivably."

He took a sip of his rejected tea and set down the cup, carefully this time. "As for why we didn't tell you, it was an ugly business. We didn't want to burden you."

I bit my lip. "When I was younger, maybe—but afterward? It wasn't as if she disappeared from your life. She called on us a few days ago, Papa."

"I'll tell you why," Mama said. "She came to see Bert."

"See . . . Bert?"

Papa started to speak, but my mother silenced him with a look. "Alice—or rather Muriel, if you insist—couldn't support a child. Who would have an unmarried mother as a maid or a shop assistant?"

"But, Mama—"

"Bert's not related to Granny-Cook. Not by blood, at any rate," she said. "Your father and I invented the story to account for the boy's presence in our home. We had to tell Granny-Cook that Alice was Bert's mother, though we didn't share our suspicions about the Beldenfield case. And Phoebe knows nothing."

I pushed back my chair. "What are you saying, Mama? Bert's not the child of Granny-Cook's nephew? The man whose wife died and who then died himself of some fever?"

My parents gazed back at me, both visibly disturbed. Had they *lied* to me? From my earliest years, they'd taught me that few things were so bad as a lie deliberately told. Outright untruths between the members of a family weakened the bonds of kinship and grew into monstrous edifices of deceit. Or so I had always believed.

"The woman we knew as Alice brought Bert to us soon after the report of Muriel Dane's drowning," Mama said after a pause. "Your father and I couldn't bear to subject him to the parish authorities, nor could we denounce his mother to the police. We kept silent, and we kept him."

I walked to the window and leaned my head against the glass.

"So the witness who claimed to see Muriel drown herself and her baby lied. Do you suppose she bribed him?"

"It's possible," my mother said.

"Why didn't you and Papa adopt Bert?"

"Questions would have been asked," my father answered. "It seemed better this way. Safer."

"For the first few years of the boy's life, we saw nothing of his mother," Mama said from behind me. "Then we started bumping into her around the neighborhood. She'd stop by to have a chat with Granny-Cook, encouraging her to gossip. We put a stop to the visits for a time. But I . . . couldn't bring myself to turn her away. Muriel was meek as a lamb, no danger to anyone." She cleared her throat. "Sometimes she'd leave a posy of flowers on the doorstep."

"Come and sit down, Esther," my father said.

"You should have told me." The glass was cool against my hot forehead.

"Yes, we should have," my mother said. "Your father thought . . . no, that's not fair. *We* thought we were protecting you. And Bert needed his chance in life." Her voice dropped lower. "You're going to make me say it, aren't you? Your father did it for me because I asked him to. I couldn't bear to think of another child, a boy, lost as my own Christopher had been. I feared Bert would be taken from us too."

I spun around. So that was it. Shame flooded me as I identified the memory that had eluded me earlier. How could I have forgotten? My long-desired baby brother, Christopher, had died as an infant when I was eight years old. My mother's lost expression tonight revived the aftermath of this bereavement when she had wandered the house. A ghost. No energy to play with her little daughter, barely any will to dress herself in the morning or help out with Papa's work. Gradually, things improved, and I'd managed to block most of this period from my mind. In truth, I'd given little conscious thought to the brother I only recalled as a mewling bundle in Mama's arms. I had assumed that her grief was laid aside like a flower pressed in a book.

"Christopher? Oh, Mama. I'm sorry. I should have realized."

"We had every right not to tell you about Bert, Esther," my father said. "We will testify at the inquest and be done with this matter."

This was the tone seldom heard from him. The one that meant he was standing on his male authority and would be obeyed.

Poor dear, I thought. *Doesn't he know his own wife and daughter better than that?*

The shadows had lengthened. Mama rose to draw the curtains and light the lamps. Intent on her task, she glided around the room, the gaslight glowing around her. Her eyes showed sadness yet also a hard-won tranquility, as if routine comforted her. My heart squeezed with love for both my parents. Leaving the window, I went to stand in the middle of the hearthrug.

"We owe Bert the truth, Papa," I said. "She's his mother." I swallowed hard. "That's why Muriel was so desperate to reach us. Besides warning us, she needed to see her son."

My father got to his feet. "I'm sure you're right. But we can't get involved for Bert's sake. Does that satisfy you?"

We confronted each other across the carpet. Though I hated to upset him, I couldn't let this go. "No, Papa. Until we find out who killed Muriel, isn't Bert at risk too? Thank heavens you didn't inform the police about him."

"But I did. That's why I went to Scotland Yard today. Your mother and I decided that, under the circumstances, we couldn't keep the full story from Inspector Jessup. He's a good fellow. He's promised to keep Bert's history quiet for the present to give the police time to investigate. When it becomes necessary, I myself will talk to the boy."

The front bell sounded, and Papa, grim-faced, went to receive his patient.

At dinner, I tried not to disrupt the fragile peace. No one referred to the inquest, which would be held the next morning. Instead, we discussed Prince Albert's illness before moving on to more domestic matters, such as Granny-Cook's complaints about the kitchen range. This was Mama's way of preparing my father for the necessity of buying a new one, if not in time for Christmas, then early in the new year.

As he liked to do, Bert carried up the dishes from the kitchen and lingered to listen to the conversation, asking several intelligent questions about Prince Albert and showing off some warm stockings Mama had mended for him. I sensed my parents' watchfulness as I chatted with the boy. Did they think I was silly enough to blurt out what I knew? It was true that I was trying to trace Alice-Muriel in Bert's familiar features. All I saw was the child we loved with his beakish nose and mischievous grin.

When we rose from the table, my mother sent Bert up to bed.

I said to my father, "Shall we hear the end of our friend Mr. Quigley's tale?" I was referring to a book about an English clergyman's journey to the goldfields of Australia, which I'd been reading aloud.

My father smiled at me. "That Quigley is a tedious fellow. Yet he evokes the landscape well."

My family gathered around the fire in the parlor. After several hours of Mr. Quigley's descriptions of friendly Aborigines, mixed with fantastical tales of gold nuggets the size of oranges, I grew sleepy. I said goodnight to my parents and went upstairs to bed. In my room, I sat down at my dressing table to find a gift awaiting me. A pile of yellowed newspaper cuttings tucked under my jar of night cream. I had no doubt of the source—these were my own gold nuggets, courtesy of my mother. A peace offering of sorts. Eagerly, I began to read, holding each cutting up to my candle.

The reports spanned a few weeks in 1850. On 21 June, a few months after his fashionable wedding to the heiress Lydia

Travers, Percival "Perry" Beldenfield had been discovered in his father's library, his skull smashed by the fireplace poker. Though no one saw the female assailant enter through an unlocked back gate and an open French window, the victim's bride came face to face with her in the garden as she fled the scene. The perpetrator, it seemed, was Muriel Dane, who'd once been employed by the victim's father, Sir Percival Beldenfield. After Perry Beldenfield impregnated her, Muriel had been ousted from Portman Square soon before her lover's grand marriage took place.

Reading between the lines, I saw that Muriel figured as the woman scorned. The police soon located the murderess' lodgings in Southwark. Then came the news of a witness. A man called Finch Norwood testified that he'd seen Muriel Dane, baby in arms, leaping into the Thames a few hours after Perry's death.

I reached the last cutting. Here, Mama had underscored one detail in black, the ink fresh and a little smudged. How had Perry Beldenfield's bride identified his killer? According to the underlined passage, Mrs. Beldenfield had described the bonnet Muriel wore at the murder scene—"green silk with pink roses and a black ostrich feather." Moreover, the witness Norwood had confirmed this description.

I put the cutting back in the pile and neatened the stack, as though that could help me organize my thoughts. The witness had lied—Muriel hadn't drowned herself. Which meant that Norwood couldn't corroborate Mrs. Beldenfield's account of the bonnet. Suppose that when he came forward with his information, the authorities asked him whether the woman he'd seen on the bridge was wearing a green bonnet, and he'd simply agreed. The detail would have strengthened his lie and got the police off Muriel's scent.

But, stranger still, I knew that the dead woman *had* owned such a bonnet, which she'd been wearing when set upon in the churchyard eleven years later. Could this be a coincidence? Since Alice-Muriel had worn this bonnet, or one like it, while committing a crime, it would be an incriminating possession. Why not dispose of it after Perry Beldenfield's murder?

I stared at my reflection in the dressing-table mirror, aware of the breath moving in and out of my lungs. My eyes looked huge and deep, and shadows danced across my face. My gaze held doubt —too many unanswerable questions. I was alive. Muriel was dead, beyond all help. She could not harm anyone, and no one could harm her, except in reputation and memory. What would Muriel Dane say about these damning reports?

The flesh-and-blood woman in the mirror gave herself a mocking smile. Time to go to sleep. Then I realized something I ought to have noticed before. The nice, warm bed reflected in my glass was empty, and Fosco was missing from his usual throne. Letting him terrorize the neighborhood would be a huge mistake. I groaned.

"Blasted animal," I said to my image.

After thrusting my feet into some shoes, I threw on my shawl and took up my candle. I went down to the basement kitchen, where all was dark except for a halo of light from the banked range fire. I unlocked the kitchen door and stepped outside into the tiny area, hunching my shoulders in the frigid air. Trying not to slip on the ice, I mounted the stairs.

At the top, I paused to appreciate the glow of the street lamps visible through a light mist. All seemed deserted. I looked first one way, then the other. No Fosco in sight. Was he digging up back gardens? Possibly. Depositing gruesome gifts on people's doorsteps? Very likely. Battling his feline enemies? Undoubtedly. The other day, I'd encountered one of the local strays missing half an ear.

"Fosco?" The candle in my hand flickered. The chain of lamps stretched away from me, little orbs of civilization. "Fosco," I said again.

No reply. Instead, the darkness stirred, and a figure separated itself from the dense blackness on the opposite side of the road. A man in a top hat and greatcoat. His scarf fluttered as he moved toward me, his footsteps loud in my ears. He stopped, his hand going to his pocket, and I heard a scratching noise. Light flared to encircle his face. He held a cigar at his lips, which he puffed so that bars of light danced over him. Bright and dark, the picture always shifting so that individual features were picked out. A chin, a nose, a pair of eyes under a high brow.

The impression faded, and I saw him with more clarity. A youngish man of medium height with a proud bearing. He took the cigar out of his mouth. As we regarded each other, I thought about retreating down the stairs but didn't. I had the feeling he would speak to me, as a stranger might stop a passer-by to ask for directions. Before either of us could move, the air came alive with a gust of wind, extinguishing the match before it could scorch his fingers.

I stepped back until I felt the area railing at my back. There seemed no reason to connect this random passer-by with Muriel Dane. But I was on edge. This was staid Bloomsbury. The gentleman would have looked more at home strolling out of a club in Mayfair. What was he doing here?

"Are you lost?" My tone challenged him.

"No, I beg your pardon. I am often out late walking. I apologize for disturbing you, ma'am."

For his own inscrutable reasons, Fosco—damn the animal—chose that moment to prance up to the gentleman on his large paws. The cat pressed against the stranger's legs.

"You smell my dog, don't you, boy?" the man said, smiling. He lifted his head to stare at me again. "Good evening, madam." Touching a hand to his hat, he went on his way.

When he was gone, I scooped up Fosco, who gave a yelp of protest. With my twenty-pound beast in my arms, I returned to the kitchen. I set the thrashing cat on the floor and bolted the door. Fosco sent me his pleading look, begging for a morsel of food.

"You must be joking," I said.

Samuel Godwin had wanted to see the surgeon's house for himself. He'd been loitering across the street, gazing up at the windows, when he heard a woman's voice calling someone—her cat, as it turned out. Sounding annoyed, she stood next to the area stairs, having just ascended from below. It darted across his mind that perhaps she could tell him more about the death the newspaper had reported, though how could he question a woman alone in the dark? He fumbled for his matchbox and lit his cigar while he debated what to do. Then came that moment when they looked at each other across the pavement, and he wished even more strongly that he could talk to her. Instead, he left her.

He roamed south for a while, then eastward, his feet settling into a rhythm. It was bitterly cold, and the damp numbed his cheeks. Several times, he paused to wipe his streaming nose or tighten his greatcoat. The movement of his limbs soothed him—simultaneously a stimulant and a narcotic—and he felt a sense of ease in his dreaming mind. He could lose himself, gain himself, and tire himself out so that he was sure to fall asleep the minute his head touched a pillow.

Never alone in the dark, he was part of a fellowship of nightwalkers. Nomads who traveled through London while others snored in their beds. All the varieties of street people had grown familiar to him. Men glimpsed in doorways, the occasional policeman tramping his route, pathetic women who looked at him, dazed and hopeful. Ragged children who slept under shuttered market stalls or huddled in alleys under pieces of sacking. Cabmen trundling along in their vehicles, wheels clacking. As Godwin moved among them, the restless pulse of a city of millions thrummed in his veins.

He knew that, unlike him, most of the people had no choice in their wandering. If anyone bothered to ask *them*, they would not welcome him; they would sooner laugh at his caprice or pick his pocket. He was as alien to them, as he was to the inhabitants of his uncle's luxurious mansion. Which, come to think about it, was what had drawn him to Muriel in the first place. When he was only nineteen, she'd become the center of his existence. He'd been a young man, trying to resign himself to the legal career his uncle had chosen for him. Muriel had intuited his unhappiness. She'd been his friend and something more. Night after night, he'd lain awake in his bed as he imagined flying with her to someplace far away, just as his mother and father had once escaped to Italy to make a new life.

His thoughts drifted. He was back in the library at Beldenfield House. He was bent over Muriel's chair as she stared up at him with those doomed eyes, not unlike those of the street women. The humiliating words of love were pouring from his mouth . . .

Irritated, he took a last puff on his cigar and crushed it under his boot. Fool that he was, he'd have married the girl in the teeth of Sir Percival's opposition, even after the debacle with his cousin. That had been an anxious time for the Beldenfields. Sir Percival had been deep in the negotiations for Perry's marriage to Lydia Travers, and no scandal with a servant could be allowed to interfere. Then, one morning, it was over. Godwin had come down to breakfast to be told that Muriel was gone, expelled from the house like a bad smell.

Stupid girl. She should have chosen him.

Eventually, Godwin found himself at London Bridge. He stood for a while, mesmerized by the reflection of the lamps in the inky expanse of the Thames, thinking of the suicide victims pulled down into its polluted depths. It seemed Muriel had been spared that fate. After a while, he crossed to the Surrey shore. He had no intention of going to the graveyard where Alice Denton had been attacked. He just wanted to see the streets Muriel Dane had once walked. Why had a pregnant woman gone to live in one of the worst slums of London? Had Perry lied to him when he swore she would be cared for? The child she was to bear would be a Beldenfield.

On the other side of the river, the yeasty smell from the breweries greeted him. He walked on, passing a prison, a madhouse, several forlorn churches, and endless rows of decrepit tenements. Nothing left of Muriel he could detect. Weary at last, he crossed back to the other side of the Thames via Westminster Bridge.

As he made his way toward his bed in Portman Square, he recalled the woman he'd encountered outside the surgeon's house. She had to be the man's wife or daughter, and she would have known Muriel. She could have heard the last words of the dying. Years ago, Godwin had been convinced that a foolish episode in his life was over for good, and he'd been wrong. He would not be fooled again. Muriel Dane might be dead, but there was still the matter of her child.

Chapter 8

The inquest took place in the back room of a pub not far from St. George's church. As my father and I approached the chairs set aside for witnesses near the front, I saw a number of other women in attendance, including the landlady Mrs. Carver, who shot me a venomous look. I also located the clergyman Cornelius Walsh, along with Inspector Jessup from Scotland Yard. A few of the journalists seated in their own section watched me as I passed, but most of them were staring at a gentleman who sat on a carved oak settle against the wall. I didn't get a good look at him until I took my seat.

It was the man who'd been outside my house the night before.

In the light of day, he had a beardless, olive-skinned face, curling black hair, and sharply cut cheeks. Not handsome exactly, too individual for that. I noted a pair of side-whiskers that formed two parentheses emphasizing his wide brown eyes. He was in his late twenties or early thirties, I judged, and he seemed absorbed in his thoughts, a little disdainful of his surroundings. One thing seemed obvious: this gentleman didn't fit Rose's description of the man who had searched Muriel's lodgings.

Before I could nudge my papa to get his opinion, the proceedings were called to order. The coroner droned through the preliminaries. Afterward, the jury trooped off to the next room to inspect the body. Upon their return, Mrs. Carver took a seat at the table. The gentleman on the settle held up a gold quizzing glass, aiming it at the landlady's chignon hairpiece, which resembled a dead animal atop her head. I repressed a smile.

"You were the victim's landlady, madam?" the coroner inquired in his ponderous way.

"Unfortunately, sir. She got herself killed before I could evict her. I have to watch myself, don't I? I was left a poor widow nine years ago."

"Indeed, ma'am. The woman was an unsatisfactory tenant?"

"She was. Refusing to account for herself. Late on her rent a time or two. You know the sort of female, sir, and not what I like to see in my house. I run a decent Christian establishment, sir. No goings-on, if I can help it."

"Hmmm," the coroner said. "That puts a different complexion on the case. Did you ever see her with a man?"

"Can't say I did, sir. Bit of a dowdy. Not much there to appeal to the gentlemen." She trilled a grating laugh.

"Any reason to suspect her of dishonesty? Associations with low people?"

Mrs. Carver shrugged. "Wouldn't surprise me. You'll find her past won't bear much scrutiny. Not my place to say more than that."

"You can't tell us what her business was at St. George's?"

"Up to no good, I warrant." She paused. "I can't abide secretive women, sir." This the woman said with a straight face even as she neglected to inform the court about allowing Muriel's so-called friend to ransack her rooms.

After the landlady had flounced away, my father took his place at the witness table. He established his credentials and related the story of the victim's appearance at his house.

"She was your patient, sir?" the coroner said.

"In a manner of speaking." Papa looked red and uncomfortable. Protecting Bert would be his main concern, but I knew the evasions pained him.

"Explain yourself, Mr. Hardy."

He obliged by describing his dealings with the woman known as Alice Denton, revealing his suppositions as to her past. A frown descended on the coroner's brow when he learned that the dead woman was alleged to have committed a murder under another name, and he promptly decided she was undeserving of his concern. Mention of the Perry Beldenfield case sent the journalists into a frenzy of note-taking, with more glances cast in the direction of the gentleman on the oak settle. I wondered again who he could be.

At length, the coroner shook his head. "A most lamentable affair, Mr. Hardy. I cannot understand why this conspiracy is only now coming to light. Why didn't you report your suspicions?"

"I would have, sir, had I any proof. I feared making a false accusation."

"Nonetheless, you had a duty to the law. If you are right that Muriel Dane was alive until this week, what befell the baby you delivered? Was it a boy or a girl?"

"A boy, sir."

Before the coroner could pose another question, Inspector Jessup intervened. "We are investigating that aspect of the affair, sir, and will report back to the court should we discover anything relevant to this inquiry."

My father's expression relaxed, though I didn't think anyone else noticed.

Next was the medical evidence. Papa detailed it, but all the coroner said was, "Couldn't the victim have fallen and hit her head? A seizure, perhaps? Might she have been intoxicated?"

"No smell of spirits about her."

"A robbery gone wrong? Someone struck her down to shut her mouth? Seems logical enough. The lower classes are often violent."

Papa's face set. "We found money in her purse, sir."

"No indication the woman had been interfered with?"

"No sign of sexual assault, no."

Papa was dismissed. The police surgeon testified as to the postmortem findings, which were similar to those my father had reached. Then came Inspector Jessup. He informed the jury that his constables had questioned the residents in the vicinity of the church, including in the criminal district called the Mint. At this, the jurymen shuffled in their chairs. I knew what that meant. They grew more and more convinced of Alice-Muriel's guilt, past and present. The jurymen's hearts were not moved by her story any more than the coroner's was.

"As for this Alice Denton," the coroner said, "your theory is what precisely? Even if she was, in truth, Muriel Dane, what are we to make of that?"

"We don't know, sir," Jessup replied.

"Muriel Dane once lived among criminals and scoundrels," the coroner mused. "Perhaps she had involved herself in further villainy, and someone killed her for it." He coughed. "I assume you will seek confirmation of the dead woman's identity, Inspector?"

"We'll do our best, sir."

The cab driver Billings repeated his testimony, and then it was my turn. Billings stepped away from the table, looking so relieved to have his ordeal over that I grinned at him. One corner of the cabbie's mouth lifted in response. He touched his hat and left me to face the rows of spectators.

I spoke of the victim's appearance at the door, along with my attempts to revive her. It never occurred to the coroner to ask my opinion. I figured merely as the daughter of the house who happened to be on hand when death came calling. That had to be why my temper got the better of me when he interrupted me for the third time. I broke into one of his long-winded remarks to say, "If she went to the churchyard to meet someone, she wouldn't have expected danger."

The coroner squinted at me. "Since no one knows the reason, I don't see how your observation is of any use, ma'am."

I had been debating with myself about whether I should mention the handkerchief Billings had found. But Jessup and the cabman had both omitted this detail from their accounts, and I decided I would too. Now that I knew of Bert's connection to the case, I was wary. Did I want to elucidate any more than necessary? I did not. The coroner's self-satisfied countenance, not to mention the reappearance of the gentleman from last night, had decided me. But I opened my reticule to take out the spectacles.

"I found these when I visited the churchyard where the assault occurred. The constables had missed them."

Inspector Jessup strode over to pluck the spectacles from my hand. "Evidence, Miss Hardy. I'll take those."

I drew breath to press on—and stopped when I caught my father's eye. A warning. So far, we'd gotten off lightly, and Papa wanted to keep it that way. The gentleman on the settle was watching me too, his gaze amused. Flustered, I missed the coroner's next remark.

Before I could ask for it to be repeated, Inspector Jessup spoke in a dismissive tone designed to put me in my place. "As I said, we intend to persevere, sir. We must hope that other witnesses will surface or that our inquiries in the Mint will bear fruit."

The coroner gave a curt nod. "That'll be all, Miss Hardy."

Mr. Walsh, the clergyman of St. George's, came next. The coroner treated the soft-spoken vicar with rude condescension, and Mr. Walsh was soon disposed of. A quarter hour later, the coroner adjourned the proceedings for a fortnight to enable the gathering of evidence.

As I accompanied my father to the street, I kept glancing over my shoulder, trying to discover what had become of the gentleman. "Papa, did you notice the dark-haired man sitting against the wall?"

"Can't say I did. Why?"

"I saw him outside our house last night. What do you suppose he wanted?"

Papa looked alarmed. "Are you certain, Esther? He's probably one of those blasted journalists. We'll be lucky if we get out of this affair without our reputation in tatters."

"I don't believe he's a journalist." I bent to retie my bootlace, annoyed that I still hadn't spotted the man.

"Stop stalling," my father said. "I have patients waiting."

"Yes, Papa." My every sense remained alert. Finally. The gentleman had emerged, part of a cluster of people flowing out of the tavern. Two of the journalists broke from the pack and started to chase him. He increased his pace, soon boarding a carriage with arms on the side panel. The coachman cracked his reins and drove off.

Back at home, I retired to the parlor and built up the fire. I threw myself into a chair and sat, pondering. I was far from satisfied that the police would seek justice for Muriel Dane. But what could I do? I'd had no opportunity to speak to the Scotland Yard inspector after the inquest, so I dashed off a note to inform him about the man who'd searched Muriel's rooms. Let Jessup see what he could get out of the landlady.

Eventually, my mother came in to draw the blinds and turn up the gaslight in the wall sconces. I sat on in silence and pretended not to observe the inquiring looks Mama sent my way. When my father came in for tea, I put in an occasional word so he would not think I was coming down with something and insist on peering down my throat.

After a while, I excused myself. In my bedchamber, I lit the lamp and picked up my pen to begin a long overdue letter to a school friend. The phrases came smoothly, though I had no idea why I corresponded with this person other than habit. How much of life was lived this way, like chickens scratching over the same patch of ground until they died?

I shook off the morbid thought. There *was* something I could do. I could call on Perry Beldenfield's widow in Portman Square. She was the witness who had established Muriel's guilt, and I wanted to hear the widow's story.

CHAPTER 9

Portman Square lay north of Oxford Street in Marylebone. The next afternoon, I walked to my destination, my ears ringing with costermongers crying their wares, organ grinders making their usual din, and the never-ceasing racket of wheels on cobbles. I smiled at a man who thrust a handbill at me even as I sidestepped him. It was a gray December day with more rain threatening and a hint of sleet in the air.

I arrived to find myself dwarfed by an expanse of grand buildings. This area was populated by aristocrats and City bankers, along with nabobs who'd amassed their colossal wealth in India or the West Indies. To these people, I was nothing. To gather my courage, I dawdled in the square, admiring the facades of the mansions and peeking into the central garden with its trees and graveled walks. When I was ready, I made my way to the porticoed entrance of Beldenfield House. Sucking in the deepest breath I could manage in a corset, I plied the knocker.

The door opened. An aged butler intoned, "May I help you, miss?"

"I'd like to see Mrs. Beldenfield if she's at home to visitors."

Doubt creased his seamed face. "I'll have to inquire, miss. Would you be so kind as to state your business?"

"A confidential matter relating to the death of a mutual acquaintance," I said with as much aplomb as I could muster.

"I don't think—"

I hurried on with a fixed smile. "It would be most helpful if you would take my card to your mistress."

The butler gave me another uncertain look before accepting the card in his liver-spotted hand and easing the door closed. I heard his feet shuffling away.

To my surprise, he soon returned to usher me into the entrance hall. After he took my pelisse, he conducted me across the marble floor and through an archway into a bright space, where a dramatic double stairwell rose to the upper stories. The butler waited as I put back my head to gape at the dome far above. Then he conducted me into a reception room off the hall.

Lydia Beldenfield rose from a chair near the hearth. In her early thirties, she was dressed in a black silk gown with white lace at the wrists. She wore her chestnut hair in a high knot with side ringlets that bracketed a pale, intense countenance.

"Good afternoon, Miss Hardy," she said. "You wished to speak to me?" She gripped my calling card in one hand—the card on the back of which I had scrawled two words: *Muriel Dane*.

"Thank you for seeing me, ma'am."

Lydia let the card fall to the table and gestured toward a damask sofa. Once we were seated, I discreetly examined the sea-green curtains at two tall windows, the porphyry columns in the corners, and the ornate ceiling with its lush mythological scene. Breathing in stale air perfumed by the vase of hothouse roses on the table, I swallowed my nervousness.

"Your calling card gave me a start." Lydia released a brittle laugh. "You may begin by telling me who you are and why you're here."

I held her gaze. "I came to tell you Muriel Dane did not take her own life after your husband's death, but appears to have been killed a few days ago under mysterious circumstances. She was using the name Alice Denton. You, of all people, have a right to know her fate."

"Indeed? How is she your affair?"

"My father is a surgeon, Mrs. Beldenfield. She died under his care."

The lady's expression shifted. She touched her jet necklace with the charm in the shape of a teardrop. "I confess I did read something about this in the newspaper, though I'd always believed that Muriel Dane drowned herself long ago. Have you any proof she didn't?"

"Nothing definite, ma'am."

"You are aware she *murdered* my husband in cold blood? I would have liked to see her hanged for her crime. If someone has removed her from the world, I can only say good riddance."

Before I could respond, Lydia darted a glance at me and thrust out her right hand. A black enamel and gold mourning ring encircled her third finger. "This ring never leaves my finger, Miss Hardy. Shall I tell you what the inscription says? *Heaven has in store what thou hast lost.* I've never fully recovered from my loss, and I don't suppose I ever shall. So don't ask me to feel any sympathy for that wicked creature."

"Yes, ma'am, I understand." I could feel my color rising. And yet, in fairness, could I blame the lady? As a virginal girl, Lydia would have married Perry Beldenfield in perfect ignorance of his relationship to Muriel. The shock of his demise so soon after her marriage must have been extreme.

"My father-in-law, Sir Percival, had employed the girl in an act of charity." Lydia's words spilled out. "People told lies about my husband . . . afterward, but I've never doubted him for an instant. He had a noble nature. Everyone loved him—how could they help it? Our romance was the talk of the season."

"Why would Muriel do such a dreadful thing to the son of her benefactor?"

Her eyes flashed. "She must have been mad. Oh, I don't deny

she fell in love with Perry, but I'll never believe he reciprocated her feelings beyond mere flirtation."

"Muriel Dane—" I broke off, reluctant to add to the lady's distress. "Muriel Dane bore a child, ma'am."

"I know what gossip reported," she said. "Still, other men could have been interested in the girl. Another servant, perhaps?"

I kept my polite mask in place, thinking that she rejected reality. No one could doubt her grief for her husband, though I wondered what role wounded pride played in all this ostentatious mourning. I glanced at the mantelpiece where an alabaster and gilt clock ticked away the hours. Did Lydia Beldenfield spend her days confined to rooms like this, imagining what might have been?

"I am sure you're right, ma'am," I said. "You met Muriel Dane in the garden on the day of the murder? It's lucky she didn't try to harm you too. Did she say anything?"

Lydia looked down at her lap. "We don't speak of that day, Miss Hardy. The past should be the past, or so my father-in-law believes. I . . . I strive to heed his wisdom."

Not much of an opening to introduce the topic of Muriel's green bonnet or, for that matter, the handkerchief with the monogram "NFN." I was about to make the attempt anyway when the sound of a raised voice reached us through the open door—a man speaking at full volume.

Lydia's hazel eyes widened, and her dress rustled. "There's nothing more I can do for you. You'd better go."

The man went on berating the person or persons he was addressing. I couldn't hear the words, but the ugliness was unmistakable. My hostess stood up in a sweep of skirts, brushing agitated hands down her body. She yanked the bell-pull to summon the servant.

As the shouting continued, we sat in rigid silence until a slight, brown-haired girl in a maid's uniform appeared at the door. "Yes, ma'am?"

"Why are you answering the bell, Dulcie? Where's John?"

Dulcie kept her eyes on the carpet. "Sir Percival's talking to him and Mr. Thompkins, ma'am."

The hectoring note in the gentleman's voice made my pulse race and aroused a sick feeling. Lydia, however, gave no sign she'd heard her father-in-law, merely speaking to the maid a little louder. "Then you must show this visitor out, Dulcie."

Glad to escape, I rose and thanked her. "Good day, Mrs. Beldenfield." I curtsied.

As soon as the maid and I stepped into the hall, the scolding reached us more clearly. My steps slowed, and I caught a glimpse of the scene taking place in the large dining room. A white-haired gentleman with plump shoulders and fleshy buttocks stood with his back to me. This had to be Sir Percival Beldenfield, Perry Beldenfield's father. He leaned one arm on the mahogany table, brandishing a cane in his other hand, which he poked forward as he spoke. A footman in knee-breeches and the butler who had admitted me faced in my direction. Expressions frozen, gazes blank. The footman noticed me, and a look of shame crossed his handsome features.

"You admitted this woman to the house, Thompkins?" Sir Percival roared.

The butler murmured something indistinguishable.

"How dare you, Thompkins! You are past your work, sirrah. We'll see about your retirement."

"Mrs. Beldenfield—" the butler quavered.

"Never mind Mrs. Beldenfield," Sir Percival said. "You ought to have brought the damned female to me, whoever she is. I am master here and no one else."

Dulcie looked back over her shoulder at me, her dark eyes huge. "Miss."

"I'm coming."

Dulcie led me back the way I'd come in, checking every so often to be sure I followed. We reached the entrance vestibule, and the rest of Sir Percival's diatribe was lost to me. Though I had been anxious to learn more, I hadn't counted on getting the servants into difficulties with their employer. I felt an inconvenient stab of guilt.

"Hurry, miss," whispered Dulcie.

I halted in the middle of the floor to frown in perplexity at the girl. *Why, the child is terrified of him. They all are.* "My pelisse?"

"Yes, miss." Dulcie reached into a closet to retrieve it. Before I could get the thanks out of my mouth, the maid almost pushed me out the door.

Chapter 10

A young man applying for the surgery assistant position came to tea. The candidate, one Josiah Ferris, was seventeen and pimply with a large Adam's apple that bobbed up and down as he swallowed half a dozen pieces of cake, one after the other. He gave somewhat incoherent responses to Papa's medical interrogation and shyly answered Mama's inquiries about his family, not even daring to look at me. Had he known it, this was a point in his favor since my father refused to put up with sheep's eyes being cast at his daughter over the tea-table. On the whole, I thought Mr. Ferris would do.

"A nice boy," Mama said after the candidate had stammered his thanks and departed.

"Another tender morsel for Papa to devour," I said. "Good for three or four mouthfuls at least. He ought to last six months if he doesn't eat us out of house and home first."

Not choosing to dignify this remark with a response, my father returned to his surgery, while Mama went to consult with Granny-Cook about dinner.

A few minutes later, I followed my mother down to the basement, hoping to have a word with the servants about the murdered woman. Entering the kitchen through the swinging doors, I found Granny-Cook seated with her feet in a bucket and a towel draped across her hunched shoulders. Mama, wearing a harassed expression, sat next to her at the scarred deal table, while Phoebe stood at the range, steaming a poultice. Phoebe's pretty mouth was compressed, her face flushed with the heat.

Granny-Cook was a slender woman in her early seventies with snow-white hair and small, bright blue eyes that usually snapped with energy. She also had a dreamy side that sent her to her rocking chair every afternoon to gaze into vacancy. Even Fosco seemed a different cat during these interludes—gentler, more kitten-like. He would curl up in his usual spot under the dresser, paws protruding. Granny-Cook tolerated his presence, claiming he was a good mouser. Neither cat nor serenity was in evidence today.

Granny looked up when she saw me. "Miss Esther, maybe *you* can speak to Phoebe. The silly chit will be sorry she didn't treat me with proper respect when I'm gone."

"Balderdash," Phoebe retorted, wielding her new favorite word. "Here I am making up a bran poultice for your bunions, aren't I? Who else can you get to do that? If that isn't showing proper respect, I don't know what is."

"Of course Phoebe respects you," Mama put in. "And you won't be going anywhere for years to come, Granny-Cook, though I understand that the aches and pains of age can be a bit . . . trying."

"A soak and a poultice will fix you right up, Granny-Cook," I said.

Granny-Cook lifted one of her feet from the bucket to examine the inflamed joint. Grimacing, she plunged the foot back into the warm water, but not before sending a fulminating look toward Phoebe. "Ask her—they'll be at the door soon."

"At the door?" my mother echoed. "Why, who can you mean?"

I was just as puzzled. Granny-Cook couldn't mean the undertakers coming to cart off her lifeless body? Because of her *bunions*?

Phoebe flipped the poultice in the pan. "She's been talking like a crazy person ever since we had the police in our kitchen, ma'am. Which was bad enough, I grant you. But you try getting any sense out of her! She bit my head off when I asked her what was amiss. All I did was inquire whether she happened to see Alice Denton when she went back to the market that day."

"Told you I didn't, Phoebe, just like I told the inspector." Granny-Cook's skinny bosom heaved.

Mama and I exchanged a startled glance.

"Granny-Cook didn't see Muriel . . . I mean Alice after the attack," I said. "I myself answered the front door when the cab driver rang the bell."

Phoebe shook her head. "That policeman is no fool, as anyone can see. He knew something wasn't right."

Granny-Cook addressed Mama. "Can't argue with the chit there, ma'am."

Mama closed her eyes for a moment, as if gathering her patience. "We appear to be speaking at cross purposes." She held up a hand before anyone could respond. "No, don't answer yet, Granny-Cook. Phoebe, I think that poultice is hot enough. You can help apply it, then please go upstairs and beat the hearthrug for me, won't you? I thought it seemed a little dusty."

The girl obeyed. She carried the poultice over to the older woman, stooped to lift Granny-Cook's feet from the bucket, and dried them with the towel. As the poultice was bound to Granny's left foot, the lines of pain in her brow relaxed. During this process, Phoebe's face remained downcast, but her touch was gentle, and she made certain to bring Granny-Cook a fresh cup of tea before retrieving the wicker rug beater.

"Sending me to beat a perfectly clean rug. I don't know what this house is coming to lately, and that's a fact," Phoebe muttered as she went out the door. Which Mama and I pretended not to hear.

When the maid was gone, my mother said, "Now we can chat undisturbed. We've established that you haven't been feeling quite the thing, Granny-Cook. Perhaps my husband ought to have a look at you."

"Who's to mind about my health where I might be going, ma'am? That's why I say my days are numbered." Granny-Cook sipped her tea.

"Things aren't so bad as that," I said. "We'll wrap you in cotton wool until you feel better."

Frowning at this inanity, Granny-Cook turned back to my mother. "I meant, what if I have to leave our Bert? Oh, I don't doubt you and the doctor would look after the boy, Mrs. Hardy. But he's used to me, and the poor child has lost enough. Perhaps I'd better say no more in present company, ma'am."

Mama gave her an encouraging smile. "You can speak openly in front of Esther, Granny-Cook. Mr. Hardy and I have told her the truth about Bert, as we ought to have done long since."

I was determined to be equally generous. "You and Papa had good reasons for your secrecy, Mama." Joining them at the table, I added, "Yes, do tell us what's wrong, Granny-Cook. Did Inspector Jessup frighten you with his questions?"

Our cook bit her lower lip. "I suppose he did, Miss Esther. And with good reason—people are starting to talk. When I went to the shops today, the tongues were wagging. The baker's boy was going on about some journalist fellow asking questions about the family."

"What sorts of questions?" I asked.

"The kind of folk we are and who lives in our house. Questions about Alice Denton too." Granny-Cook tugged at her cap.

"It'll die down in a few days," my mother said. "I don't think we have anything to worry about. In any event, you mustn't exaggerate the problem. It's not good for you."

"No, ma'am. It's just . . . this affair has Phoebe in a twitter too, as you saw for yourself."

Mama nodded. "I think she feels excluded. I'll have a word with her, Granny-Cook. It's time she knew about Bert. I trust her completely."

"Maybe so, ma'am. But sometimes, that girl lacks every one of the wits the Lord blessed her with. She's got me thinking the worst too."

Mama and I glanced at each other again. Our servants mostly got along well, though Granny-Cook was sometimes hard on Phoebe when her efforts didn't rise to the cook's standards. Phoebe might respond with hours of the silent treatment or take the rebuke in stride and sing at her work ten minutes later. One never knew.

"Phoebe does enjoy her high drama." I reached over to pat Granny-Cook's hand. "She's been worse since she stopped walking out with her young man."

"To be sure, miss. She burst out crying and scurried out of the kitchen when I scolded her yesterday. Made me scorch the potatoes, I was that riled. How would *you* feel if you expected to be dragged off to prison?"

"The authorities have no reason to arrest you," Mama said in bewilderment.

"I wish you'd convince Phoebe of that, ma'am. She acts like maybe I popped that woman over the head myself. When Inspector Jessup was talking to us, Phoebe kept giving me such looks. I wanted to shake her until her teeth rattled."

"How utterly absurd to suspect you," I said.

Granny-Cook drew a shaky breath. "Well, I suppose I'd better tell you ladies all about it. Phoebe has a bee in her bonnet because she knows that Alice Denton and I had words. I good as lied to the police about it too." Embarrassment registered on the older woman's face. "Truth is, I finally told Alice to clear off. I shouldn't have acted without your permission, Mrs. Hardy."

"When was this?" my mother said in a hollow voice. No doubt she was envisaging another confession to Scotland Yard.

"Thursday last, before the business in Southwark, ma'am. Alice came down to my kitchen and tried to dictate terms. I wasn't having it, and you can't blame me, even if she was Bert's mama."

I leaned my elbows on the table. "Yes, I spoke to her at the door that day. What did she want, Granny-Cook? It could be important."

"Why, she said she was grateful I'd done right by the boy and warned me to keep him close." Her pause was ominous. "While I still could."

Mama stared at her in horror. "Oh, Granny-Cook. We never told you the whole story. Her name wasn't Alice at all—but rather Muriel. Muriel Dane. She was once accused of killing a man."

"Lord sakes, ma'am. I didn't think she was that bad. She ought to have left the boy alone long ago. What good could she ever do for him? It was selfish, that's what. I sent her off with a flea in her ear and felt dreadful when I heard she'd been murdered. And I was scared the police might look in my direction if they found out we'd argued."

"Are you certain Alice meant to threaten you?" I said.

Granny-Cook's eyes filled. "I didn't know what to think, Miss Esther. I wasn't taking any chances." Tears leaked down her cheeks, and she dashed them away without seeming aware of them. "I was afraid to say anything. Where would I be if the police arrested me or you dismissed me in disgrace? I've no legal claim to my boy."

My mother hastened to reassure her. "That will never happen. Don't worry, Granny-Cook. If necessary, we'll mention the matter to Inspector Jessup ourselves. You won't be in any trouble."

Granny-Cook gave a watery smile, got to her feet, and hobbled toward the range. "I'm glad I got the nasty business off my conscience. Now, if you ladies want dinner on the table tonight, you'll have to excuse me. Besides, Bert will be home soon. He mustn't see me like this."

～

Mama and I went our separate ways: Mama to smooth things over with Phoebe and I to help my father with his correspondence. After dinner, Bert and I played a game of beggar-my-neighbor for an hour. Then I threw down my cards and escaped to my bedchamber, where I brushed my teeth and gave my hair its one hundred strokes. Once I'd bundled myself into a flannel night-gown and put on heavy woolen socks, I climbed under the bedcovers to wait.

Ten minutes later, the visitor I had been expecting arrived. Wearing a frilly nightcap, my mother slipped into the room. Her face, smeared with night cream, showed that hopeful look that said she was eager for a chat.

"Are you awake, Esther? Where's Fosco?"

"Granny-Cook must have let him out to do his business."

"He'll deposit his filth on Miss Meadows' garden path. Why didn't you lock him up?"

"Would you prefer he topple my ink bottle or score my bedroom door with his claws?"

"That cat is menace enough to suit his name," Mama said.

I could not disagree. Count Fosco was the oily villain in Wilkie Collins' *The Woman in White*, which we had read the prior winter. The fictional Fosco was an Italian aristocrat. His namesake was an enormous gray-striped feline who'd shown up at the kitchen door, meowing piteously until I weakened and fed him some scraps. I had soon learned that the two Foscos had much in common. Both were stout and slyly intent on their own purposes. Both had a fondness for birds, which, in the cat's case, resulted in the pitiful creatures being left half alive on our doorstep. And the cat's origins were as mysterious as the count's. I could not fathom how a gutter animal had become so sleek. For all I knew, my Fosco's origins were aristocratic too.

I lifted the blanket. "Never mind, Mama. Fosco can fend for himself. Get in bed with me. The tip of your nose is quite blue."

Padding across the carpet, she kicked off her slippers and climbed in.

"Mind, no cold feet on my legs," I said. "And no face cream all over the sheets."

With twin sighs of pleasure, we snuggled under the covers and turned in unison toward each other.

Mama studied me. "This has all been rather extraordinary, hasn't it?"

That was an understatement, I reflected, as I traced my finger over the bow under my mother's chin. So much had changed in just a few days, and I felt like a different person. I knew that my mother had been worried about me. Who knew better than a mother when one's daughter required occupation and a change of scene? But the choices for any woman like me were limited, for what could she do but seek a teaching post? I scoffed inwardly, imagining a schoolroom full of spoiled brats whose parents had taught them to despise their governess. That would really be putting the fat into the fire. Instead, I was playing detective.

"I wish Granny-Cook had extracted a more intelligible tale from Muriel. I don't believe she meant to threaten anyone, do you?" I said.

"Do you think she intended to tell the Beldenfields about Bert?"

"The son of an accused murderess? They'd want nothing to do with him."

"A child with Beldenfield blood," Mama reminded me. "What kind of monster visits the sins of the parents on an innocent?"

"Muriel deprived Mrs. Beldenfield of her husband and prevented her from having his children, Mama."

As accurately as possible, I described the grieving widow and her bellicose father-in-law. Unfortunately, my impressions sounded muddled and contradictory. My mother listened as I shared my speculations about Muriel's bonnet and the mono-grammed handkerchief—we were no closer to grasping the signifi-cance of either. There was also the gentleman from the inquest whose role in this affair remained a mystery.

"Do you suppose he's a Beldenfield connection?" I said.

"A relation or a family friend?"

"Perhaps he can tell us more about Mrs. Beldenfield. She still wears a mourning ring on her finger. Surely a woman of her wealth and social position could have left her past behind. She was so young when Perry Beldenfield died."

The candle flame flickered in my mother's eyes, and I glimpsed something hidden and raw I would have preferred not to see. "Your father always says that if anything ever happens to him, I'm to go on with my life," Mama said. "He doesn't approve of lengthy mourning. I wonder if I'd have the strength."

"Of course you would. Besides, Papa's as strong as a horse. To return to the fair Lydia, she must have hated Muriel more than anyone in the world. A good motive for murder."

Mama shook her head. "I can't see a lady like that having the nerve."

"Why not? She might have avenged her husband's death. Or Sir Percival could have killed Muriel himself. One of them could have met her in the churchyard."

"What about Perry Beldenfield's murder? Is it possible—" My mother interrupted herself, then continued. "I was debating whether Sir Percival could have killed his son in a rage. Yet that doesn't seem at all likely, dear. Perry was Sir Percival's heir, a promising young man for whom he'd just arranged a brilliant match."

I leaned my cheek on my hand. "You're right, Mama, but what if Perry had refused to give Muriel up and his father feared a scandal? Sir Percival has a horrible temper."

I was about to develop this theme when a yowl split the silence—*Fosco*. Many Londoners seemed to find cats disgusting because of their role as rat exterminators. I didn't know anyone besides our family who kept one as a pet. At times like this, I wondered if Fosco was worth it.

"What did I tell you?" my mother cried. "That cat will awaken Papa, who needs his rest. He's been fretting about this Muriel

Dane affair, and we have the decision to make about Mr. Ferris as well. You'll have to go down."

My flesh shrank at the prospect, but a second piercing yowl quickly followed the first. What in God's name was the animal doing this time?

Mama kicked me under the covers. "Esther, he'll rouse everyone on the street."

I threw back the covers, disloyally enjoying my mother's gasp as the chill air hit her. For the second time in as many days, I donned my dressing gown and boots, lit a second candle from the first, and left the room, saying, "Wait for me. Don't you dare fall asleep in my bed."

Downstairs, as soon as I cracked open the area door to the outside, I saw that the weather had worsened. Thick fog swirled so that I couldn't see more than a foot in front of me. I stepped into the mist's clammy embrace and groped my way up the stairs.

Gaining the street level, I peered into the gloom. Useless. The nearest street lamp emitted a sickly yellow glow that made it impossible to see much, and my teeth had begun to chatter. Picturing Mama upstairs in her warm cocoon, I was about to give up my mission when I heard a low, feral growl. Crouching, I swept my hand in ever-widening circles until I bumped up against something solid and human. A trousered leg. I was so amazed I dropped my candle. Fosco hissed. I grabbed for the cat and managed to snatch a tuft of fur before I felt the animal streak away.

"Confound it!" shouted Bert's high, clear voice. "Got me good that time."

I stooped to pick up my extinguished candle. "You frightened me, boy. What are you doing out here?"

"Same as you," he said.

"I warned you to leave Fosco alone," I scolded. "Let's go inside before we freeze. We won't catch him tonight."

"I can get him, miss." But Bert accompanied me down the stairs and into the kitchen.

The room was pleasantly warm, lit only by the banked fire in the kitchen range. A tendril of fog that had accompanied us into the house dissipated into the coal-scented air. I relit my candle, and Bert and I examined each other like two conspirators. He pushed up his sleeve. A long scratch snaked up his wrist and forearm, sluggish blood welling. He prodded his wound and rubbed his hand on his coat.

"Granny-Cook will be furious that you left the house," I said.

I was about to fetch the medical supplies. His next words stopped me. "Dark doings, miss. A woman put to bed with a shovel. And . . . *him*."

Suspicion flared. "What were you really doing outside?"

"I saw a man from the window and wanted a better look."

"Saw *who*, Bert?"

"I don't know, just a man. I couldn't see much. Maybe he thinks we killed Alice. Or he killed her himself and is drawn back because of his guilt."

"Alice wasn't set upon in our house. You've been reading too many penny bloods."

Bert rolled his eyes at my smug tone. "I watched from the window until it got too foggy. Then I went down to make certain he'd gone. When I was coming back, I tripped over your cat, miss. Thought I'd do you a favor and collar the animal."

There had been altogether too much interest in us since Muriel's death. If Bert had seen a night-watcher, could it have been the gentleman I caught lurking outside the house the other night? Or even the man who searched Muriel's rooms? Our address had been in the newspaper . . .

I sighed. "How could you be so reckless, Bert? I'll have to tell Granny-Cook and my parents about this in the morning."

The boy looked as though I'd kicked him or, worse, destroyed his faith in humanity. His dark eyelashes fluttered as he scowled at the floor. In a year or two, he would lose his cherubic face and sweet voice. He would be apprenticed to a tailor or perhaps a law office, an unsuitable career for a gallant boy who hated confinement. And I would miss him.

"You shouldn't do that," Bert finally said. "They'll say you've been encouraging me."

I went to get a basin of water, some linen, and a sticking plaster. "You'll disgrace yourself in your lessons tomorrow if you stay up so late," I said as I set to work on the scratch. "Promise to let me manage Fosco, as well as any mysterious night-watchers, in the future?"

"I'm not going to school tomorrow, Miss Esther. One of the boys has got . . . *dipterium*, and your papa's keeping me home."

"Diphtheria. Nonetheless, you must mind me." I grasped the boy's wrist to emphasize my point. "I'll box your ears myself if I catch you out of bed at night a second time."

CHAPTER 11

I was dusting the consulting room the next morning when Mama appeared in the doorway. "Are you finished, Esther? Mrs. Jardain should be arriving for her appointment."

Mrs. Jardain was a nervous young woman who was pregnant with her first child. These days, she saw the doctor anytime she experienced so much as a twinge.

"Coming, Mama," I said.

My mother lingered as I swirled my dust cloth a few more times. Mama, pink-cheeked and well rested, wore the blue merino dress I liked, the one that erased her years. Her thick, unruly hair, which as yet showed no gray, was arranged in a coil at the back of her head. *She ought to be chipper*, I thought a little sourly. She'd been sound asleep in my bed when I went back upstairs the prior night and had not returned to her own room until dawn. Now she watched me with an expectant expression.

"Yes?" I said with a lift of my brows.

"A boy delivered a message for you." My mother took a piece of paper from her apron pocket. "He gave it to Phoebe."

I crossed the carpet to snatch the message. I read its few lines, written in a wavering hand with many misspellings. "It's from Rose, Mama. A gentleman called Samuel Godwin has written to the landlady Mrs. Carver about the arrangements for Muriel. He intends to call in Burton Street this morning at ten."

"Is he the same person who searched her rooms?"

"I don't think so. According to Rose, Mrs. Carver's caller was not of that class."

Silence fell.

"What should we do?" Mama asked.

"*We*, Mama?"

"Well, I suppose I mean you." She stuck her nose in the air.

I amused myself by ticking off the emotions crossing my mother's face. Irritation. Trepidation. Excitement. Trepidation again. And under it all, I could read her never-spoken fear that every time her daughter walked out the door, there was always a very small chance she would not come back again. Mama had lost one child. Why not another? Nor did it matter how old I got. That would never change.

"What are you going to do?" she said.

"Take my walk in that direction," I said gently. "Then come straight home and tell you all about it."

When I stood in the entryway, putting on my cloak and bonnet, Bert popped up from the basement.

"Ready, miss?"

"Ready for what?"

"I heard your mama telling Mr. Hardy you had an errand this morning. She'll want me to go with you."

"Not today, Bert."

My complications were multiplying like fleas on a goat. Bert had been unusually naughty the last few days, perhaps because he viewed Alice-Muriel as an eccentric stranger whose death he found compelling for unknown reasons. Well, she was his mother. Was it possible he sensed a bond between them? Or was he just caught up in recent events? I had warned my parents about the watcher outside our house the night before, though my papa was inclined to attribute the incident to Bert's fertile imagination.

"I've finished my chores," Bert said in the same wheedling tone. "Granny-Cook wants me out from under her feet since I didn't go to school today. Please, miss." He fixed melting blue eyes on mine, and I had a glimpse of how he might appear in ten years, young ladies hanging on his every word.

"Maybe next time. I'm just going to speak to someone for a few minutes. You'd be bored." Steeling myself to disregard his crestfallen face, I departed.

I made short work of the walk to Burton Street despite the slush and mud. I'd decided to avoid the rude landlady and instead knocked at the kitchen door. If I also hoped to get a look at this Mr. Godwin, that would have to depend on circumstances.

Mrs. Carver's cook opened the area door. Her hands were covered in flour, her cheeks red from the heat of the oven. "Rose isn't here, miss. The mistress sent her on an errand. Can I give her a message?"

Reading curiosity in the woman's eyes, I hastened to say, "Nothing important. A small matter in regard to our conversation the other day. My name is Esther Hardy. Perhaps Rose might call at my father's house sometime? She has my direction."

After thanking the woman, I turned away. What next? Mr. Godwin was not due to arrive for another few minutes, so I positioned myself at the window of the greengrocer across the way. The shopkeeper had made his display festive for the Christmas season with tired greens and wrinkled holly berries. As I waited, a woman with an enormous shopping basket, a man with a tray of muffins, and two boys chasing a hoop came by.

I was stamping my chilled feet to restore my circulation when my glance fell on a gentleman with a dog at his heels. I watched him as he walked down the street with a loping grace, his hair curling over his collar. Tan overcoat, unbuttoned. Top hat in his hand rather than on his head. A restless countenance dominated by those parenthetical side-whiskers and eyes that seemed to sweep everywhere at once, taking in the people, the buildings, the sky.

He stopped to smile at a tiny girl who'd darted out from a doorway to pet the dog, a lovely cocker spaniel with a glossy ginger coat and drooping ears. It seemed the gentleman felt my interest, for he looked up at me by the grocery window. His face lit with recognition. He said goodbye to the child and swerved toward me, dog in tow.

The accusing words flew out of my mouth. "You were outside my house the other night. I saw you at the inquest too."

"This meeting is fortuitous, Miss Hardy," he said. "I'm calling on Muriel's landlady to discuss the funeral and the bestowal of any property. I went to the morgue to identify the body and saw the clergyman of St. George's this morning. The churchyard is closed to new burials, though Reverend Walsh has made an exception. He offers a corner where Muriel may be at rest."

The flood of information overwhelmed me. He spoke as if we'd already met, as if we resumed an earlier conversation.

"Who are you, sir?" I demanded.

He grinned. "I got ahead of myself, didn't I? I am Samuel Godwin, nephew to Sir Percival Beldenfield. I believe you visited my cousin-in-law, Mrs. Beldenfield."

So that was it. My mysterious gentleman was indeed a Beldenfield. Why was he making the arrangements for Muriel Dane? Didn't he loathe her like the rest of his kin?

"You're Perry Beldenfield's cousin, sir? I've read about his murder."

"You and everyone else in London."

"There's no longer any doubt? Alice Denton was, in truth, Muriel Dane?"

His eyes darkened. "None whatever, Miss Hardy. You see, I knew her well."

Both of us froze at the sound of running footsteps. Then Bert was at my side, eyes ablaze with determination.

Drat the boy. Where had he come from? He'd followed me here, and I hadn't even noticed. Fine detective I was. This was too much—the boy deserved a spanking or, at the very least, a thunderous scolding.

"Wicked, disobedient child." I reached for his arm. "We're going home. This time, I'll make sure Granny-Cook punishes you." I needed to get Bert away from Mr. Godwin, though I was angry about the lost opportunity to pursue my inquiries.

The boy evaded my grip to plant himself in front of me. The dog began to bark as Godwin regarded us, clearly perplexed. As he looked Bert over, my unease grew.

"Who's that, miss?" Bert pointed at the gentleman.

"You appear to think I mean your mistress harm." Godwin reached down with a gloved hand to restrain his pet. "Quiet, Lola."

Lola subsided, eyeing me with a baleful expression.

"This is our cook's boy," I said. "He's appointed himself my protector."

Godwin glanced around the peaceful street. "And do you require such protection, ma'am?"

"That was you outside our house last night, wasn't it? What did you mean by it?" Bert said.

I felt myself blush. "Bert!"

"No, Bert," the gentleman replied, his tone grave. "It's true that I passed by your house a few days ago and met Miss Hardy in the street. I often take long walks at night when I can't sleep. Last night, however, I was tucked up in my bed. What did you see?"

"A man in the fog. He got away."

"So you couldn't haul him off to the constable? How ungenerous of him to escape." He smiled at Bert but sobered almost at once. "It does seem important to discover who it was and what his motives may have been. You think the incident connected to the recent murder?"

"Bound to be. You believe me, sir?" Bert flashed a look of triumph at me. Obviously, my papa's skepticism had bruised his feelings when he told his tale at breakfast.

"I do. It's sensible of you to keep watch over Miss Hardy," Godwin said.

Although I was wishing Bert anyplace else, my lips twitched. It was comical to see the boy's animosity dissipate like a puff of smoke. He was flattered at being consulted, and there was also the dog. Bert had dropped to his knees to stroke the silken ears, seeming to decide that any fellow who owned such a magnificent creature could not be an out-and-out villain. I was much less certain of that—the gentleman's manners were entirely too charming. And the dog was yapping again.

"She doesn't like you, miss," Bert said.

"I'm afraid Lola doesn't always appreciate grown-up young ladies and their skirts." Godwin pulled on Lola's collar, but not before the spaniel had left a line of spittle on my boots.

"We mustn't keep you, Mr. Godwin," I said. "Bert's granny will be wondering what's become of him."

Godwin's shrewd glance rested on me, and he nodded. He was quick; I would grant him that. He'd intuited that I didn't want him to speak of Muriel Dane in front of the boy. "I have a proposal for you, Miss Hardy," he said. "I'd planned to tie up Lola outside the lodging-house while I complete my business. It occurs to me that she would be much happier if Bert took her for a stroll. Will you allow the boy to escort Lola to Charlotte Street, and I'll come collect her in, say, an hour? Perhaps you would be at liberty to receive me for a few minutes?"

"I'll look after Lola, sir." Joy suffused Bert's face.

Godwin's lurking smile was back. "She won't bite you, ma'am."

"I'm not scared of your dog," I said.

～

Escorting Lola made Bert's day. When we got home, he dashed off to display his prize to Granny-Cook and Phoebe while I ran around like a madwoman, tidying the parlor. No chance to warn Mama about our visitor as she was busy helping my father in the surgery. I built up the fire, hid my papa's old slippers under the sofa, and put *Les Trois Mousquetaires* in its place behind the cushion in case Mr. Godwin happened to disapprove of ladies reading adventure novels.

True to his word, Samuel Godwin rang the bell less than an hour after we'd parted. When I opened the door, Miss Meadows' housemaid was scrubbing her stoop. The maid drank in every detail of Mr. Godwin's appearance, and I saw another face pressed against the window of the house across the street. In an hour, it would be all over the neighborhood that Esther Hardy had a gentleman caller.

"Come in, sir," I said. "My parents are busy at this hour, but won't you come upstairs to the parlor? Bert and Lola are down in the kitchen."

Godwin stepped into the hall with its aroma of camphor and the carpet worn by many feet. Mama's voice reached us through the closed surgery door. She was talking to one of the patients, who seemed a little deaf. I took Godwin's coat and shiny silk topper and hung them on the coat tree.

"I trust Lola has behaved herself," he said. "Was that your cat I saw in the street when I passed by the other night?"

"Fosco can defend himself, sir."

He grinned. "Count Fosco, eh? Perhaps you're right."

In the parlor, Godwin took the chair I indicated. I noticed him making a discreet inspection and found myself viewing our world through his eyes. I was a woman a few years short of thirty in a brown dress with a modest hoop and pagoda sleeves. Attractive enough but out of fashion, both the dress and the woman. Mr. Godwin absorbed our somewhat shabby furnishings, my mother's overflowing mending basket, and the rows of well-thumbed books in the alcove bookcase. Not to mention the poorly embroidered fire screen that had been one of my less successful projects and the grinning-goblin fire irons I'd stumbled on in a shop and insisted on buying. The man missed nothing. I pictured him in his luxurious Portman Square mansion and felt like the crow to his swan.

"We have much to discuss," he said.

With an effort, I threw off my tongue-tied shyness. "Did your business with Mrs. Carver prosper?"

"I learned nothing beyond what we heard at the inquest. Mrs. Carver agreed to dispose of Muriel's belongings."

"And picked your pocket for the privilege?"

"Afraid so. I checked for important papers but found nothing."

"The police must have removed them, sir. Or it could have been the 'friend' who searched her rooms the evening of the murder before the authorities arrived."

His brows went up. "You are well informed, Miss Hardy. Who was this person?"

"I have no idea. And yet I wonder if his name might be Finch Norwood—he was the witness who supposedly saw Muriel jump in the Thames. He once lied for her sake."

"In which case, I must tell you that a scoundrel insinuated himself into my cousin-in-law Mrs. Beldenfield's presence a few days before Muriel's death. He told Mrs. Beldenfield he was prepared to offer proof her husband's murderess was still alive. She tossed him out after he demanded a large sum. What if it was the same man?"

"Blackmail?"

"Of a sort, Miss Hardy. Mrs. Beldenfield is a wealthy woman. That's why when you yourself called in Portman Square, also in regard to Muriel Dane, I'm afraid my uncle assumed the worst about you." Godwin tilted his head, and a gleam appeared in his dark eyes.

I couldn't put my finger on just what it was about his behavior that seemed so different from any other gentleman I'd ever met. "I'm sorry to have provoked Sir Percival," I said, my tone demure.

"Provoking my uncle is easily done." Godwin's good humor died with his next words. "Could this man be Muriel's killer?"

"Perhaps." I was too caught up in the conversation, too excited to hear what Godwin thought about the case, and very near to forgetting we'd just met. "Wouldn't a blackmailer need her alive if he hoped to profit from her capture?"

He considered that. "I suppose you're right. At all events, we must hope the authorities will uncover word of the fellow in the rookery near the church."

"You intend to inform Scotland Yard about this development?"

"Yes, and give Inspector Jessup a description of the man. How else can the police hope to solve the crime?" He leaned back in his chair, seeming in no hurry to depart. "I've been wanting to ask you, Miss Hardy. Why did Bert suspect me of sinister motives merely for passing by your house the other night? I'd read the story about Muriel's death in the paper. I admit I was . . . curious. But I hesitated to speak to you in the dark."

"I was looking for my cat. As for Bert, he has a vivid imagination, sir."

"I don't like it. From what you've just told me, someone is still interested in Muriel. Bert was right—the situation could prove dangerous." He paused. "Boys of that age can be a handful. By the way, how old is the child?"

I tensed. "We'll leave Bert to his granny and my father." To distract Godwin, I detailed my dealings with the cabman Billings, along with describing Reverend Walsh's encounters with Muriel Dane. "Back then, her life seemed to have taken a turn for the better. How tragic she returned to the church years later and was murdered."

Godwin dangled his arms between his knees, a faraway expression stealing over his face. "Were you with Muriel at the end? Did she say anything to you, Miss Hardy? Anything at all about who did this to her?"

"She . . . was in a stupor, sir." Which was true. Muriel Dane had taken her secrets to the grave.

"A shame."

I frowned. "You mystify me, Mr. Godwin. Muriel is accused of murdering your cousin. You could consign her to a pauper's grave and spit on it afterward. Yet you attend her inquest and make her funeral arrangements."

He sucked in a breath. "I want the matter settled. For everyone's sake, but mostly for my cousin. For Perry."

How was that supposed to happen? Perry Beldenfield had been dead for over a decade.

"I don't believe the matter can be settled unless her killer is caught and punished," I said. "Whoever she was, whatever she did, she did not deserve a violent end."

"Selfish acts unleash an uncontrollable evil."

"Sir?"

"That's what Perry said to me. I assumed he was referring to his own selfishness in destroying Muriel's innocence."

"She returned the favor, didn't she? I mean, she destroyed *him*."

Godwin tapped his toe on the carpet and rubbed one finger down his cheek, as if speaking of the dead woman disturbed him in some profound way. Wherever his thoughts took him was not a pleasant place. He stared over my head.

I prompted him. "The evil your cousin spoke of found Muriel herself. Some would call that justice, Mr. Godwin."

"Justice? No, never that." He looked at me, his eyes somber. "You must be wary, Miss Hardy. I fear evil isn't through with us yet."

Chapter 12

I lost my chance to press Godwin on the meaning of this extraordinary statement when the door opened and Mama came in. He rose at once to greet her. She welcomed the visitor with a spring in her step, beaming cordiality. No one would call my mother an ambitious woman, but she unconsciously responded to any youngish gentleman in my orbit. Even a man connected to two murders, which, according to Mr. Godwin posed a threat to all of us.

I was well aware that ever since the Benedict Caxton affair, Mama had burned to stick a finger in the eye of my former betrothed. Over her one "medicinal" glass of wine in the evenings, she sometimes daydreamed about walking into Caxton's church on the arm of an impressive son-in-law. I always countered that it would be too cruel to inflict one of Benedict's sermons on this mythical person. As I compared Benedict to Samuel Godwin, the solution to my earlier conundrum leapt to my mind. Benedict was abrasive, lordly, and dismissive of any opinions not his own. Godwin, though of a much higher position in society, behaved as if he actually wanted to hear a woman's views. Dangerous.

Mama recalled me to the present. "Esther, why haven't you

rung for tea?" She flew to the bell-rope to remedy the oversight. "Did I hear a dog barking?"

Godwin smiled. "That's my Lola, ma'am. Your boy is minding her in the kitchen. She won't disturb your husband's patients?"

"Not at all." Begging him to be seated again, she responded to his questions about her family. She told him about her childhood as a farmer's daughter in a Yorkshire village, where she'd met Theodore Hardy, the son of a London jeweler who'd been apprenticed to a local surgeon.

"We were young, and neither side of the family approved of the match." Mama gave a rueful laugh. "Not that we let that stop us. Oh, we struggled in the early years, Mr. Godwin, until my husband's career was better established. But I've never regretted my choice."

"Your husband is a lucky man, ma'am."

At my mother's prompting, Godwin spoke about his own family. His father, the Italian music teacher, and his mother, the English girl, sister of a baronet.

Smooth, Mama, very smooth, I thought, as she extracted information from our guest, who seemed far more relaxed with her. Phoebe brought in the tea-tray with macaroons on our best china. The girl glided to the table with a stately step, though excitement oozed from her pores. Mama sent her away and poured the tea herself.

"How old were you when you lost your mother, Mr. Godwin?" she inquired when we were seated at the table.

"Four years old, ma'am. Unfortunately, I have but few distinct memories of her. Her hair tickling my face while she held me. Her laugh and the silly clapping game we used to play. Little more than that. She died of consumption."

"And your father?"

He shrugged. "Still alive in Italy, I presume. He does not write to me."

Mama's hand twitched, as if she would have liked to pat his arm. Thankfully, she restrained herself. After a short silence, she went on in a nonchalant tone. "Did your mother reside with your uncle in Portman Square before her marriage?"

He nibbled a macaroon. "Yes, my mother—Sophia was her name, ma'am—managed Sir Percival's household and served as his hostess back in the day when he used to give grand parties. He believed she was content. I suppose she fell in love, though it happened rather quickly, I gather. She was just eighteen when she and my father ran away."

"I hope your parents were happy in the time they had," Mama said.

I drank my tea, content to observe. More and more, I couldn't account for Mr. Godwin. He seemed not to care that he spoke of personal topics to strangers, addressing my mother in an eager voice, leaning forward to answer each question almost before she finished asking it.

"My uncle didn't bargain on his heir dying so young," he said. "Or on being left with a half-Italian nephew who can't inherit the estate. He once intended to have me trained in the law so I'd have some profession. Perry's death changed everything, Mrs. Hardy. I'm an idle sort of fellow these days."

Mama smiled in sympathy. "You must miss your cousin, sir."

"If it hadn't been for Perry, I'd have stowed away on a ship bound for Italy long since. I confess I would like to discover what befell his child."

I observed the moment when the problem of Bert rushed back to my mother. Not only did Bert have another family, but a wealthy and well-connected one at that. She widened her eyes, murmured something appropriate, and changed the subject.

Mama and Mr. Godwin were discussing a shared interest in music when his face brightened. "As it happens, I will host a small concert in Portman Square on Saturday, ma'am. Singers will perform glees, and we'll have a pantomime skit, capping off the evening with a supper. I'd be honored if you and your family would attend."

He cast a mischievous glance at me. Was this supposed to be

my chance for further detection? The gentleman took a lot for granted.

"That sounds delightful." My mother seemed as taken aback as I was. "I'm afraid Mr. Hardy's practice has been short-handed. He's often busy in the evenings." Her gaze swung toward me. "However, my daughter and I would enjoy the outing. Do you agree, dear?"

"Thank you for the invitation, sir," I said. "Yes, it sounds like a pleasant diversion."

He bowed from his seat. "Your presence will enliven the occasion, Miss Hardy."

Godwin finished his tea and made conversation for another five minutes. When he rose to depart, I flew to the kitchen to retrieve Lola, ignoring her indignant barks. The gentleman soon settled the issue by shouting for her down the stairwell.

"I'll see you on Saturday?" he said, while Lola fawned over her master as if they'd been separated for an eternity.

"I hardly think your uncle will approve."

"But I do, Miss Hardy." Godwin frowned down at his great-coat, started to button it, and stopped. "I've begun to realize that grief can harden into something that festers. Perhaps the Belden-fields would benefit from a . . . fresh perspective." He moved to the door. "Will you come, Miss Hardy? Saturday, eight o'clock."

"Eight o'clock," I agreed.

Godwin stooped to adjust his dog's collar. "You've spoiled my trousers, Lola." In another of his swift mood changes, he grinned at me. "Nothing new in that."

After the door had closed behind them, I went slowly upstairs. Would my mother wish to attend Mr. Godwin's soiree once she heard about his warning of dangers ahead? Remembering that bleak expression in his eyes made me thoughtful until more practical considerations intervened.

I had no gown to wear to the concert.

∾

Sir Percival Beldenfield came into the library at Beldenfield House. His cheeks with their prominent veins were wind-reddened, his white hair tousled. He drew off his driving gloves, tossing them onto the table. "There you are," he said to his nephew.

Samuel Godwin sat in an armchair by the crackling fire with Lola asleep across his feet. For once, his memories had been peaceful as he petted his dog and sucked in the familiar aromas of leather and linseed oil. Here, in this quiet room, Muriel Dane's ghost had become as much a part of the furnishings as the rows of gilt-edged books and the statuary busts. Those soft blue eyes that had looked at him with compassion. The way she put aside the yellowed family papers that consumed her hours and rose gracefully when she saw him. The way her delicate hands left streaks of dust down her skirt.

May I help you with something, sir? Were you looking for your uncle?

He never was. He would fumble for excuses to explain his presence. A book he wanted to read. An urge to relax in one of the cushioned chairs. An impulse to discover if Muriel knew whether the first post had arrived. Or the second, third, or fourth. Any reason at all to linger by her side.

Now Sir Percival peered at him in suspicion, his leonine head sinking over his chest, too heavy to hold erect. As usual, Godwin's idleness annoyed him. "Did you see the police?" he said. "Was it Muriel's corpse?"

"Yes, uncle."

"Good. That's over and done with. Look to the future, eh?"

Godwin shook his head. "I think we must be prepared for the wretch who harassed Lydia to cause further trouble. He's unlikely to give up so easily, and since he can no longer hope to profit from Muriel's arrest, he may try to sell his information to the papers. It's a titillating story, you must admit, sir. Muriel Dane evaded the authorities for a decade."

Alarm showed on Sir Percival's face. "Nonsense, Samuel. How can the blackguard be any threat?"

"And Muriel's child?"

"What does the bastard child of a murderess have to do with us? Besides, Muriel probably disposed of the brat like she murdered my son."

"We've never understood what drove her to it. Don't we need a better explanation, Uncle Percival? I know how much you loved Perry—"

"That's enough."

This was delivered in the cutting voice that had once made Godwin shrivel. Hearing that note, Lola lifted her head and whined. Godwin put his hand on her back, keeping his gaze steady on his uncle. Sir Percival's chin thrust out, and the cords of his neck strained against his collar. He was looking much older these days, though it seemed to Godwin that he clung to his power like a drowning man.

"Perhaps you're right, sir." Godwin edged his leg closer to the dog.

"Certainly I am. Today, I've had a brisk walk to my club along with a drive in the park," Sir Percival boomed. "Have you made the plans for your musical gathering? I take it we are to welcome your favorite bohemians on Saturday?"

"You did leave the guest list to me."

Sir Percival forced a smile. "I wanted to please you, my boy, and put Lydia on her mettle as hostess. I do not complain. As usual, you take me up too readily."

"I should inform you, sir, that Miss Esther Hardy and her mother will be among our guests. Miss Hardy is the lady who called seeking information about Muriel Dane. Her family befriended Muriel years ago. At all events, I met Miss Hardy by chance and extended the invitation."

"What on earth possessed you?" The baronet exhaled a gust. "The young woman is not of our class and a busybody to boot.

As it is, we must confront any revived gossip about Perry and Muriel."

"Which is why I invited Miss Hardy. We show the world we have nothing to hide—right, Uncle? She and her family are not to blame for what happened."

"It was a damned odd thing to do. But why should that surprise me?" As if he didn't trust himself to say more, Sir Percival moved toward the door. "What's done is done, and we must put a good face on it."

"A reasonable philosophy." Godwin was aware that his meaning would escape his uncle. He wasn't being sarcastic. It was just that he understood how Sir Percival thought. To be "reasonable" was to uphold appearances at all costs. Even if that made you heartless. Especially if that made you heartless.

"Well, I'm off." Sir Percival turned back to regard Godwin with evident perplexity. "Lydia would remind me that a rest ought to be next on my agenda. You know how she fusses over me these days. I tell her I still have a bit of spirit left."

"Plenty, I would say."

"I won't last forever, Samuel, and it's past time we resolved matters. Lydia deserves as much, since you've raised expectations. She's not getting any younger either, particularly if you hope to get a healthy son or two off her."

Godwin's eyes strayed to the burgundy brocade drapes, drawn back to make the most of the thin December sunlight. The reds and greens of the floral carpet appeared dulled—it wasn't the same one that had been here in Perry's time. That one had been replaced . . .

"We have time yet, Uncle," he said. "Lydia has just begun to emerge from her grief. I won't rush her."

"Damn it, boy. You've always had a morbid turn of mind to match your eccentricities. I can't leave you much of an inheritance. What do you imagine you'll do when I'm dead? More than that, you have a duty to me."

This was the simple truth. The title and the entailed estate, including the mansion in Oxfordshire and Beldenfield House in London, would go to another nephew, the son of Sir Percival's estranged younger brother. Perry's marriage to the heiress had been essential to the family fortunes, just as Godwin's marriage to the same woman was necessary for himself. As Sir Percival was fond of pointing out, a man required comfort and security in his old age.

But couldn't his uncle grasp the crassness of commanding him to marry his cousin's widow in the room where Perry had been murdered?

CHAPTER 13

On Friday morning, Mama carried a large box into my room. "Look at this." She dropped the box onto the dressing table with enough force to vibrate the creams and powders.

I was sitting cross-legged on the bed as I jotted queries about Muriel Dane in my journal. I put down my pencil, resigned. Whenever my mother wore that particular gloating expression, I was generally in for a whirlwind of maternal enthusiasm. "What are you up to, Mama?"

"I've found you a dress for Mr. Godwin's concert." She pulled the lid off the box, rustled the tissue paper, and stood back, beaming. I joined her at the dressing table.

She lifted out the gown with reverent hands so that I could marvel appropriately. Worn with a crinoline and trimmed with rosettes and bows at the hem, it swept down in a fall of salmon-pink satin. It had a somewhat narrower silhouette than the current bell shape. A good thing, as far as I was concerned. I'd given up wearing the widest of crinoline hoops one saw in the shops since it was no fun to be swiping objects off tables or charring my skirt when I swished it too close to the fire. Not to mention the threat to life and limb.

Laying the gown over the chair, Mama stroked the satin. "Miss Meadows was at great pains to emphasize the Bond Street label, Esther. Unfortunately, the previous owner put on flesh after the birth of her first child. Miss Meadows purchased the dress for a song and sold it to me. Wasn't that kind?"

"She didn't want it for herself?"

"I don't think it suited her," said my tactful mother. "We'll get on well at Mr. Godwin's concert, I in my gray silk, you in this." She pursed her lips, reflecting. "Somehow, I don't think your gold locket works with that neckline. Shall I lend you my pearl and chain?"

"I put myself in your expert hands, Mama."

"Let's see how it looks. Try it on."

Before I could comply, Papa knocked and walked in, holding a letter. The faces we turned toward him must have looked guilty because he said, "Where did that come from?"

"It's for the concert. A gift for Esther," Mama said. "You won't believe the bargain I struck, Theo."

"Very pretty."

"It is, isn't it?" She patted the dress again.

Papa brandished his letter. "Speaking of this concert, your Mr. Godwin has been obliging enough to write to me. He informs me that he and his cousin-in-law, Mrs. Beldenfield, will look after the pair of you since I don't wish to attend. If we're agreeable, he'll send the cabbie Billings to collect you and have the driver wait to carry you back. Godwin says Mr. Billings can be trusted."

I laughed. "Mr. Godwin must've located Billings at the cab stand I told him about."

"The gentleman thinks a great deal of himself, doesn't he? Making arrangements for my womenfolk," my father grumbled.

"Gracious of him, don't you agree?" Mama said.

Papa coughed. "What will you ladies do among the rich folk? Not to mention being forced to sit through a clutch of caterwauling singers. Not my idea of fun."

"We go for Bert's sake, dear." As she spoke, Mama crossed to the door and shut it. "Remember that Sir Percival Beldenfield is Bert's grandfather. Don't we owe it to our boy to learn something about the family?"

"It never did Muriel a speck of good to be associated with the nobs." Papa glanced at me. "I suppose you intend to poke around tomorrow night?"

"Why else would we go?" I retrieved my journal, anxious to recruit my parents to my detection efforts. "Do you care to hear my ideas? They are swimming around in my brain at this very minute."

"Not particularly," Papa said. But he sat down on my bed, folding his arms in front of him.

Mama perched next to him while I remained standing in front of them. I almost laughed aloud when I realized that my mother's face showed the hushed, attentive expression I recalled from recitations at school prize days.

I lifted one finger in the air. "Firstly, did Perry Beldenfield end his affair with Muriel before his marriage? Mrs. Beldenfield declines to acknowledge that her husband and Muriel ever had any serious relationship at all. I think we must discount that view."

"Had he any sense, Beldenfield would have made a fresh start," Papa said. "A new bride to please, a scandal to scotch, and a position in the world to uphold."

"That's what *you* would do, dear," Mama said. "A man of wealth and questionable character can conceal a mistress."

"Insightful, Mama." I smiled at my parents. "You highlight the problem all truth-seekers face. We can only evaluate any possibility through our own limited perspective. It can be difficult to imagine why someone else behaved as he did. Even if Perry Beldenfield had parted with Muriel, why abandon the mother of his child to destitution and crime?"

"Didn't Reverend Walsh mention that someone gave her financial assistance? Perhaps it was Perry who helped her," Mama suggested.

My father yanked his watch out of his waistcoat pocket. "I've got five minutes until my next appointment. What's your second question, Esther?"

"We know that the supposed witness to Muriel's suicide, one Finch Norwood, perjured himself. Who was he? Could this be the man who rifled through Muriel's rooms at Mrs. Carver's lodging-house? The same man who recently called on Mrs. Beldenfield to sell information as to Muriel's whereabouts? Rose, Mrs. Carver's maid, told me that Muriel was expecting a letter from someone. Which makes me wonder whether she was involved in some secret business."

"Norwood once helped Muriel escape the police," Mama said. "Would he betray her?"

"There you go." I waved two fingers. "Mrs. Beldenfield may have misrepresented his intentions." I gasped. "Papa—the man who fetched you to deliver Muriel's infant in the Mint. What was he like?"

"It was a long time ago. I seem to recall a little gamecock sort of man, not very clean. Unhygienic beard down his shirt front."

"If it was him, what do you think he'll do now?" I asked.

Papa stroked his chin. "We can't answer that question. How can we predict?"

"I agree. Stick to the facts," my mother said.

"Fair enough." I raised a third finger. "Don't forget the handkerchief Billings found in the churchyard. We still don't know whose it is or what the monogram signifies. Do the initials 'NFN' belong to the murderer? Is there any connection to the Beldenfields? Mrs. Beldenfield would deny anything to protect her husband's reputation, and Sir Percival is unlikely to cooperate with any inquiries. My best approach is to ask Mr. Godwin tomorrow night. Take him by surprise, as it were."

"And hope he doesn't toss you and your mother out on your ear," Papa said.

"I have a feeling he won't. His mind seems . . . inquisitive," I said.

"What else, Esther?" Mama said.

"Ah, my final question relates to Muriel's bonnet." I tucked my thumb and held up four fingers.

"You mean the one you failed to turn over to Inspector Jessup?" my father said.

"It's safe on the shelf in my wardrobe, Papa. I have a notion Scotland Yard won't care two pins about feminine frippery."

Staring at me with her mouth open, Mama jumped up from the bed. "Miss Meadows' remark about the Bond Street label on the dress—" She trotted to the wardrobe and emerged with the green bonnet. Turning it over, she peered inside, holding it close to her eyes. She said in a breathless voice, "It has a label too. We ought to have noticed that before."

My father frowned. "That's it, Nan. You'll be fitted with spectacles and actually wear them this time. I'll handle the matter."

"Let me see." I took the bonnet from her. "*Mrs. E.B. Robson, 239 Regent Street, London,*" I read aloud. I squeezed my mother's waist. "Well done, Mama."

"What can it matter where Muriel bought the bonnet?" My father took his turn inspecting the label too.

"Because we can attempt to trace its history," I said. "Mrs. Beldenfield's testimony depends upon it. Why would Muriel wear an incriminating bonnet to meet her killer in the churchyard years later? According to Rose, she dug it out of her trunk on her last day."

Mama nodded. "Why keep such an ill-fated thing?"

"Perhaps this was Muriel's avenging fury bonnet," Papa said. "To be worn anytime she planned to crack someone over the head. However, someone got to her first this time."

Mama and I said together, "That's not funny."

Papa looked sheepish. "You're right. Murder is no joke. All right, how's this? Mrs. Beldenfield's testimony is both confirmed and unconfirmed. Confirmed because Muriel *did* own a green bonnet, which makes her look very guilty indeed. Also unconfirmed because Finch Norwood lied about seeing

Muriel in said bonnet when she supposedly drowned herself. Thus, we have only Mrs. Beldenfield's word that Muriel was wearing the bonnet in Portman Square on the day of Beldenfield's murder. Understand this puzzle, and you understand both crimes."

"Precisely," I said.

Mama and I had often read about the entertainments of the titled and wealthy in the newspapers. Windows ablaze with light, carriages thronging the pavement, ladies and gentlemen streaming into ballrooms to rotate like whirligigs. *The Countess of Farnworth will give a grand ball at her residence in Grosvenor Square on Saturday* or *Sir C. Scott entertained a fashionable company to dinner at his mansion in Eaton Square*, we were reliably informed.

So it had been a strange feeling to see Mr. Godwin's concert mentioned in one of the gossip columns this morning as likely to be a "crush." This time, we would see for ourselves. But in all likelihood, our host would be occupied with his other guests, leaving us to hover at the edges, a pair of wallflowers. The thought made me smile. We should get a good view of the natives from there.

When Billings pulled up in Portman Square, a footman opened the coach door for us. The servant's wooden expression gave no sign he'd noticed our descent from a hired vehicle.

"I'll be round the back, ma'am," Billings called to my mother.

"Thank you, Mr. Billings," Mama said.

We took deep breaths and proceeded to the entrance, where another servant ushered us into a cloakroom and took our outer garments. We waited in the marble-pillared vestibule as the butler conducted another lady and her husband up to the drawing room. He returned; Mama gave our names.

"Ah, yes. Mrs. and Miss Hardy." A faint smile flickered across the butler's long face as he assessed us.

I saw no trace of the tremulous servant I'd heard Sir Percival browbeating. Tonight, the butler was a dignified figure with a ramrod posture.

"My name is Thompkins, madam," he said to Mama. "Mr. Godwin asked me to watch out for you and Miss Hardy. Right this way, if you please."

My pulse quickened as we ascended one side of the double staircase. I gripped the banister so I wouldn't trip and nearly bumped into my mother when she craned her neck to gaze up at the magnificent dome. We reached the landing, and Thompkins announced us, though few seemed to hear him. We thanked him and stepped into the drawing room.

The massive chandelier blazed with such intensity that I blinked. My gaze landed on tall windows lined with luminous sea-green drapery and moved to the gilt-framed portraits of Belden-field ancestors placed on the wall at uniform intervals. The blues, peaches, and lilacs of ladies' gowns shimmered in the gaslight, a contrast to the dark sheen of gentlemen's suits. Mama pulled me forward just in time to avoid some newcomers on our heels.

I followed my mother across the crowded room, concentrating on my crinoline lest it brush against the other guests. In my overexcited state, I couldn't make any sense of the cacophony of voices. I felt awkward amongst these confident, chattering people. I was sure my slippers were the wrong shade for my dress, and my pink bows made me feel like a Christmas package. Or Little Bo-Peep. My footsteps slowed, and Mama glanced back over her shoulder. She sent me a sharp nod, picked up her skirts, and sailed onward, rather in the vein of a mother duck floating regally across a pond with one duckling in her wake. We passed a series of low couches and chairs covered in gold brocade. A lady in a purple turban peered at us over her large fan. The gentleman she was with whispered in her ear.

Godwin and Lydia Beldenfield stood together about halfway down the room. Our host was talking to someone as we approached, so we greeted Mrs. Beldenfield first. I was intrigued to observe that the widow wore a half-mourning gown of silk tulle with sequins in a shade of mauve that made her skin look sallow. A magnificent diamond pendant glittered at her breast. Her light brown eyes with their reddish lashes appeared shadowed.

"Miss Hardy. How pleasant to see you again," she said, extending her gloved hand.

"Thank you, ma'am. May I present my mother, Mrs. Hardy?"

"It was kind of you to include us in your entertainment tonight, ma'am," Mama said.

"Not at all." Lydia Beldenfield looked toward the woman with the large fan, and her lips tightened.

"Is something wrong?" I asked on impulse. We had a moment or two before the next guests reached us.

Lydia hesitated, then spoke in a hurried tone. "It can be no secret from you, Miss Hardy. It's this business with Muriel Dane —some additional paragraphs in the newspapers have been published. We must weather the storm. It's just that it's . . . unpleasant."

"People are often insensitive, ma'am," I said.

"Indeed," Mama said. "Though if they've been reading today's papers, they ought to be more worried about the health of the Prince Consort." While the most recent intelligence in *The Times* had announced some mitigation in the Prince's symptoms, my father had not been reassured. All of England hung on the bulletins from Windsor Castle, the royal family's current residence.

Lydia's expression relaxed. "We're all praying for him. I would not wish widowhood on my worst enemy, let alone our dearest queen, whose marriage is an example to the nation. One does not soon recover from such a loss, however compelled we are to put on a brave face to please our friends."

"Is it painful for you to mingle in society, ma'am?" Mama asked.

"Oh, no. I'm glad to lend my support to Mr. Godwin. My father-in-law is old-fashioned, I'm afraid." She smiled. "There are several famous portrait painters in attendance, as well as an author or two. Not our usual set, but Mr. Godwin requires a hostess. I do hope you'll enjoy the concert."

"Most obliging of you." Mama picked up her skirts to move away.

Godwin, who had finished his other conversation, started to welcome her and would have included me, except that Lydia laid a hand on my sleeve to detain me.

Her voice dropped. "You met Mr. Godwin at that woman's lodgings the other day, didn't you? We—that is, Sir Percival and I —are concerned he may be a bit too—" She broke off in confusion.

"Curious about Muriel's fate?"

"We do hope the authorities will soon arrest the perpetrator. But you must understand that Muriel Dane was the kind of female to stir up trouble among young men. Far better to let ghosts sleep, don't you agree?" Lydia seemed to steel herself before continuing. "You seem like a sensible woman, Miss Hardy. I ask that you not encourage—"

No time for more. Another guest approached, waiting to be greeted.

Inwardly cursing the interruption, I joined my mother and Samuel Godwin. He looked distinguished in his black cutaway coat and pleated white shirt front. Like the rest of the men, his dress was simple, though his waistcoat was a striking emerald color. His gaze flickered over me, and my cheeks warmed. Was my dress too fussy for the occasion?

Godwin shook my hand. "May I compliment you on your gown, Miss Hardy?"

"Thank you, sir."

"I wanted to tell you that Inspector Jessup from Scotland Yard called on my uncle to give his report yesterday. He made a favorable impression. Still, Sir Percival doesn't wish to rake up old sorrows. He may press you to drop your inquiries."

Lydia Beldenfield has already done that, I thought.

"I'll be discreet, sir."

"Will you, I wonder? No, I meant no insult, Miss Hardy. Quite the contrary."

As we stared at each other, the lines of tension around his mouth deepened. Mrs. Beldenfield was right. Mr. Godwin cared —but about what or whom? He'd loved his cousin Perry, it seemed. But had he also been in love with Muriel Dane? The possibility made my spirits sink.

This will not do. The gentleman was an enigma. And yet I was acutely aware of an attraction to him. I wouldn't call it romantic at this point. It had more to do with a feeling of like to like, of friendship and understanding. For some inexplicable reason, I was convinced that Samuel Godwin, too, looked upon this array of well-dressed, pampered guests and held himself aloof. This *had* to be an illusion born of wishful thinking. An illusion that made me read a message in his eyes that couldn't possibly be there.

CHAPTER 14

———

After completing our circuit of one sumptuous chamber after another, Mama and I headed for the music room to find seats for the concert. Conversations swirled around us. People spoke of the glees to be performed by some of the male guests and a promised Christmas pantomime. Also, there was gossip about Prince Albert's health, along with a squabble about the merits of a famous racehorse. And a great deal of angry discussion about recent political tensions with the Americans, who, while embarked on their own civil war, had sparked a diplomatic incident with England by arresting two Confederate envoys on a British ship. I heard nothing about the old scandal of Perry and Muriel until we paused under a potted myrtle tree, and two voices reached our ears.

"Surprised to see the widow here," a gentleman with gray hair and a limp, white mustache remarked.

"Bit of a cold fish." His companion had a bored gaze and a moist mouth. "Looked right through me when we were introduced."

"You mean to try your luck with her, Talent?" said the first.

"Not I. Word is Sir Percival means for Godwin to step into his cousin's shoes. No idea why it's taken him and Mrs. Beldenfield so long to make a match of it."

"Godwin's an odd egg, isn't he? Not entirely—" The gray-haired gentleman halted, searching for the word.

"He'll fall in line," the younger man said. "They always do when there's a pot of money at stake."

"Lucky for Sir Percival his daughter-in-law has bankrolled him all these years. She's got a pretty little fortune of her own, you know. And trustees to guard the coffers until she remarries." The gray-haired man chuckled. "Always wondered what really happened to that poor sod Perry Beldenfield. What's the world coming to when a man can't have his bit of muslin on the side without getting himself killed? What do you make of this new business about the murderess turning up her toes?"

"Thought she was dead already."

At this tantalizing moment, the two men drifted away. I had felt my mother's eyes on me as they discussed Mr. Godwin. Perhaps it shouldn't have surprised us that Godwin's name was linked with that of Lydia Beldenfield. And also, apparently, with Muriel Dane. If he was now on the brink of marriage to Lydia herself, no wonder she didn't like his interest in the dead woman. Yes, it made sense. Godwin and his cousin's widow had lived together for years. But the idea of him relying on Lydia's wealth made my lip curl. Why hadn't he made an independent life for himself? Would he marry the widow to please his uncle—or to line his pockets? Smiling in reassurance at my mother, I laid a hand on her arm and drew her into the crowd.

In the music room, we found our places. Next to a grand piano sat a harp. A trio of musicians tuned their instruments as the chairs rapidly filled up. We had been waiting for about five minutes when Sir Percival Beldenfield came down the aisle. I studied him from under my lashes. He was a portly man, saved from obesity by his height. I didn't think he'd ever been hand-some—his features were too coarse for that. The gentleman exuded arrogance and undeniable charm, though he moved stiffly as if his joints pained him. As I watched him calling out jovial greetings to acquaintances, I wondered about his relationship to Lydia Beldenfield. Despite her money, she hadn't fulfilled the role of wife and breeder of heirs. How did he treat her behind closed doors?

When Sir Percival reached our row, he stopped. "Good evening. As we aren't standing on ceremony tonight, I hope you'll forgive the lack of a proper introduction. Percival Beldenfield at your service. You're Miss Esther Hardy, are you not? My nephew pointed you out." He gave a wide, wolfish smile that made me squirm in my seat. The gentleman spoke in ringing tones that must have carried around the room, and his bow was masterful. Graceful for so large a man, it carried a whiff of contempt.

I inclined my head. "Yes, sir. I'm looking forward to the concert." I indicated Mama. "May I introduce my mother, Mrs. Hardy?"

He offered Mama a marginally deeper bow. "An honor to meet you, madam. It's easy to detect a resemblance to your daughter."

"How nice of you to say so, sir." She sounded nervous.

"Not at all, Mrs. Hardy. A mother imparts far more than looks to her offspring. Manners and morals are also important."

Did I detect a hidden, or not-so-hidden, barb in this? I did, though Sir Percival exuded an almost overpowering geniality.

"I tried my best, sir," Mama said after an uneasy silence. "My daughter has a mind of her own."

I nudged my mother with my elbow. "Unjust, Mama. I was always a model student."

At this, Sir Percival laughed outright, and the heads of several people swiveled in our direction. "Miss Hardy proves my point. How barren we gentlemen would find our existence without feminine wit and beauty to grace our lives."

He bared his teeth a second time, displaying a set of strong, white teeth, artificial. Then he leaned over my chair. "My nephew has told me of your interest in recent events in Southwark. Bad business all around. I had a word with that police inspector. Good man. He promised us results in a few days. No one can ever bring my son back, but I confess it will be a relief to have the matter resolved."

"I did not realize that an arrest is imminent, sir."

"I have it on good authority it is. You and your family need not worry, Miss Hardy. It must've been a shock to discover you'd been harboring a fugitive."

Mama sat up straighter. "We did not 'harbor' Muriel Dane, as you put it, sir. She was a free agent. Mr. Hardy's line of work brings him into contact with many people."

"Some better left to the rubbish heap, eh?"

Again, he'd spoken too loudly, and I noticed for the first time that the dowager with the large fan sat in the row behind us, head at half tilt as she strove with all her might to listen.

My face got hot. I didn't like the way the baronet had spoken to my mother. We were invited guests, whatever our social status. One might suspect that my next words were the result of poor self-control. They were not. I hadn't meant to confront him. Now I looked Sir Percival in the eye. "May I inquire, sir—did Inspector Jessup ask you about a handkerchief monogrammed with the letters NFN?"

The baronet's good humor fled. I stared at the bulging veins on his nose as he lifted his head to glare at me. He slashed a hand through the air, just brushing the puffed sleeve of my gown. "What nonsense is this, Miss Hardy?"

"The monogram on the handkerchief found in the churchyard where Muriel Dane was assaulted, sir."

"Ah, I see what it is. You imagine you alone can succeed while the police will fail. A slip of a girl like you? I'm sure your family cannot wish you to expose yourself like this."

I kept my voice level. "We owe Muriel something since she died in our house, Sir Percival."

He turned to Mama. "What about you, madam? As the wife of a rising professional man, shouldn't you be more mindful of your husband's interests? Scandal can do nobody any good. A pretty girl like your daughter ought to be enjoying her beaux and finding herself a nice young man to wed, don't you agree?"

"I do indeed, Sir Percival." Mama darted a quelling look in my direction.

He went on addressing my mother, as if I had become invisible. "What a pleasure it has been to meet the wife of a medical man. It occurs to me that your husband might take a crack at curing my rheumatism, eh? My other sawbones does nothing for me. Yes, I'll consider consulting Mr. Hardy. Once we've put this sordid affair behind us." He bowed and passed on.

I sat there fuming, trying to ignore the eyes that bored into my back. The baronet's message was clear. Sir Percival Beldenfield knew what his patronage could mean to my father's advancement. Cooperate, and he would stand as our friend. Refuse, and we would have an enemy with the power to destroy lives and careers with one flick of his finger.

~

"Should we leave?" Mama seemed shaken by the encounter. In truth, I was too, though I didn't choose to show it among these people.

"Not yet, Mama. The concert is starting."

The room hushed as a pretty girl came forward to play the harp. But I was studying Lydia Beldenfield seated with Godwin near the front, his chair drawn close to hers. At one point, when three gentlemen strode to the stage to roar out a bawdy song, he grimaced, then grinned at Lydia unrepentantly. She smiled back, looking younger and freer than I had ever seen her.

For the finale, Godwin himself took part in a pantomime skit. Pantomimes were a Christmas tradition, with Londoners often attending the theaters in the West End to enjoy these extravaganzas. This skit presented a tale about the Harlequin and his lover Columbine, who were fleeing Columbine's tyrannical father,

Pantaloon. A Fairy Queen "transformed" the players into their roles, and Pantaloon appeared as a pompous man with a pasted-on gray goatee. Godwin played the role of the clownish servant. In his cap with brightly colored streamers and a blousy white peasant's shirt thrown over his suit, he soon had the audience in an uproar as he lifted his mask to tell sly jokes and chased the hapless lovers, both played by young men. Poor Columbine was about to be married off to the fop she detested when the Fairy Queen reappeared to engineer the happy ending.

The absurdity relaxed me. I laughed with the rest, calling out, "He's behind you" and "Watch out!" I was fascinated by the way Godwin leaped and pranced, tossing aside pieces of his costume and donning new ones, becoming a rival lover or a cook or even a bear, complete with a bearskin. He tore handkerchiefs from pockets, tripped the lovers with his boot, and even jumped through a flaming hoop, making the audience gasp. A few of the more boisterous guests hooted and whistled at the players.

During the final round of applause, I noticed that Lydia's chair was empty. Scanning the room, I spotted her by the refreshment table. Lydia conversed with the teenaged maidservant whom I recognized from my last visit. The maid held out a folded piece of paper. Lydia opened it, read its contents, and put a hand on the table, as if to support herself. The maid said something but was waved away. Lydia slipped across the room to the French windows, where she stood for an instant with her back pressed to the glass. Then she turned and went out onto the terrace.

CHAPTER 15

"I'll be right back," I whispered to my mother.

Mama was watching the performers take their bows. "Shush. I think they're doing an encore."

I crossed the room and stepped out onto the terrace. As soon as the frigid air struck my arms and neck, I wished for my cloak but didn't hesitate. This was the very reason I'd wanted to attend Mr. Godwin's concert in the first place—to make further discoveries. Had Lydia come out into the winter's night to meet someone? There had been something furtive in her movements.

Pausing to get my bearings, I discerned the other woman at the bottom of the shallow steps that led down to the garden. Lydia glanced right, then left, before moving down a path lined by laurels. I dashed after her. Ahead of us loomed a structure of latticework woven through the bare branches of an enormous tree. In summer, trellis and tree together would provide a leafy bower in which privacy flourished and secrets could be told. Now it looked like an iron cage. Lydia came to a halt under this latticework, the path at her feet covered by intricate shadows thrown by the moon.

As I approached, she swung around to face me, and panic contorted her features. I forgot that this was the daughter-in-law of a baronet, for she seemed like a frightened child in need of help. I made a beeline for her.

"Go away, Miss Hardy," she said.

I could taste the cold on my lips, feel it reaching down my throat. My voice shook a little. "Come back inside where it's warm, Mrs. Beldenfield."

"You'll make things worse."

"I saw the little maid hand you a note. Who was it from?"

"I can't tell you. I won't tell you. You must leave me."

"Answer my question and I'll go."

"Dear God, can I trust you?" Lydia said through chattering teeth. "I mean, really trust you? I . . . have no one."

No one? What of the lady's protective father-in-law and attentive cousin Samuel, a suitor for her hand? Her luxurious drawing rooms with every whim satisfied by an army of servants? Her fashionable friends and fawning acquaintances?

"I'm listening," I said.

"I swear I'll satisfy you. It's just . . . I need to be alone for a few minutes. Shall I meet you inside in a quarter of an hour?"

I gazed into eyes like dark holes. A man would have labeled the note in her voice hysteria, and it probably was. "What's upsetting you, ma'am?"

"Go away, Miss Hardy."

"Not unless we go together." How could I leave Lydia alone when I didn't understand the situation? Should I run for Mr. Godwin?

"I don't want you." She twisted her hands and hunched her body as if to shield herself. "Go away," she repeated, barely audible.

I spoke, my tone gentle. "What is it? Tell me before we both perish from the cold."

Lydia's head shot up, and she gazed wildly around. "Did you hear that?"

"Hear what?" I had been paying little heed to the sounds around us. Now I listened to the distant hum of voices from the concert and the creaking of the massive branches above our heads as the tree shifted in the wind. From a long way off, a street player's barrel organ shrilled. Then my ears caught a new sound—a rustle.

"He's watching us." Lydia reached for my hand. Her fingers felt like ice through the glove.

Suspicion gripped me. "Who are you expecting, ma'am?"

"A man." She hurried on in the same agitated way. "The one who came before. He threatened me. He'll go to the papers with his story. He . . . he may even kill me, Miss Hardy, like he must've killed Muriel Dane. He'll tell lies and more lies about my husband, and everyone will believe him."

"Is he *here*, Mrs. Beldenfield?"

It was too late. The sounds became more distinct. Footfalls coming nearer. A few more beats of time passed before a figure stepped out from behind the hedge.

A man stood in the middle of the path about six feet away, blocking our retreat. His dark clothing blended into the hedge, but his moonlit cheekbones stood out like blades. A voluminous beard covered the lower part of his face and spilled onto his neckcloth. The man wasn't a guest or a gentleman. He held himself all wrong, his bowler hat tilted too low. He looked at Lydia Beldenfield, then at me. Danger sizzled in the air.

"Who's this?" he said with a jerk of his thumb in my direction. "You were told to come alone, Mrs. Beldenfield."

Lydia faltered. "I couldn't help it. Indeed, I could not."

"Say what you have to say to both of us," I said. "Better yet, if you have business with Sir Percival, you can knock at the front door like anyone else."

"Don't antagonize him, Miss Hardy." Lydia clutched my arm.

The man sucked in his lips with an unpleasant *phtt* sound. "Hardy, eh? That won't do, miss. *You* won't do."

I stared back at him. "I have no idea what you mean."

"Not much escapes me, missy. Got my ear close to the ground, I does. You was in the papers. Testified at the inquest too."

I was shivering in my evening gown. This mean little knave, comfortably swathed in a greatcoat, knew far too much about me and my family. Lydia Beldenfield, shrinking at my side, was useless in this crisis. I struggled to think. There was the long beard my papa had described. Could this be the Finch Norwood who'd known Muriel in the Mint and falsely reported her suicide? The same man who'd ransacked the victim's rooms after she was attacked? Had he *murdered* her too? Anything seemed possible.

"Well?" He glanced over his shoulder toward the house.

"What you say is true," I said cautiously.

"My business with this lady won't wait." His voice carried a husky note that rose to a higher pitch at the end of each sentence. A nasty kind of throat clearing, as if he had perpetual phlegm.

I tried to sound bold. "What business, sir? State it and be gone."

Lydia's shoes crunched as she shifted on her feet. She looked into the man's leering face, and her eyes fell to the ground. "I'm perfectly willing to satisfy you. Let Miss Hardy go."

He grinned. "You won't like what happens next if I blow the gab. Maybe I'll have a word with the scribbling men. Got a lot I could tell the papers about our Muriel. Don't I know all about her and her brat?"

"What do you expect us to do for you?" I said.

"Be *quiet*, Miss Hardy." To my astonishment, Lydia went right up to the man. She reached behind her neck to detach her diamond pendant and thrust it at him. "This bauble should fetch a pretty penny. Will you go?"

The pendant disappeared into his pocket. Another feral smile. "Most obliging of you, ma'am. You tell Sir Percival and his nevvy that I mean business."

"Get away from him, Mrs. Beldenfield," I cried.

She raised a shaking hand to her face and addressed the man. "I have nothing more to give you tonight. We'll be missed, and someone will come. Go away."

"That gewgaw is just the first installment. You'll hear from me."

Laughing, he lunged toward Lydia, who stood with her arms half outstretched, as if pleading with him. Somehow, she evaded him to fly down the path, her slippers sending up sprays of gravel.

I tried to follow, but Norwood—for I grew more and more convinced of his identity—grabbed my shoulders with both hands. I screamed. He was strong, surprisingly strong, despite his slight stature. His hands encircled my neck and pressed hard. I started to choke.

"Stop your screeching," he said. The pressure eased.

"Leave me alone, Norwood," I croaked through a throat on fire. I saw his eyes widen and knew my guess had been right. What a fool I had been. I had no idea why I'd taunted him with his name. It just . . . popped out. A lantern bobbed toward us in the darkness, and a dog was barking. The spaniel Lola. Footsteps approached.

Godwin's voice floated over the garden. "Miss Hardy?"

Norwood released me. "Watch yourself, girl. I ain't so fond of inquisitive young ladies." I felt a yank at my gold chain. He was gone.

I stood there, trembling and trying to catch my breath. Then Godwin was at my side, still wearing his cap with streamers. He pulled me close. Lola, barking madly, pursued the intruder.

Godwin stripped off his jacket and wrapped it around me. "Who was that man? Are you hurt? Don't worry, Miss Hardy. We'll catch him. Bertrand and John will go after him." He motioned to two strapping footmen, who had come panting up.

"Take me back to the house, Mr. Godwin." I looked around for Lydia Beldenfield and located her by the window, flanked by her father-in-law, the butler, and a huddle of curious guests.

Among them was my mother, who saw me and ran toward us. I wanted to go home.

"Who was that?" Godwin repeated.

I answered him through my dizziness. "Finch Norwood."

Samuel Godwin took Esther and her mother into the library. After he guided Esther into an easy chair, he held a snifter of brandy to her lips. The lace at her neck was torn, and the bruises on her neck would soon be livid. He gazed into her dazed brown eyes, feeling sick.

"Down, Lola," he said when the dog put a paw on her knee.

All his fault. Godwin had invited Esther for his own selfish reasons, and this was the result. The most galling aspect of the affair was that two women had been attacked and robbed on his uncle's property while he capered like a clown. His dog had taken a bite out of the intruder's trousers, but the villain had escaped. Now Godwin could hear the hum of voices as the guests departed in their carriages. The tale would be all over town by morning.

Esther bent to fondle Lola's ears. She looked up again, and the dazed look was gone, as if she'd exerted her will to banish it. "Is this the room where your cousin died?" she said with an innocent air that might have made him smile under other circumstances.

"Esther!" her mother said. "Haven't you done enough for one evening?"

"It is indeed, Miss Hardy," Godwin said. "Your mother is right. Drink a little more brandy." He looked at the small figure in the muddied gown with its frills and bows that didn't suit her in the slightest. It didn't matter what she wore. When she spoke to him, there was something in the very timbre of her voice that made him want to go on talking to her. And, after tonight's scare, he admired her pluck even more.

Esther coughed as she swallowed the spirits. "When Papa

hears what happened, he'll lock me in the house until my hair goes white."

Nan Hardy's chin wobbled. "I'll throw away the key myself. Your bruises will be spectacular, dearest."

"He . . . took your necklace, Mama."

"Never mind about that," Mrs. Hardy said. "We must go home to your father at once."

"Please, wait a few minutes until Miss Hardy has recovered," Godwin urged. He didn't want the Hardys to leave, not yet. Darkness never bothered him, but tonight, it seemed alive with menace. He considered accompanying them in the cab, then remembered Lydia upstairs under the care of her maid. He needed to talk to her—tonight, if possible.

Echoing his thought, Esther said, "Mrs. Beldenfield seemed greatly distressed, sir. You may need to summon a physician."

"First thing tomorrow, if she isn't better."

She held his gaze. "I don't understand why she meant to confront Norwood alone. I saw your maid hand her his note."

"I've spoken to Dulcie," Godwin said. "The man had the effrontery to call to her from the terrace. The girl ought to have brought the note to our butler. She's young. The villain told her to deliver it straight into Mrs. Beldenfield's hands, and Dulcie was too much of a mouse to defy him."

"Did you see the note?" Mrs. Hardy asked.

"Yes, ma'am. A crude threat I will turn over to Inspector Jessup. It stated that the writer possesses damaging information about Perry Beldenfield. I imagine this Norwood read about our entertainment in the newspaper and saw his opportunity with so many guests and their servants on the premises." He paused. "This is theft, as well as assault and extortion—Lydia confirmed it was the same man who called on her before Muriel's death."

"Mrs. Beldenfield surrendered her necklace without a murmur, sir. Mine was torn from me," Esther said.

Godwin took her brandy glass and set it on the table. "You must permit me to replace your property myself, Miss Hardy."

She nodded, then winced at the pain. Whining, the dog nestled against her knee more firmly. "Lola's changed her mind about me," Esther murmured. She knuckled the sensitive spot behind the dog's ears. "None of this makes any sense, Mr. Godwin. As far as the world is concerned, Muriel Dane and Perry Beldenfield had an affair. Muriel found herself pregnant and murdered her lover in a fit of jealousy when he married someone else. Isn't that bad enough? What more could there be?"

"The child," he said with certainty. "Norwood must know something about his fate. A murderess' child who bears the blood of a baronet's son. Makes a good story for the papers, doesn't it?"

Esther's hand stopped stroking Lola.

"It was one thing when we all assumed Muriel and her son had drowned in the Thames," he continued. "But that's not what happened, is it? Muriel has been killed, possibly by this man or by one of the other criminals who hatched the conspiracy."

"Norwood is a common thief and blackmailer," Mrs. Hardy said. "Is he likely to be Muriel's killer too? Only a brazen fool would kill a woman, then emerge from the shadows for blackmail. He'd be eager to avoid the noose around his neck."

"I thought of that, ma'am. He might need money to disappear, so preying on Mrs. Beldenfield could be his final card to play." Godwin ran a hand through his hair, which was flopping on his forehead as usual. "Norwood must realize she won't want the matter raked up again. This morning, Sir Percival caught a journalist sniffing around on our doorstep."

"You aim to protect the Beldenfield name?" Esther's scorn lashed him.

"What more can I do for my family, Miss Hardy?" He got up to give the fire a savage poke and turned back. "Are we convinced that the blackguard was indeed Finch Norwood?"

"I am," said Esther. "He reacted to his name when I addressed him. Muriel must have met him in the Mint, and he helped her stage the fake suicide."

Godwin covertly scanned both ladies. "What of Muriel's son? Where could he have been all this time?"

He pretended not to notice the glance that flashed between them.

~

It was after midnight. Mama and I were in Billings' cab. As we bounced along in the dark, Mama had her arm around my shoulders. Light coming from the street lamps we passed cast feeble beams into our retreat.

"This has gone far enough," she said. "Papa and I couldn't bear for something to happen to you."

"But, Mama, none of us will be safe until that man is caught and the truth is known." I whispered to save my voice.

"No more now."

I drifted off to sleep despite the cold, despite the jolting of the coach, despite the palpable fear that accompanied us. A few minutes later, I sat up. "What was that? I thought I heard bells." I shook my head. "No, there's nothing."

"You were dreaming, dear," Mama said.

But my sense of foreboding refused to be banished. If bells were drifting out into the night, they could mean only one thing. A message to the city and to all of Great Britain and the Empire beyond. The tolling of bells at this hour and in this manner had to signify an invasion of our shores—or a death of national significance. The former seemed impossible.

I gaped at my mother in horror. "Do you think it might be Prince Albert?"

Chapter 16

A dreary dawn. Curled around a snoring Fosco, I had lain awake for hours, stupefied by a feeling that cut deep. Never in my life had I encountered violence of any kind. The moments with a man's hands around my throat had been brief, but they'd shocked me. Had I treated these murders like a game, the means of alleviating a spinster's boredom? If so, I was repaid.

In the gray light, I rose to dress in a shapeless gown, one I'd thrust to the back of my wardrobe because it made me look years older than my age. At least it had a high neckline that hid my bruises, which were a medley of black and green this morning. Once ready, I popped open my locket to study my parents' faces. Clicking it shut again, I added the locket to my ensemble.

Papa was at the breakfast table, reading the newspaper. "Good morning, Esther."

"Any bulletin about the Prince's condition?"

"Nothing as yet. If it's typhoid fever . . ." He got to his feet. "Unbutton your dress. I want to take another look at your neck."

I rolled down my collar, and he studied the bruises, his expression forbidding. "Oh, Esther." More cheerfully, he said, "No permanent harm done. You'll be sore for a week."

"I was lucky, Papa."

"Lucky? That rascal probably killed Muriel and perhaps had something to do with what happened to Perry Beldenfield too. I'll send word to Jessup. They'll pick up Norwood and put an end to this mess."

"Yes, Papa."

"Sit down and I'll serve you some breakfast. Is your throat too sore for coffee?"

He poured me a cup, which I accepted. I'd never needed coffee more.

On that Sunday, we went to church as we always did. I soon discovered that I'd been right about hearing bells in the night. There *had* been a massive peal at St. Paul's, along with a gathering crowd to listen. A peal that would soon spread to every church in the nation. This morning, the streets hummed with the news of Prince Albert's death at Windsor, which had been wired to London late the prior evening. It seemed that the earlier bulletin about his improvement had been unduly optimistic, and his condition had deteriorated.

A pervasive gloom had descended on the capital. We encountered Londoners in groups, reading aloud from the newssheets, quicker to publicize the tragedy than the papers. Many people wept; others stood by, their faces slack with dismay.

Granny-Cook held Bert back when he would have darted off to talk to a newsboy, who bellowed, *"Death of His Royal Highness, the Prince Consort,"* at the top of his lungs. Disappointed, Bert waved at his friend.

Once ensconced in a pew, I heard gasps when the Prince's name was omitted from the traditional blessing for the royal family. A few of the parishioners were just learning about his death, and the buzz intensified as the collection plate was passed. My dear former betrothed, Benedict Caxton, was in his element. Standing at his black-draped lectern, he managed to imbue his sermon with such portentousness that many parishioners fished for handkerchiefs and sobbed. I looked at Caxton's handsome face, then at his wife, Elizabeth, sitting placidly nearby with her perfect infant in her arms—and felt nothing.

After church, we ate our cold meats to save the servants from Sunday labors. Papa put up his feet to read the papers—the afternoon editions had a black border and carried accounts of the Prince Consort's final hours. Mama sat with my father. I went down to the kitchen, meeting Phoebe on the stairs.

"Terrible news from Windsor," Phoebe said.

"Indeed. Granny-Cook will be feeling especially sorry. I'll go sit with her."

"She'll like that, Miss Esther." Phoebe leaned over to give me an impulsive hug. Mama's quiet word about Bert with our housemaid seemed to have had a good effect. Common sense had reasserted itself, and Phoebe and Granny-Cook were thick as two peas in a shell again.

The kitchen welcomed me with the smell of barley soup, mingled with the reek of the liniment Granny-Cook used for her lumbago. On this occasion, she sat hemming a dish-towel, a melancholy expression on her face. No doubt she was thinking about the Prince whom she'd admired, so much so that Granny-Cook had renamed Muriel's baby in Albert's honor. Today, she kept glancing at the shelf on which she kept her precious creamer jug that commemorated Victoria and Albert's wedding in 1840. She heaved a gigantic sigh and motioned for me to sit down.

We had been sitting quietly in the rocking chairs near the range for a quarter hour when Bert erupted into the room.

"Mr. Hardy says I can't go see Tom and Jack," he announced. "I won't play marbles on a Sunday, but I could at least talk to my friends. Find out what they think about the Prince."

"Wouldn't be seemly," Granny-Cook said. "We're in mourning."

Bert plopped himself down at our feet. "I'm sorry about it

and all, but it's not like we ever met Prince Albert. And just because I happen to be named after the fellow . . ." Breaking off, he leaned against his granny's legs, his face discontented.

"Now, Bert." Granny-Cook tapped the back of his head with her thimble. "You be a good boy and do what the doctor says. He knows what's right, better than you and me."

"He wouldn't let me go yesterday either. And that was before the Prince died."

"Listen, Bert," I said. "My father wants to keep you close to home for a while. I explained that to you before."

"Nobody ever explains anything to me."

"Bert!" said Granny-Cook. "You go read your Bible. Or sit quiet and give a body a rest."

It seemed the Bible did not appeal. Bert sat on, keeping company with his boy thoughts, while Granny-Cook and I retired to ours. The dreamy expression returned to Granny-Cook's face, and I wondered what she thought of besides the royal family. As far as I knew, there had never been a husband in the picture for her. Granny-Cook enjoyed her courtesy "Mrs. Kipling" and seemed untroubled by what her life might have been. Wherever she went when she escaped into her dreams, she always emerged refreshed, ready to pluck a chicken or knead a dough. Soon she rose to resume her work. I heard her moving around in the scullery, muttering to herself.

Bert took Granny-Cook's chair. "Miss Esther, there's something important I don't know about the dead lady, isn't there?"

"What do you mean, darling?"

"I'm not stupid. She came to see me, didn't she? I . . . I could just tell, Miss Esther. She used to follow me in the street when I was walking home from school."

"Did she ever speak to you?"

"No, she just . . . looked. Once I put out my tongue at her, and she laughed."

I had only one possible reply. "You're not imagining things,

Bert. My father will explain the matter to you when the time is right. Will you trust us?"

He lowered his voice. "Granny-Cook never did talk much about our family."

Tears gathered in my eyes. "We love you dearly and couldn't do without you. That's all that matters, right?"

As if the emotion in my voice had embarrassed him, he nodded and jumped to his feet. "I have a new magazine in my room. But I'll read a few Bible verses first just in case Granny asks me."

"A splendid plan," I said.

On the following day—a Monday as gloomy as the Sunday had been—we resumed our normal activities. Papa was beset with an unusual number of patients, many of whom, male and female alike, chose this time of national crisis to develop palpitations or pains in the stomach. After breakfast, Mama and I lingered at the table, reading the papers. I summarized the articles for her benefit while she drank her tea.

"Life is over, Mama. According to *The Morning Post*, 'the eclipse of death is this day on every home in England. More than that: a shadow has been cast over the world.'"

"Stop it, Esther." Mama spluttered into her cup. "This truly is a calamity."

"I feel for the Queen most sincerely. I don't mock *her*, Mama. Still, it's a bit much for the newspapers to praise Prince Albert now he's gone. A pity they didn't always appreciate him when he was alive."

"They were hard on him, poor man." After a pause, she added, "Do you feel up to a shopping expedition this morning? I've made my calculations, and I think we can afford a few black ribbons to trim Granny-Cook's and Phoebe's caps. A ribbon for Bert's sleeve will suffice, don't you think?"

"Artificial flowers, collars, and black-bordered handkerchiefs," I recited as I pointed to a large advertisement. "Are you sure we don't need those as well? This man of business will supply ready-made mourning at five minutes' notice or made to measure in five hours. The merchants haven't wasted much time."

"And why not? We need their wares."

I pushed back my chair. "Fine, Mama. I'll do my duty by queen and country and battle the throng on Regent Street."

"Take Phoebe with you and come straight back, dear." The front bell rang. She rose to hurry toward the door.

But I stopped her, saying, "I know what you're doing. Thank you."

Mama looked back with raised brows. "What do you mean, Esther?"

"Sending me into the world so I don't develop any silly fears."

"What hazard are you likely to encounter beyond ladies fighting you to the death for a bolt of cloth?"

An hour later, I summoned Phoebe to collect our pelisses. On our way out, we encountered my father's patient Mrs. Jardain, back again in the waning days of her pregnancy. Emerging from the reception room, the expectant mother didn't look as if her consultation had reassured her. Her face was peaked, and she had smudges under her eyes. Still, she greeted us with a friendly smile and sallied forth to her carriage.

Phoebe and I followed in her wake. All of the houses, including ours, had their blinds lowered as a mark of respect for the Prince. Mama had added a black border to the brass plaque that advertised my father's surgery.

Phoebe pointed at the bandbox I carried over my arm. "What's that, miss?"

"You'll see. It's for one of my errands."

I always enjoyed outings with Phoebe. The maid was an ener-getic walker and a lively companion. She kept up an easy flow of conversation, glowering at any young blades who dared to ogle her, which happened often, even on such a mournful day. We soon completed Mama's business. I purchased the requested black ribbons and was free to turn to my other purpose.

On the pavement, I drew Phoebe to one side, handed her the parcels, and pried up the lid of the box. Next, I removed my hat pins and hat. I took out Muriel Dane's bonnet and settled it on my head, tying the strings under my chin. It fitted me well enough, but felt . . . wrong. Though I wasn't superstitious, I couldn't help but think I was inviting bad luck by wearing a garment associated with two murders.

Phoebe gaped at me as if I'd lost my mind. "Why do you have that? It's not—"

"My style? You're right about that, Phoebe. We are conducting a little experiment with this bonnet today. Your part is to keep silent and nod in the right places. Agreed?"

"A bit of investigating, miss?" Phoebe's eyes were round. "I never heard of such a thing."

"Me neither. I have no idea what will happen."

A bell tinkled as I opened the door of the establishment of Mrs. E.B. Robson of Regent Street. I'd been a little afraid the milliner's shop might have gone out of business in the years since Perry Beldenfield's death. But here it was, one among endless similar places in London with plate glass windows, a long wooden counter across the back, and a wealth of hats and bonnets on display. These were strewn on the counter, stacked on shelves, and displayed on racks. Two ladies leaned over the glass case against the wall, examining a jumble of silk flowers, gauze for veils, and artificial fruits. Another customer peered at herself in the ornate looking glass against the wall, a silk scarf tossed over one shoulder.

Phoebe stopped in front of a table near the front. "Look at this, miss." She stroked a fox fur muff and hat presented in a gold foil box.

A clerk was assisting another customer a few feet away. Was this the milliner Mrs. Robson herself? She was a willowy woman of middle age with a dewy complexion and an aura of competence. Gracious and impeccably dressed. Noticing us, she motioned at another shopgirl in a crisp apron, who smiled at me. *Too young*, I thought.

The shopgirl sauntered over. "What may I do for you this morning, madam?"

"I have a question or two. I'll wait for your proprietress, if you don't mind. Is that Mrs. Robson?" I inclined my head toward the older woman.

The girl stiffened. "It is. I am qualified to demonstrate our wares, madam. Let me show you a few of our newest creations." She launched into her patter, whipping one hat after another before us.

I listened with half an ear as I eavesdropped on Mrs. Robson's conversation. Shopping brought out the demon in some people, I mused. Such customers forgot to hide their true natures. The masks came off, and they stood revealed in all their nasty, greedy glory.

This particular lady—a buttoned-up sort of female with mean eyes—had decided that the prices charged in the establishment were exorbitant, for I heard her saying, "Lord's sake, what a shocking amount for a piece of material and a bit of lace. Highway robbery, I call it."

The lady repeated this remark in a loud voice several times, as if the repetition might somehow alter matters. Mrs. Robson tolerated her with inflexible politeness, but after a minute or two, she excused herself. She came out from behind the counter, her face plastered with a smile. Her gaze flew to the top of my head and held. The smile died.

Rudely, I cut off the young shopgirl in mid-sentence. "Excuse us, miss. The proprietress is free."

With Phoebe behind me, I swept forward. "Good day. Mrs. Robson, I presume? I've come to inquire about a bonnet."

Though she couldn't help staring hard, the milliner's answer was composed. "Yes, madam. Certainly, madam. Can you provide further details? Is it for yourself or possibly for a Christmas gift?"

"I haven't decided yet. Do you have one like the one I'm wearing?"

She hesitated. "It's not in the current mode, madam." Seizing a bonnet from a stand on the counter—a concoction of black silk with a modest plume—she held it out. "This might be more suitable in a time of mourning."

"I'm interested in this one." I pointed at my head. "Am I correct, ma'am, in thinking you recognize the design? It bears your label."

"Really? That must've been ages ago." She spoke to the air over my shoulder. "We sell so many different styles, madam. I cannot help you."

"What a pity. Did you design it yourself by chance? This would have been in the year '50. In May or June?"

Mrs. Robson gave an unconvincing laugh. "You can't expect me to recall a bonnet I may or may not have sold over a decade ago, ma'am. While I pride myself on an accurate memory of names and faces, I cannot claim superhuman abilities."

"You did sell it. It bears your label." I glanced at Phoebe, who was obeying her instructions to the letter. Phoebe stood like a soldier half a step behind me with her lovely, long-lashed blue eyes fastened on Mrs. Robson's face. She nodded every so often to underline my words, which was strangely effective. A muscle in the milliner's cheek began to twitch.

"I must trace it," I said. "Any scrap of information would be useful. Who purchased it, for example? A lady or a gentleman? Would you be so kind as to consult your records?"

"I cannot help you, madam." Mrs. Robson picked up the bonnet I had rejected and restored it to the stand.

"You have an excellent reason to recall this particular design," I insisted. "This bonnet was worn in the commission of a murder and described by several witnesses. Perhaps you read the reports in the newspapers and recognized your own work along with the name of the purchaser? That can't have been pleasant for you."

"Really, madam. There must be countless green bonnets with

roses in London at any given time—and gentlemen to purchase them. I might have sold hundreds like this."

Chagrin crossed her face as she realized her mistake. She sucked in a breath and looked around as if seeking an escape. At that moment, we heard the bell tinkle, and two more customers entered.

"Who was the gentleman you referred to?" I said.

"I can do nothing further for you, madam. Good day." Mrs. Robson turned away to greet the newcomers.

"Whatever she knows, she's not telling," Phoebe whispered.

"We'll see about that." I bowed to the new customers, a pair of ladies. "Excuse me. My business with the proprietress is not quite complete. Would you mind waiting?"

I ignored their huffing and addressed Mrs. Robson again. "If you would only consult your records, I won't take up any more of your valuable time, ma'am. Muriel Dane—do you have a record of a purchase made by her or on her behalf? Any reference to Perry Beldenfield of Portman Square? The name Godwin? Or Finch Norwood? You do recall the *murder* in the year 1850? It's a matter of justice for an unfortunate woman. I wouldn't bother you otherwise."

The conversations in the shop died away, and every eye was on us. The surly lady who had complained about the prices dropped the artificial flowers in her hand to edge closer. The two customers standing nearest stared at me, mouths agape, as the milliner's flush deepened to an alarming hue.

"Miss Garvey, look after our customers for me," she said to the shopgirl, who seemed frozen in place. "I'll be back shortly." Mrs. Robson disappeared into the back.

Phoebe and I exchanged a look. It had occurred to me that the bonnet could have been a lover's gift from Perry to Muriel, and I hoped Mrs. Robson might offer some clue as to what it had meant to the dead woman. Had Muriel preserved it for sentimental reasons despite its incriminating history? As I waited, I believed that the answer to this question was within my grasp. I smiled at everyone around me, already savoring my victory.

Mrs. Robson was back. "I did check, madam, and I regret to tell you I have no records from that year. I discarded them some time ago, never dreaming they could be needed. I cannot oblige you."

This time, she turned her back on me to escort the waiting customers to a display on the other side of the shop. Disappointment tasted bitter. The milliner had won, and I had lost, though at least I'd gained two valuable bits of information.

The bonnet's purchaser had been a gentleman—and Mrs. E.B. Robson of Regent Street was a liar.

CHAPTER 17

When Phoebe and I got back to Charlotte Street, we found Billings' cab parked outside the door.

"Good day, miss," the cabbie called, lifting his whip to greet me. It was tied up with a bit of mourning crape in honor of Prince Albert.

I smiled at him. "We've been shopping, Mr. Billings."

"I'm to drive you anywhere you need to go," the cabman replied, his jaw jutting. "After what happened at the party, Mr. Godwin thought it best, miss. Paying me handsome too."

What to make of this? It wasn't Godwin's responsibility to ensure my safety. "I'm not going out again today, Mr. Billings. You must be eager to pick up other fares."

When Billings merely smirked at me, I looked at him, confused. Then the door of the cab opened, and I saw Samuel Godwin himself seated inside. He wore an embroidered black waistcoat under a black suit. His face showed none of its usual animation, and he had dark circles under his eyes as if he hadn't slept.

"What are you doing here, Mr. Godwin?" I said.

"Miss Hardy, how are you this morning? Are the bruises painful?" He glanced at my stylish oval-crowned hat. I was glad I'd removed Muriel's ugly bonnet as soon as Phoebe and I left Mrs. Robson's shop.

"Not much, thank you. Were you waiting for me?"

"I'd like to speak to you. Billings and Debby won't mind a rest."

"Debby? Oh, you mean the horse."

"Indeed. That queenly steed," Godwin said.

Billings chuckled.

"Should I tell your mama where you are, miss?" Phoebe's eyes sparkled at this unforeseen development.

"Please do, Phoebe." I sent her back to the house with our parcels and got into the cab. Above our heads, Billings started a conversation with Debby, who whickered back. This, I realized, was the cab driver's way of signaling he would try not to listen to our conversation.

At first, Godwin was quiet, and I felt awkward with him in the enclosed space. He said tentatively, "Bad news about the Prince."

"Yes, the Queen must be distracted with sorrow."

He shifted his weight on the seat. "You've recovered from your ordeal the other day, Miss Hardy? I owe you and your parents an apology."

"You worry too much, sir. I don't need you or Mr. Billings to act as nursemaid."

He tugged at his necktie. "Don't you see it was my fault? If I hadn't invited you to my concert, you wouldn't have been in harm's way."

"Why did you? Invite me, I mean."

"I told you why. Because . . . because I thought your presence might provoke a reaction. There's something very wrong in Portman Square. I've ignored it as long as I could." He directed a searching glance at me. "Let's have plain speaking between us, Miss Hardy. Muriel Dane is at the root of our trouble."

"You blame her?" I heard a defensive note in my voice.

"Not exactly." He frowned. "Let me explain. From the first,

I've felt I could talk to you. An inexplicable but undeniable tug of sympathy. Which is why I'll tell you the truth, even if you question my good faith."

I contemplated my scuffed boots. Godwin had expressed my own feelings with disarming frankness. No wonder this man always put me off balance. "I have no reason to doubt you, sir."

"You may think otherwise when I confess that I was once in love with Muriel Dane myself. Sometimes, I think I love her still."

"Mr. Godwin?" I had guessed this much from Lydia Beldenfield's hint at the concert, yet my first thoughts were not entirely kind. The gentleman's name was linked to Mrs. Beldenfield's. Well, why shouldn't he marry an heiress whether or not he cared for her? The world would call it a brilliant match. Anyway, it did no good to love a ghost. In my book, you had to respect the dead and cherish your memories, but your primary debt was always to the living.

"I was three years younger than Perry," he said with a flickering smile. "Cloddish and spotty and selfishly absorbed in my first calf-love. How could I expect an angel to notice me when my cousin was around? I was unprepared when Muriel left my uncle's employ in disgrace."

"How long before Perry Beldenfield's murder was this?"

"In February, a few months before his marriage to Lydia Travers. My uncle was concerned lest the scandal reach Lydia's trustees before the marriage settlements were finalized. Gossip among the servants had reported Muriel's 'illness,' and Perry had been observed meeting her in private. I thought him cruel. Fortune's darling, who took what he wanted, never mind the cost. I would have wed Muriel out of hand, family be damned. I was even prepared to lend Perry my support if he did the honorable thing by her." He slid another glance at me. "I prefer to let people become . . . themselves, Miss Hardy. If they comprehend what that means. Many people don't."

"Did Perry tell you where she'd gone?"

"He turned on me in a fury when I asked him. Perry! The

sweetest-tempered man who ever lived. He swore it was all over with Muriel and told me never to mention her name again."

"What of Mrs. Beldenfield? Did she know?"

His shoulders hunched. "Not until her husband was dead when the whole sordid tale came out. Perry and Lydia had postponed their wedding journey until later in the year and settled in Portman Square. At first, they seemed happy, like any other newly married couple. Then Perry's behavior changed. He snapped at anyone who addressed him and argued with his father. I assumed Muriel was making difficulties."

"I pity Mrs. Beldenfield in that situation."

He nodded. "She'd brought so much to the marriage, a fortune her father had made in trade. Textiles, I believe. From what Lydia has since confided, her papa was an ambitious man, and the Beldenfields suited his ideas of grandeur. You can imagine how great a shock Perry's death was to her."

"What about the day of the murder?"

"I was poring over my detested law books in my bedchamber. The first I knew of what happened was when our butler knocked at my door. My uncle had just returned from his club. He went into the library and discovered the body."

"And Lydia Beldenfield?"

"In the garden among the roses. That's when she encountered Muriel."

"You didn't see Muriel?"

"No. Any other questions, Miss Hardy?"

"Not at present." I needed time to consider so I could understand my annoyance. His depression of spirits was infectious, and I didn't want any part of it. If this feeling had something to do with Godwin's dealings with two separate women, I didn't choose to admit that to myself.

He was watching me, his dark eyes on mine. "Perhaps you're asking yourself if I could have murdered my cousin Perry or even Muriel in a jealous rage. You've decided not to trust me. I sensed your reserve when we were with your mother in the library the other night and before that as well. There's something you haven't told me."

"I have no idea what you mean, sir."

"Lydia mentioned that Norwood spoke of a child. I'm afraid she still deludes herself that Perry wasn't the boy's father. Nonetheless, we must get to the bottom of the matter. I owe as much to Perry—and Muriel."

The silence seemed to suck up the air in the coach. In my agitation I removed one of my gloves, balled it up, and squeezed it into a crumpled wad. "You fear the boy is in danger?"

"He's not under Norwood's thumb, if that's what you mean. No, I'm certain the child is safe." When I didn't respond, he went on inexorably. "After all, the surgeon who delivered Muriel's son was your papa. Who better to adopt the boy?"

I turned toward him, a pulse beating at my throat. "How long have you known?"

"It would be more accurate to say I had my suspicions. I asked myself why Muriel, mortally wounded, was so desperate to reach your house and why you were so tenacious in your inquiries. Also, when I met Bert outside Mrs. Carver's lodgings, I spotted the resemblance. He has the look of a Beldenfield. The decided nose and deep-socketed blue eyes."

"Bert is a healthy boy with a family to love him and my father to settle him in a profession once he's grown. He's far better off with us," I said, not bothering to disguise my anger.

Godwin took my hand to uncurl my clenched fingers. My glove dropped into my lap. He looked into my eyes as he smoothed his hand over my skin in a warm and delicate gesture. When he was finished, he let his fingers lie over mine. "You and your family have done a magnificent job with Bert, Miss Hardy. But you must grant me the right to take an interest in the boy. He is, after all, a Beldenfield."

I knew what my father would say to that, and he would be right. "What about your uncle and Mrs. Beldenfield? Inspector

Jessup knows where Bert is. We are very much afraid he will tell them."

"I'll have a word with Jessup. Any consideration of Bert's future can wait until Norwood is arrested."

"Yes," I agreed, relieved. Slowly, I disengaged my hand. "Since we're laying our cards on the table, I have something to ask you too." I unclasped my reticule and pulled out the sketch I'd drawn of the handkerchief's monogram. Once I'd explained its origin, I said, "Inspector Jessup has the handkerchief itself. Didn't he show it to you?"

A lock of Samuel Godwin's dark hair had fallen across his cheek so that I couldn't read his expression. He bent his head to study my drawing. When he answered, his voice was as cool as mine had been. "No, Miss Hardy. He saw my uncle when he came to Portman Square. This is the first I've been told of it."

"Do you recognize the monogram NFN?"

"NFN might not be a monogram at all. Have you thought of that?" Moving so abruptly he startled me, Godwin leaned over to open the door. "I must be off, Miss Hardy. If you don't require Billings, I'll have him drive me back to Portman Square. Lola awaits her airing."

Bewildered by the abrupt dismissal, I climbed out of the cab and stood blinking in the sunlight. "Wait. May I ask, Mr. Godwin —will you attend Muriel's funeral on Thursday? Papa prefers that Mama and I stay at home. My father will represent us."

"I'll be there. Good day to you." He pulled the door shut, banged on the ceiling of the hansom, and the cab drove off.

Samuel Godwin and Theodore Hardy were the sole mourners at Muriel's funeral. After the ceremony in the church, they accompanied the vicar to the graveside, which was tucked away in the corner under the Marshalsea Prison wall. They bowed their heads and tossed in fistfuls of earth when the time came, Hardy's face stern. Godwin was not surprised by the disapproval that emanated from him, for Esther's father had every reason to wish anyone connected with the Beldenfields in Hades. But what more ailed the man? The surgeon looked haggard, eyes dull with fatigue, clothing disheveled.

Afterward, Godwin greeted the vicar. "A moving service, Mr. Walsh. I appreciate all you've done for Muriel."

Reverend Walsh bowed. "Thanks to your generosity, sir, a sinful woman has avoided a pauper's grave. The monument you purchased from the undertaker will be installed in a day or two."

"Thank you, Mr. Walsh. Miss Hardy told me of your efforts to befriend her. The mark of a true Christian."

"*Judge not that ye be not judged*," Walsh quoted as he pondered the mound of dirt at his feet.

"We think alike, sir." Godwin's attention had strayed toward the surgeon, who was charging down the path without ever having spoken to anyone. "Will you excuse me?" Godwin said to the vicar. "I'd like a word with Mr. Hardy."

"Pray give my regards to Miss Hardy's father."

"Glad to." Godwin hurried away, calling out, "One moment if you please, Mr. Hardy."

Hardy swung around to face him, reluctance evident in his knitted brow and dilated nostrils. "I mustn't tarry. I have appointments."

Godwin held out his hand, which the surgeon took in a brief grip. "I am Samuel Godwin," he said, smiling. "It's a pleasure to meet you, sir."

"I know who you are."

"I won't detain you. I merely wanted to express—"

The surgeon exhaled. "Your regret at having drawn my daughter into peril? I can do without any such apology. Today especially."

Hardy lifted his hat and would have departed. Godwin said, "Please wait, sir. Is Miss Hardy recovered from the encounter with

Norwood? When I saw her a few days ago, she seemed her normal self. But I'd like to be assured of that."

"She's well. At home with her mother."

"I can only apologize that she came to harm while under our roof."

Hardy glared at him, then seemed to catch himself. "No, it wasn't your fault, Godwin. Esther chose to leave the house that night. I suppose it's better that Mrs. Beldenfield didn't face Norwood alone. And yet—"

"I agree with you, sir." A silence fell as Godwin discreetly examined the other man. Up close, Hardy's distress was obvious. What had brought so bleak an expression to the brown eyes that reminded him of Esther's? What was the source of the emotion Godwin sensed roiling beneath the clipped speech? More than fatigue. More than irritation with an interfering stranger. "You don't look well this morning, Mr. Hardy. Is there something I may do for you? Will you allow me to call you a cab, or will you share one across the river?"

"I require no assistance from you, Mr. Godwin. The fact is, I came here today from the deathbed of a young woman. I'm not myself, though that's no excuse to vent my spleen on you. I tried everything humanly possible to save my patient, and I failed."

Godwin stepped closer. "What happened?"

Hardy looked away. "A mother is dead along with her babe, and her husband is left a widower. The delivery went damnably wrong—the child was too large. Poor Mrs. Jardain hemorrhaged before I could stop it."

Words of comfort would be useless, Godwin knew. "So you attend the funeral of a woman you once saved from a similar fate?"

The surgeon snorted. "A lot of good my assistance did Muriel Dane in the end. Someone murdered her on this very spot."

Godwin cast a look around the quiet churchyard. The vicar had gone back into the church, and they were alone. The sun that straggled through heavy clouds outlined the wrinkles on Hardy's forehead, making it possible to envisage what he would look like when he was old. As the surgeon lifted his hand to rub his neck in an absent gesture, Godwin caught sight of a blood splotch on his sleeve and shuddered. Collecting himself, he said, "Before you go, has Miss Hardy told you about our conversation the other day? About Bert?"

"She has." He sounded wary.

"Then you must know I don't mean the boy any harm."

"I know nothing of the sort!" Hardy exploded. "Say no more about Bert on this occasion. Let the child's mother rest in peace awhile before you consider uprooting him from his home. Can you do that?"

"As it happens, sir, that is my plan. Will you do me a favor in return and answer a question or two?"

"Go on," the surgeon said.

"The birthplace of Muriel's child—was it nearby?"

Theodore Hardy's face assumed a faraway expression as he retreated into memory. "She had a room on Redcross Street at an institution assisting women giving birth to illegitimate offspring. But I'm afraid the charity did not extend to anything so frivolous as a doctor. She was left to fend for herself once her pangs began."

"She had no friends?"

"Most of the women had been prostitutes, too busy trying to survive. The men who ran the place had their own designs."

"Men like Finch Norwood?" Godwin said. "Perhaps he met her at this institution."

"I expect you're right. Her room overlooked a graveyard for single women. A filthy and odorous place. Much worse than this one."

Godwin listened to the description, Hardy's precise voice conjuring up a picture he would have preferred not to see. A patch of ground set aside for the outcast dead. Paupers and low women, often Irish, interred there. Scattered bone fragments littering the ground. Misery, disease, and death.

"The site was a sanitary nightmare," finished Hardy, too tired for anger now. "It's since been closed. In any event, Muriel survived, and I saw nothing more of her until she knocked at my door with her son in her arms. She thrust our Bert at me and begged me to keep him. My wife took one look at the child . . . Well, we would have adopted him officially had we not feared provoking further speculation."

"Bert was fortunate, sir."

"After reading the accounts of Perry Beldenfield's murder, we had our doubts about Alice Denton. We chose the welfare of the child and his mother over justice for your cousin." The surgeon sighed. "I won't apologize for that."

Godwin nodded. "I see how it was. I'd have done the same."

Another snort. "You're not married, Godwin. I imagine that one day, you truly will understand. I must go. I need a bath, a shave, and breakfast in that order if I'm to face my patients today. The ones who are still alive."

"One more question, sir. Did Muriel explain why she'd gone to the Mint in the first place?"

"Not really, though I had the impression there was more to the story than we thought."

Dread. That was what Godwin felt. A dark suspicion had awakened inside him, and he didn't know what to do. He stood where past and present mingled, half convinced that if he dreamed of Muriel, he could see what she'd seen, hear what she'd heard, in this churchyard. If memory could attach to a place, could it also float free, like the gossamer strands of a spider's web adrift in the air? Ruptured, seeking a haven in some new consciousness? After all the years since Godwin had first laid eyes on Muriel Dane, he wanted to capture any stray wisps of the stuff and wind them around his fingers.

When he got back to Portman Square, Thompkins was on hand to take his coat and hat.

"Good afternoon, Mr. Godwin," the butler said.

"My uncle and Mrs. Beldenfield?"

"In the library, sir."

Godwin raised his brows. Lydia tended to shun the library, saying it revived sad memories. The butler, seeming to catch this thought, added quickly, "A matter of business to transact, I believe, sir."

Nodding, he thanked Thompkins. But halfway across the vestibule, he turned back. "Any letters for me today?" Godwin had decided to make one final attempt at writing to his father in Italy. It was too soon to expect a reply. Yet he asked every day.

The butler bowed. "I believe there's one on the salver on the library table."

Godwin regarded the elderly servant. "I've been wanting to ask you something about my cousin's death, Thompkins. Do you recall that day?"

Startled eyes flew to his. "How could I forget it, sir?"

"You met my uncle in the hall when he returned home. Did he go directly into the library? How soon afterward did he summon you to my cousin's body?"

An anxious look flitted across Thompkins' face. "It couldn't have been more than a few minutes, Mr. Godwin."

"What of Mrs. Beldenfield? I saw her in the garden from my window. Were you aware she'd gone outside?"

"No, sir, I wasn't," the butler quavered, his chin trembling.

"You yourself neither saw nor heard Muriel Dane, am I correct? None of the other servants saw her, either?"

"It was Miss Dane."

"What makes you so sure?"

"I don't understand why you're asking me these questions, sir. I'm afraid my memory isn't as sharp as it once was. You'll want to speak to your uncle."

"I suppose I will," Godwin said. "One more thing, Thompkins. On Saturday afternoon, nearly a fortnight ago, I myself was engaged with friends. But I wondered whether Sir Percival or Mrs. Beldenfield went out?"

When the butler gaped at him in consternation, Godwin gave in and thanked him. He took himself into the library to find his uncle and Lydia bent over the large rosewood table in the center of the room, a document spread before them.

Lydia, dressed in a dove-gray gown that suited her coloring, had a pen in her hand. The gaze she turned on him was clear. She smiled a welcome. "I'm glad you're back, Samuel. Was the funeral grim?"

"At least it's over. I suppose we may congratulate ourselves that the Beldenfields have done the decent thing by Muriel Dane."

"Were you the sole mourner?" Lydia asked. "No journalists, I trust."

"Fortunately, the papers didn't sniff us out. Miss Hardy's father attended." Godwin nodded at the papers. "Did I interrupt you?"

"Merely some business with my banker. A paper for me to sign. We're finished." Lydia set aside her pen and handed the document to Sir Percival, who dropped it into a drawer, which he locked.

"Shall I ring for tea?" Lydia said. "Oh, you have a letter on the salver."

Catching sight of the London postmark, Godwin knew at once that the letter would be something trivial, a note from a friend or an invitation to dine. He pushed aside his disappointment and let the letter lie. Taking a seat, he addressed Sir Percival. "Will you and Lydia join me for a cup of tea, Uncle? I'm parched after my drive."

Agreeably, Sir Percival deposited his bulk in the armchair next to him.

As Lydia moved to the bell-rope to call the servant, Godwin said, "You're looking well today, sir."

Sir Percival leaned back, crossing his booted feet. "The

weather cooperated long enough for me to take Lydia for a drive this morning. Fresh air always bucks me up."

Young Dulcie entered the room. She kept her eyes averted and scurried off to do her mistress' bidding. Lydia busied herself at the table, capping the ink-well and tidying a pile of correspondence. The tea came. Lydia poured out for them, her movements graceful.

"Sit down, Lydia," Sir Percival said, irritation in his voice. "You mustn't overtax your strength."

"I'm quite comfortable as I am, Father."

Godwin looked from one to the other, unsure what to say. Silence had become a habit. For years, Perry and Muriel had been a forbidden topic, and Godwin had learned to comply with the unspoken rule in the interest of harmony. Now it occurred to him that he'd made an error. He turned to his uncle. "Attending Muriel Dane's funeral has got me thinking, sir. You never told me what went wrong between you and Perry before he died. Did he refuse to give her up?"

Sir Percival sent a meaningful glance toward Lydia. "Let's save this discussion for another time, shall we, Samuel? You'll upset your cousin."

She gave a queer little laugh. "Don't let my presence stop you, Father. I've often wanted to know the answer to that question myself. No, really. I'm not a child." She went to the baronet's side and dropped a kiss on his cheek. "Though you do it for the best, you must stop coddling me."

As if the words were wrung out of him, Sir Percival said, "I begged Perry. Almost on bended knee, I begged him to listen to me. He was unreasonable. Your cousin didn't deserve Lydia. And so I told him. Will you leave it alone, Samuel?"

"Yes, that's what we always do."

"Why are you being difficult today?" Sir Percival said. "Now that Muriel is safely in her grave, haven't I earned the right to some peace of mind?"

Godwin froze with the teacup at his lips. "Safely in her grave? A curious choice of words, Uncle."

"Samuel!" Lydia said.

"You take me up too quickly, boy. I call that unkind." The baronet scowled at him.

"I apologize. You wish to defend the family honor," Godwin said. "After all, *never unfaithful*."

Sir Percival went on staring at him as he sloshed a little tea in his saucer. "We do what is necessary for the Beldenfields, my boy."

Hopeless, Godwin thought. He heard himself saying, "There is one thing that puzzles me, sir. Why hasn't that Norwood fellow been in touch? Why would he give up?"

Sir Percival shrugged. "The police are watching for him. The scoundrel bides his time, that's all."

"That makes sense, Father," Lydia put in. "The authorities will find him and arrest him. When they do, this will be over."

Had they so easily forgotten Muriel and Perry's child? Godwin opened his mouth to remind them and closed it again. They sipped their tea. After a while, Sir Percival went away to take his afternoon rest. Godwin was on his way out of the room when Lydia stopped him.

"You agree with me, don't you, Samuel? Perhaps I can begin to let dear Perry go. What happened to that poor, doomed female may prove a blessing in disguise. If nothing else, it's shown me that I have my own life to live. You and Sir Percival will help me." She stepped closer and lifted her eyes, swimming in tears, to his face. "That's what Perry would have wanted, don't you think?"

Godwin's arm encircled her waist. With his other hand, he snagged the handkerchief in his pocket and handed it to her. His feeling of hopelessness deepened. "He would want you to be happy, Lydia."

She dabbed at her face, then returned his linen with a comical grimace. "Don't worry. I'll stop crying before I look a fright. But I was wondering if you'd care to show me Italy one day soon? I know you've always wanted to travel."

Chapter 18

I did not spend that Thursday of Muriel's funeral at home but rose earlier than usual to don a plain black gown. No jewelry, I decided, putting away my locket. After making sure I had money in my reticule, I packed a small bag with a comb, an umbrella, and a book of poetry. Next, I tossed in extra hat pins in case the day grew blustery. Lastly, I collected my hat and winter cloak, then went down to the kitchen to add a bottle of cold tea and some bread and cheese to my bag. This earned me curious looks from Granny-Cook, Bert, and Phoebe. However, when Bert asked a question, Granny-Cook frowned him down.

With everything arranged, I went to breakfast.

Five minutes later, Mama entered the dining room and immediately homed in on my bag. "Are you going somewhere?"

"A small errand, Mama. I'll be back by three o'clock."

"Does it have to do with Muriel's bonnet again?" she asked.

I had told my mother about Mrs. Robson's slip of the tongue, which had provided fodder for a pleasant hour of speculation over tea the prior day.

"Not this time."

Mama's glance fell upon Bradshaw's railway timetable folded under a saucer. "You're taking the *train*?"

I explained where I was going and why. Mama responded with all the reasons why my father would disapprove and added that he couldn't be asked for permission since he had yet to return from Mrs. Jardain's lying-in and Muriel's funeral. I reminded my mama that any danger to worry about today was more likely to be focused on the funeral taking place near the Mint. Besides, I was a grown woman and determined to have my way.

Mama sat down opposite me. "What can you hope to accomplish, dear?"

"It occurs to me that it would be nice to get word of Muriel Dane from someone not named Beldenfield or Godwin." In truth, I was willing to try anything. At an impasse in my inquiry, I had remembered Reverend Walsh's story about Muriel's friend, the nursemaid at the manor house in Stoke Poges. It seemed worthwhile to attempt to locate this woman.

"That's all? Nothing to do with proving to Scotland Yard that you can solve these murders before they do?"

I smiled. "Nothing's stopping Inspector Jessup. He can investigate anyone he likes."

"I'll have to go with you." My mother tapped the railway timetable, a distracted look on her face. "Though I can't imagine how your father can spare me today of all days, what with him being so occupied with Mrs. Jardain, the charwoman coming in to do the heavy cleaning, and the new surgery assistant starting. It will also take time to teach Mr. Ferris our ways. Dear Papa lacks the patience."

"No, Mama. I couldn't ask that of you."

"But if your father doesn't like the plan—"

I myself was losing patience. "My journey takes me less than an hour outside London. I'll take the train from Paddington to Slough, and it's a manageable walk to the village."

"Let me ask you something, dear. What will you do if I forbid you?"

I made a face, though I did feel a qualm. My parents never denied me anything, and it struck me that my behavior toward them had been somewhat churlish. "I'd ask you to reconsider your decision and try to persuade you I was right."

"Thought so." Mama resumed eating her eggs, murmuring to herself as if she conducted an inner debate, or perhaps rehearsed what she would say to Papa. "Why shouldn't my daughter visit a country village if the whim takes her? What kind of civilization is this if a woman can't travel a short distance on her own?"

"Very true," I said meekly.

A few years ago, my parents and I had read a book called *The Englishwoman in America* about Isabella Bird, who traversed America and Canada, having many adventures. I started to remind Mama of this example but stopped as I caught the sardonic glint in her eye.

She poured herself another cup of tea. "I do have one condition, dear. You'll make this last attempt, which I hope will set your mind at rest. After that, you'll leave the matter to the police and stop worrying your papa. Are we agreed?"

"That sounds fair," I said, even as I doubted my ability to honor any such pact. Ignoring a pang of guilt, I returned to my breakfast.

"It's for your father's sake," Mama continued. "He won't want you to turn into one of those bold, brassy creatures we are constantly warned about. Independent young ladies—mostly American, I admit—who smoke and flirt the day away."

"Never, Mama."

"At least we don't need to worry about how you'll get to Paddington."

"Mama?"

She sipped her coffee. "When I looked out the front window earlier, I saw Mr. Billings parked outside. You can ask him to drive you to the station."

~

Billings acted as if I were headed into the wilderness, instead of traveling less than twenty miles outside London aboard the most significant invention of the modern era. Wearing a grumpy look, he deposited me at the depot and promised to meet my return train. After I purchased my ticket and found the platform, the guard ushered me into a compartment. I relaxed in the blue cloth and leather seat.

I had my book up to my nose under the illumination of the carriage's one lamp when the door to the compartment opened. A woman swathed in a gauzy black veil and sagging wool skirt hobbled in on the guard's arm. She had a traveling rug draped across her shoulders and a cane tucked under her arm. A faint, sour smell wafted in with her.

"Here you are, madam," the guard said. "If you'd be so kind as to release me, other passengers require my assistance."

She dropped the guard's arm without a word of thanks. The railway official withdrew, locking the door behind him. The woman sat down right across from me, her petticoat brushing up against my gown. A bell sounded, and a whistle shrieked. Then came the cacophonous *chuff chuff chuff* as the carriage jerked forward.

I decided that it would be silly to permit my unwanted companion to spoil the journey because I loved traveling by train —the speed, the loss of control, as the fire-breathing iron monster hurtled forth into an uncertain future. My father disagreed with other medical men who claimed that such speed was unhealthy for human beings. No harm in it, my papa always said. Good for the blood to be a little stirred. I smiled to myself and shifted my legs closer to my body. But I felt the old woman's gaze on me and, with some uneasiness, observed an odd bulging around the material of her veil. It was as though something had sprouted under her chin, visible through the semi-transparent material. I looked away.

"Should I lower the window, madam?" I asked. Without waiting for a reply, I leaned over to yank down the sash, then regretted my hastiness when a piece of soot landed in my eye. Blinking, I groped for my handkerchief.

"Take mine." The woman's voice cracked on a husky note that made me peer at her again uneasily. The extended hand held a bit of cloth, and, without thinking, I stretched out mine in return. A vise grip closed around my fingers. The handkerchief drifted to the floor of the carriage. Unmarked linen, very dirty.

"What are you doing? Let go of me," I cried as my fingers were crushed to the point of pain. I blinked out the bit of soot blinding me, and the hand holding mine came into focus. Sinewy and furred with black hairs. My fellow passenger plucked off his veil and tossed it aside, a sly grin on his lips. It was the man with the billowing beard. Finch Norwood himself.

I cast a panicked look around. Was there a communication cord to alert the guard? I couldn't see one. I felt sweat dripping down my neck, and my heart thundered in my ears, almost as loud as the noise of the train. Until we reached the next station, I was trapped. Even if I could exit the carriage, this train had no connecting corridor. The only escape—no escape at all—would be to climb onto the exterior footboard and cling for dear life.

With this thought, I noticed that our elevation had gradually increased, and a peek out the window revealed a glimpse of a Doric temple on the grounds of a cemetery. I struggled to recall the timetable I'd consulted earlier. How long? How long until the next station?

Norwood spoke over the rattling din. "Caught you with your drawers down, didn't I?" He dropped my throbbing fingers and raised his skirt to reveal trousers and mud-caked boots underneath. A knife protruded from his left boot. He saw me looking at it and smiled his terrible gray-toothed smile.

"The police are looking for you. How . . . how did you find me?" I stammered.

"Scotland Yard won't catch me napping, nor will you." He wagged a finger. "Saw you get in the cab on Charlotte Street, didn't I? When I tumbled to where you was bound, I said to myself, here's a prime opportunity."

"You know where I live?" I managed.

"Weren't exactly a state secret. Acquainted with your papa from way back, ain't I?"

The cooler part of my brain struggled awake. Of course he knew Papa. I was certain Norwood had been the one who fetched my father to attend Muriel Dane when Bert was born. It wouldn't have been difficult for the man to ask around for information about a surgeon. Then I remembered Bert's story about someone watching our house.

"I'm on my way to visit my aunt in the country," I said, recognizing this for an idiotic remark.

"Tell you this, missy," Norwood said. "I won't put my head in a hangman's noose for you or no one else. The rozzers aim to lay me by the heels. How'd you make me?"

"I . . . I read your name in the newspaper reports about Muriel's supposed suicide and put two and two together."

His face darkened. "What's it to you?"

"I'm sorry, Mr. Norwood." My voice was high and breathless. "If you would tell me what you want, I'll do my best to satisfy you."

"It's like this, missy. I helped Muriel when she ran away from her gentleman. When she was fingered for murder, who told the rozzers he'd seen her jump in the river? Owed me her life, she did. Now you and your papa mean to line your pockets at my expense, eh?"

"That's not true!"

"You're getting mighty friendly with them nobs. The scribbling men at the papers too."

"No, we . . . we wouldn't do that." Twisting my head, I risked another glance outside and saw that we'd gone under a bridge to enter a cutting where an embankment towered above us, obscuring the vista.

"You give me one good reason why I should believe you. Everyplace I look, there you is. You're a sneak and a hindrance, missy—that's what you is."

The next instant he was on his feet, cane clattering to the floor, travel rug flying. He braced his arms on either side of my seat as fury poured off him in waves. The rank odor of his breath overpowered me, and he had bits of food and debris trapped in his long, matted beard. I jerked myself to one side, but he pulled me back, his features contorted. This man would kill me if self-interest demanded it. The worst part was that I kept picturing my mother's face swollen with grief, as it had been years ago when baby brother Christopher died.

He thrust his face even closer to mine. "I ain't the man to wink at what's due me. Sticks in my craw, it does. My need's a little pressing, see?"

His hands moved from the armrest to my shoulders. He shook me until bile rose in my throat. I pushed it down.

"You listen," he said, spittle spraying. "Once upon a time, Perry Beldenfield was falling all over himself for Muriel's sake. He would've paid to shut my mouth, all right. He knew things could get nasty if people heard what he'd done to an innocent gel. The gentleman had bagged himself an heiress. Wouldn't suit him to have his little peccadilloes blown hither and yon, would it? Only it went wrong, and I ain't having that a second time."

"I . . . I understand."

"I know what o'clock it is, missy. What have you been telling the police about me, eh? And what was you doing in the garden with the lady the other night?" His hands tightened, fingers pressing into the soft skin above my collarbone, still tender from the last time he'd grabbed me. "I warrant that the lady has been squealing. Maybe the pair of you think to wrap me up tight before I blow the gab."

"It was pure chance I was in that garden, Mr. Norwood. Let me go. I'm no threat to you."

"You were with Muriel at the end, weren't you? Stupid cow got what she deserved. You'll get the same if you poke your nose in my affairs." Norwood shook me a second time. "What'd she tell you about her boy, eh?"

"Her boy?"

"You ain't stupid, missy, so don't act it. Her brat. Last I saw the puny little scrap, he didn't look long for this world. Perhaps he did cock up his toes, like she said."

The implacable eyes bored into me, and I willed my gaze to remain a limpid pool of innocence. But I couldn't speak, not at first.

It was Norwood who added softly, "Your papa helped birth the whelp."

"The . . . baby died a short time later, Mr. Norwood. Of the measles."

"That so? A pity. I warrant them Beldenfields would pay a pretty penny to keep that boy under wraps, eh? Murder sure do make a stench, don't it?"

With a swiftness that stunned me, the knife was out of his boot and pressing against my throat. "You lying to me, Miss Hardy? Why shouldn't you and your papa grab a piece of the profit?"

"We . . . don't want money, Mr. Norwood. Not for Muriel's child or anyone. We don't mind if you expose the Beldenfields. I'd sooner jump in the river myself than take a farthing from them."

As I awaited my fate at his hands, I shivered with the vibration of the train. What did he intend to do with me?

<h1 style="text-align:center">CHAPTER 19</h1>

We had reached the station. Norwood bent to retrieve his cane and traveling rug, which he tucked under one arm. Next, he restored his veil. As we waited at the compartment door, I could feel a sharp object poking my back. His knife.

"We's getting off this train, missy," he hissed in my ear. "You ain't going to say a word to no one. Nice young lady helping the crone onto the platform, that's you. You peach on me, you get my steel. Got that?"

"Perfectly," I said, teeth chattering.

"Stop that. You's going to smile as if you likes it."

All I could do was nod. I could hear footsteps approaching and a babble as other passengers exited their compartments.

The same guard appeared at the door. He looked at me, ignoring Norwood. "Pleasant journey, miss?"

I pasted a smile on my face. "Very pleasant." But my expression must have been ghastly because the conductor gave me a sharp look, though he was too indifferent to bother further. He completed his business and went on to the next compartment.

Norwood and I made our way to the platform.

"What now?" I said.

"You stay at home like a good girl, and nothing will happen to you. Cross me again, you're dead."

He gave me a vicious shove that sent me careening into a lady in a magenta gown. Down we went in a tangle of limbs and skirts, the woman crying out as she landed. Fortunately, she cushioned my fall, or I might have been hurt or even tumbled onto the tracks. As it was, I scraped my knee and banged my elbow.

The lady's husband rushed to the rescue. "Good gracious, my dear. What's this?" He addressed me. "What the deuce do you mean by this, madam? Remove yourself from my wife's person at once."

I managed to extricate the hem of my dress that had been caught under the lady's ample rear end. Ignoring the red-faced husband, I said to her, "I'm so sorry, ma'am. Are you hurt?"

"No . . . no, I don't think so. Just startled."

I got to my feet, a little disoriented myself, mostly with relief. I reached down a hand. "Let me help you, ma'am."

"You've done enough," the husband said.

The stationmaster and a group of gawping people had gathered around us. I scanned the crowd, but Finch Norwood had melted away as though he were a bad dream.

"What happened, miss?" asked the stationmaster.

"I saw it," a top-hatted gentleman said. "An old woman pushed this young lady into the other lady and knocked them both down."

"Is that true, miss?" the stationmaster said. "Where'd she go?"

"She ran away," I said.

The railway official couldn't have been nicer. He escorted me and the married couple to the cloakroom to tidy ourselves, then conducted us to his office. Offering chairs, he summoned a medical officer to check us over and gave us tea and biscuits. The lady in the magenta gown was called Mrs. Forster. She insisted she was fine, only bruised. After a while, her husband warmed to me and became just as indignant on my behalf as he was on his wife's.

"Wretches like that need to be locked up," he kept saying.

"They're a danger to respectable people. Are you sure you weren't robbed, miss?"

"I'm certain, sir." I drank my tea and nibbled a biscuit.

In all the bustle, I had time to think. I told the stationmaster I'd taken a ticket for a station down the line but had felt light-headed and got off the train sooner than planned. If I gave him the whole story, I'd be stuck for hours, and who knew whether I would be believed? The last thing I wanted was for the papers to get wind of a female locked up in a compartment with a would-be ravisher. Another scandal would do my family no good and might hurt my father's reputation. The incurious guard on the train had continued on his route. By the time he came forward with his information—if he did—I would be gone.

The stationmaster sent a man to see if he could spot anyone in the area and used the telegraph to transmit a description of the old woman. But I knew they wouldn't find Norwood. He would have boarded another train back to London, having abandoned his disguise. It would be much easier for him to hide in the city.

"What do you wish to do, miss?" the stationmaster asked after he'd seen off Mr. and Mrs. Forster with thanks and bows all around. "You ought to go home."

"No, thank you, sir," I said. "Your kindness has restored me. I've decided to finish my journey."

When I returned to Charlotte Street several hours later, I waved goodbye to Billings, who had collected me from the station. I used my key to unlock the front door, stepped inside, and stood motionless as the smells and sounds of home washed over me. Camphor from the surgery mixed with the olive oil soap my father used to keep the premises pristine and a hint of my mother's rose water perfume lingering in the air. The murmur of Papa's voice as he advised a patient in his consulting room. From above, footsteps clomping, no doubt Phoebe with her bucket and mop. From below, the friendly clanking of the kitchen range. I leaned my forehead against the coat stand.

"Esther?" Bert said.

My heart sank. After what I'd just learned from my interview with Muriel's friend, Bert was the last person I was prepared to face. As soon as I looked at him in the dim light of the entry, I saw that my father had finally told him about his birth. But my parents didn't yet know the full truth, and it would be my task to explain it to them.

I tried to speak lightly. "Were you waiting for me?"

This brought Bert's head up. He stared at me with a mixture of pain and bafflement. "I've finished my lessons," he said, as if I had scolded him.

"That's good."

Bert and I sat down on the bottom stair, as we had so many times before. I couldn't recall when we'd begun this habit, but it must have been when he was about three years old. We liked to watch the comings and goings of the patients, and Bert often interrupted our conversations to run and open the front door. Usually, the boy bubbled over with the small events of his life. Not today.

Bert said, "I don't believe it."

"What don't you believe?"

"Your papa told me something, Miss Esther. People think my mother was a *murderer*." The word fell from his lips like an obscenity.

I summoned my flagging strength. "My father wouldn't lie to you, Bert. Some do believe that, though I think they might be wrong."

He raised a palm to swipe under his drippy nose. "It'll turn out to be something not so bad. Won't it?"

Or something worse. I reached over to smooth a lock of his fair hair. It would be cruel to give him false hope, for how could Muriel's innocence ever be proved? I framed a tentative reply. "We may never know what actually happened, Bert. But none of it can ever reflect on you."

He jerked away from my hand. "Well, I think my mother must have been treated very badly."

"Yes, she was." I heard the anger in my voice, and he glanced at me in surprise. "I don't have all the answers yet, Bert. But I'll make sure that the people who hurt your mother pay." It was a rash promise. I made it anyway.

A silence fell between us. He leaned forward to hide his face, arms resting on his knees. Eventually, he said, "The woman who died—my mother—I never liked her. She looked at me with eyes that were"—he paused to grope for the right word—"hungry, I guess. I stayed away from the kitchen when she was there."

Muriel Dane hadn't been able to leave her son alone even as she'd tried to protect him. Which was why she told Granny-Cook that Bert might need to leave our household. She must have been worried Finch Norwood would draw the boy into his schemes. Which was also why she asked the cab driver, Billings, to transport her to Charlotte Street after she was fatally injured. Had she wanted a last glimpse of her son? I remembered how my father had sent Bert out of the room that day and felt sick.

"I was the same as you," I told Bert. "But mostly, I didn't notice her."

He nodded and jumped to his feet. "It's time for my tea, miss. We're having a treacle tart that Granny-Cook made just for me. Because I'm not myself today."

Me neither. "Don't I get some too?"

"I always share with you, miss." He smiled down at me.

We said our goodbyes. As I went up the stairs, I was turning one curious fact over in my mind. In all of Bert's musings about his past, he had never expressed any interest in his father.

I was at the washbasin in my room, scrubbing myself from head to toe, when my mother came in.

"Thank goodness you're back," she said. "Was your errand successful?"

"Let's wait for Papa." I didn't think I could bear to tell my story twice, and I wanted to make sure Bert was out of the way in the kitchen.

"Papa's with his last patient. We've been so busy I didn't have a chance to tell him about your errand today." Mama's voice rasped. She cleared her throat. "Esther, I'm afraid there's devastating news. Mrs. Jardain's confinement went awry. She and the child are both gone."

Gooseflesh rose on my wet arms. Dropping the sponge, I turned to stare at my mother. "Oh, Mama. Papa must be so shaken."

"He is, dear. I've told him he did everything possible. He's . . . not ready to talk about it yet."

I pictured Emma Jardain's frightened face as she boarded her carriage just a few days ago. Had she sensed her looming fate? Perhaps, after all, it was better to be a "surplus" woman who could avoid childbirth in the first place.

"Don't worry. I'll explain everything to Papa," I said.

Mama nodded. "I'll leave you to get dressed. Hurry, dear. You'll catch a chill."

Half an hour later, we were drinking tea in the parlor when Papa came in and tossed the evening edition of the newspaper on the table. The signs did not look favorable. His brows twitched, and he growled when he saw Fosco curled up in his chair. I hastened to remove my cat.

"Any more news about the Prince?" Mama poured Papa a cup of tea and dosed it liberally with several lumps of sugar. She handed it to him. "We hear that the Queen will not attend the Prince Consort's funeral. Did she depart for the Isle of Wight as planned?"

"I've no idea. Something of the sort, I suppose. The Queen

won't do her weeping in public, will she?"

"Papa, I must tell you—"

"No, Esther. Let me speak first." He pointed at the newspaper, and I saw that he'd underscored two paragraphs in black ink. "Want to hear what that vile little tidbit says? I'll save you both the trouble of reading it."

Mama and I made big eyes at each other.

Papa snatched up the paper to read aloud: "*It has come to our attention that Mr. Theodore Hardy, surgeon of Charlotte Street, Bedford Square, had a more intimate connection with the late Muriel Dane than was previously acknowledged. It seems that Mr. Hardy, who delivered the accused murderess' babe, concealed Miss Dane's whereabouts from the authorities for more than ten years. Readers will remember that the child, presumed lost or dead, was reputed to be the baseborn offspring of the murdered gentleman, Perry Beldenfield, son of Sir Percival Beldenfield of Portman Square. What was the fate of this child? Would it behoove the authorities to question Mr. Hardy on the subject?*

"*Of more recent concern, it is our sad duty to report that a patient of Mr. Hardy's—a Mrs. Robert Jardain—has died after an arduous confinement. We cannot help but wonder whether, had other medical attention been provided, Mrs. Jardain might yet be alive and well with her husband and family. Does Mr. Theodore Hardy number incompetence among his faults as well as deceit?*"

"Oh, Theo," my mother said. "What a piece of malice. I'm so sorry."

"You must get the writer to print a retraction," I said. "Threaten him with a lawsuit."

"Threaten the penny-a-line man with a lawsuit?" my father bellowed. "I'm sure that'll do the trick, Esther." Calming himself with an effort, he added, "Now, what did you want to tell me? Get it over with so we can enjoy our tea."

"Papa, I don't want to add to your troubles." I broke off. *How to begin?*

Papa studied me with a glint in his eye I couldn't fathom.

My mother leapt nobly to the rescue. "Esther's done something rather daring. I think perhaps you won't like it, Theo. But we must listen to her story."

I sent Mama a grateful look. "Earlier today, I took a short journey by train to interview a friend of Muriel's. I had to go, Papa."

Later, whenever I recalled this conversation with my parents, it was the expression on my mother's face that would haunt me. Mama looked astonished, then stricken as I gave my report. My father sat in his chair, gaze fixed on the fire, almost as if he weren't listening. I stumbled over my words a little as I spoke. When I told my parents that I was inclined to believe Norwood hadn't killed Perry Beldenfield and Muriel Dane, Papa made a disgusted sound. Only twice did he interrupt.

"Did that man touch you?" he barked in the voice of a stranger.

"No, Papa. He just scared me half to death." It seemed wiser not to mention my sore fingers and throbbing elbow.

"How did he know where to find you?"

"He had our address and followed me to the station."

"Fine friends you've made, daughter."

Rummaging in the basket at her feet, Mama picked up her embroidery frame. She looked at it as if she'd never seen it before and put it back down. "I don't understand, Esther. You reported the incident to the railway officials. Why didn't you come straight home? You got back on that train? You walked alone down a country road to your destination? Are you mad?"

"Norwood showed no interest in my errand, Mama. His purpose was to warn me off, and when I got off the train, there were loads of people around. The station is but a few miles from Windsor Castle, you know. Besides, wasn't it better for me to meet Billings at the pre-arranged time rather than drive home from Paddington by myself?" This made perfect sense to me but didn't seem to persuade my mother.

"What about Bert?" she demanded. "Must we keep the boy under lock and key until Norwood has been apprehended?"

"I convinced him Muriel's son is dead. At least, I hope I did."

"Next, you'll claim this journey was worth it," she said.

My mother's bitter tone dismayed me. Even when I had done something out of the ordinary, Mama always seemed to applaud my independence. Now that this approval was in danger of being withdrawn, I understood how much it mattered to me.

"Look," I said, "Norwood is a rascal, but I'm not a fool. He's after money, whether by selling his story to the newspapers or blackmailing Lydia Beldenfield. Mama, I think I know who committed these crimes."

She shook her head. "It doesn't matter. Admit it, Esther. This has gone too far."

"She'll admit nothing, Nan," Papa said. "She'll end like Muriel Dane, dead on our doorstep." He looked at me. "Do you intend to destroy us? Is that what you want?"

It was like ingesting a block of ice. This man was not my papa. My papa had played with me for hours when I was a child, read the newspapers to me when I could barely grasp the words, fought for me like a man possessed when I had scarlet fever, never once leaving my bedside. My mother gave a cry of distress and started to speak, no doubt wanting to erase what had been said. I needed to convince my parents that I couldn't abandon this case and keep my self-respect but that I had no intention of hurting my family. Could one break the bond between people connected by blood and deep affection? No, not this one. Not if I could help it.

"The Beldenfields are rotten to the core. We've been wrong about Muriel and Perry Beldenfield from the beginning." I went to stand on the hearthrug, facing my parents. "Mama, Papa, you must let me explain what I learned today."

CHAPTER 20

———

The woman I had interviewed was named Christina Rook. Now in her late fifties, Muriel's friend was a lean woman with a face like a withered pear and an anxiety to please. Though no longer employed at the manor house, she hadn't been difficult to find. When I inquired for the nursemaid at the servants' entrance of the imposing Georgian mansion, the young woman who currently held the position had directed me to a cottage in the village.

Two of Mrs. Rook's grandchildren—a boy about Bert's age and a tiny elfin girl—were with her when I arrived. The boy was occupied with a book, though I could tell he followed every word of the conversation. In a world of her own, the little girl played with her dolly by the fire.

"Muriel wrote to me that summer," Christina Rook said after offering me a seat. "I wish I could have helped her, but—" She gestured at the scratched armchairs and dilapidated sofa, then at the children. "Fact is, my daughter—mother of these ones—never amounted to much. Married when she was sixteen. When her first man drank himself into the grave, she took up with the father of the littlest one. Neither of her husbands was ever any good, and she couldn't keep a situation for long. Now she's gone and left me with them. If it weren't for the gentleman from the big house paying my annuity, I'd be in a right pickle." Mrs. Rook reached down an absent hand to caress her granddaughter's shiny dark hair.

"Family first," I said. "Muriel asked you for money?"

"Just a loan. I don't think she knew anyone in London, no one she wanted to turn to, at any rate. Said I was sorry I couldn't oblige and wished her well, Miss Hardy. I was that shocked when I heard what she did after that. Killing a man, taking her own life and that of her innocent babe? Got to thinking that maybe if I'd sent her a pound or two when she asked, it might've been different." She flicked a glance my way, checking for criticism.

I nodded. Who could blame Mrs. Rook? And yet, when she'd refused that loan, Muriel had become Finch Norwood's prey, setting in motion a chain of events that led to two murders. Norwood had used Muriel to blackmail the Beldenfields. Twice.

"To think of her being gone this decade and more," Mrs. Rook said. "Her poor little mite too."

With an unpleasant jolt, I realized that Mrs. Rook didn't realize her friend had been alive until a few weeks ago. Living a semi-retired life, she must not have seen the recent reports in the newspaper. Nor did she seem very familiar with the circumstances of Perry Beldenfield's death.

When I explained what had happened, the woman's face crumpled. She said in wonder, "She hid from the police all that time? And someone killed *her* in the end? You've astonished me."

"I understand, Mrs. Rook. And yet Muriel's death by an unknown hand throws doubt on her guilt. Will you tell me about your acquaintance?"

"Happy to, Miss Hardy." As a new thought occurred to her, she gasped. "What's happened to her child?"

"I'm afraid he died." The lie seemed necessary to protect Bert.

Mrs. Rook bowed her head while I waited in respectful silence. At length, Muriel's friend said, "I'm glad to hear she wasn't as wicked as she was painted. I always liked her, no matter what people said, miss. She could be good fun when her spirits weren't low. Wicked smart too, with all her learning. She asked me to teach her to cook, though I'm afraid she weren't much good at it."

"You met Muriel Dane when she came to stay in the village?"

"You mean Mrs. Morgan."

"Mrs. *Morgan*?"

"Weren't her true name. But in a place like this, folk do talk. I suppose her gentleman wanted to make her seem more respectable."

I listened, saying little and offering copious sympathy while Christina Rook unfolded her tale. She seemed to find relief in having someone to confide in about a matter that had long troubled her conscience, her eyes moving from one to the other of her grandchildren as she spoke. She paused several times to admonish the girl to keep away from the fire and to remind the boy, whose name was Alan, of his chores. Alan didn't budge, as if he meant to stand guard.

Muriel had lived in a house in the village in the spring and early summer of 1850. She became friendly with Mrs. Rook, who defended her despite the chorus of "wagging tongues" that made her life a misery. No one believed she was married, despite the ring on her finger. She was nothing more than a gentleman's fancy-piece, and the villagers hadn't appreciated the selection of their village for a hole-and-corner affair. So, I thought, at least her lover hadn't deserted her when she first left Portman Square. How, then, had Muriel ended up in the Mint?

"Did her gentleman visit her?" I asked.

Mrs. Rook sniffed. "From time to time. People saw him on the platform at the station. Once, a farmhand caught sight of someone skulking in the shrubbery. None of us ever met him. I heard that a man of business handled the lease."

According to Mrs. Rook, all remained peaceful until one day a group of boys threw a clod of mud at Muriel when she was taking her walk. A day or two after that, Mrs. Rook had a scare. "I found her sitting on the edge of the pond on the estate after the sun went down. I was afraid she'd hurt the baby. Wet to the skin she was, with that big belly bursting out of her dress. I assumed she'd fallen in and managed to crawl out. But it was much worse than that. Oh, I can see her now, with her white face a-pleading with me and the water dripping down her back."

"She planned to drown herself?"

"Said as much. Thank the good Lord she'd thought better of it. I scolded her, Miss Hardy, you can believe that. I got Muriel home and out of them sopping clothes as fast as I could."

A feeling of awe crept over me. Muriel's tragedy might have ended in that pond, and everything that happened afterward would never have been. Wiped away, a new story inscribed in its place. Mrs. Beldenfield might be a contented wife still, and Sir Percival would be secure in his heir. How strange life was. To think that Muriel had decided to live instead of committing suicide, only to later be suspected of drowning herself. I said none of this to Mrs. Rook, who still seemed to fear she might be held to blame in some fashion.

I reached out to touch her work-roughened hand. "You did the best you could for your friend."

She smiled her thanks. "I thought that pretty silk bonnet her gentleman had given her was ruint for certain after she'd dunked it. But I used a bit of hartshorn to buff it and got most of the stains out."

"Bonnet? What did it look like?"

My tone had been too sharp. Alan went rigid, and the little girl put her finger in her mouth and stared at me.

Mrs. Rook looked worried again. "Why, it was green silk with pink roses and a sable plume. A gift from her gentleman. When I went to see how Muriel fared, she tried to give it to me. Said she detested the thing, never wanted to see it or him, ever again. I . . . couldn't take it."

"I see. Can you tell me why she left the village before her child was born?"

The little girl, growing tired of her doll, clambered into her grandmother's lap. Mrs. Rook arranged the child more comfortably. "I hadn't called on Muriel for a day or two. My daughter was getting up to her nonsense, and I suppose I was distracted. One morning, Muriel came to tell me she was off to London. Thanked me for my kindness, told me she'd write when she could. Made me swear not to tell *him* where she'd gone."

"Did she say why?"

Her eyes were unfocused, remembering. "No. There was something . . . not quite right about it. I got to thinking—" She drew an audible breath, seemed to consider her words, then spoke out boldly. "She was scared of him. I wondered if . . . he'd forced her to begin with. Forced her even afterward. She as good as told me so. I'd seen bruises on her arms a time or two."

My stomach gave an unpleasant lurch. *How could I expect an angel to notice me*, Samuel Godwin had said. Was he or Perry Beldenfield capable of hurting a woman like that? *No, not Godwin*, a voice inside me insisted. He'd been so young at the time, just a boy himself.

"Did 'Mr. Morgan' ever return to the village?"

"He came looking for her, all right, miss. The landlord of the cottage spoke to him. Gentleman was in a towering rage when he learned she'd gone."

"What can you tell me about the young gentleman? Muriel's so-called husband."

Mrs. Rook gaped at me. "Young? Why, Mr. Morgan wasn't young at all, Miss Hardy. Sixty if he was a day."

My parents both spoke at once. "That means—" Mama said.

"The bastard." Papa cursed again under his breath, and no one reproached him.

Coward that I was, I was glad his anger had been redirected, for I hated to be at odds with my father. Which he knew. He met my look, but I could detect no softening.

"If Perry Beldenfield didn't make Muriel his mistress, he couldn't be Bert's father," Mama said.

"You're right," I said. "Once Finch Norwood got his claws into Muriel, she had a dilemma. What if she couldn't bear to tell Norwood the truth? It's not the kind of secret a woman divulges, especially to a blackguard like that. Anyway, gossip had already named Perry Beldenfield as Muriel's seducer. That must be why Norwood approached him instead of Sir Percival. And also why the blackmailer went after Beldenfield's widow recently."

My father leaned forward. "Why would the son shoulder the father's blame, Esther?"

"Rape, Papa. It wasn't just seduction. Sir Percival abused an innocent girl in the worst possible way. That explains why Muriel was desperate enough to consider drowning herself. She put on the bonnet Sir Percival had given her because she wanted to obliterate their relationship along with her life. When she couldn't go through with it, she fled to the Mint. Then Norwood got involved, and Perry needed to protect his family's reputation."

"Men like Sir Percival never pay for their misdeeds," Papa said. "You'll never convince anyone that Muriel didn't willingly submit. Certainly not on hearsay evidence from a woman of Christina Rook's class."

I edged closer to the mantel, the fire warm on my back. Would this day ever end? I was tired and felt the beginning of a headache. "Don't you see, Papa? Muriel had no reason to harm Perry Beldenfield. It would make far more sense if she'd murdered Sir Percival. Sir Percival had a stronger motive to silence her."

"What of Mr. Godwin?" Mama said.

"He was in love with Muriel and seems to have believed Perry responsible for her ruin. Who knows how hot-headed young men might react in that situation? There could've been a flare-up of jealous rage between the cousins. And Mr. Godwin might have his own reasons to wish Muriel out of the way. I can't clear him yet." I forced myself to articulate my next thought. "He has a great deal at stake financially with the proposed marriage to Lydia Beldenfield. We can't be sure of anyone in that family."

Mama grimaced. "Horrid man."

I blinked. "Who?"

"Mr. Godwin."

"I thought you liked him, Mama. Why shouldn't he marry whom he chooses?"

"It wouldn't bother me in the slightest if he hadn't amused himself at your expense."

Tears stung my eyes. "He didn't. At least, I don't think he did."

"It's obvious Mrs. Beldenfield intends to have him," Mama said. "So what did a gentleman like him want with us? Can we be certain he wasn't using us for information about Muriel?"

"Am I so repellent he couldn't have liked me for myself? As a friend. I never thought it could be more than that." I hated the tinge of self-pity under my words.

My mother looked distressed. "Of course he likes you, dear. But I'm not sure what difference that makes if he isn't trustworthy."

I turned to my father, who was watching us with the same stony expression. "Papa, I'm sorry about the paragraphs in the newspaper and even sorrier I've been a worry to you both." I glanced at the goblin fire irons. Their grins seemed to mock me, as if they weren't too happy with me either. "Still, I must do what I can to bring this matter to a close for Muriel's sake. And Bert's."

"*You* must?"

"Yes, Papa. I'm glad you told Bert about his birth. But now we know we were wrong. Everyone was wrong. Norwood embroiled Muriel in his blackmail scheme a second time, and that got her killed."

"You expect me to inform our boy that he's the son of an aging lecher who violated youthful innocence?"

"It's awful. It makes me ill, Papa. But if Mr. Godwin tells Sir Percival and Lydia Beldenfield that Bert is alive, what then?"

The color drained from my mother's cheeks. "They won't want him. Even if they did, we won't let them near him."

I sat down on the sofa and rested my head against her shoulder.

"You've changed, Esther," my father said after a short silence. "I don't expect to get my old mope-around daughter back anytime soon. Maybe I should have a word with our estimable clergyman, Mr. Caxton. Perhaps he can persuade you to keep out of trouble."

CHAPTER 21

The next day, Papa called on Inspector Jessup at Scotland Yard to report my latest encounter with Norwood. My father returned well after the December darkness had fallen and came into the parlor, where my mother tackled the bottomless mending basket, and I crocheted a Christmas gift for Granny-Cook: a lace collar for her Sunday dress. Not very adroitly—the pattern was no help.

"They'll get Norwood," Papa announced, raising a fist in triumph. "Jessup has an informant who knows the criminal pubs and haunts in the Mint. The description given matches the one we already had. Also, the landlady, Mrs. Carver, has admitted to receiving a 'gratuity' from him to search Muriel's rooms." He glanced at me. "Jessup is convinced of his guilt."

"Norwood murdered Muriel?" Mama asked.

"Seems like it," my father replied. "A man like him lives by violence. The word around the rookery is that he lured her into the churchyard. Jessup thinks Muriel got in his way somehow, perhaps by threatening to denounce him to the police. Didn't you tell me Norwood said something of the kind to you on the train, Esther? About Muriel deserving what she got?"

"Yes." I winced as I jabbed my palm with the crochet-hook.

Muttering a curse, I dropped the collar in my lap, glared at it, and picked it up again. "Inspector Jessup's theory doesn't hold water, Papa. Didn't Norwood need Muriel alive to put teeth in his blackmail?"

"Unless he has letters or other documents to sell." Mama snipped off the thread on the sock she'd just darned and tied the knot. "Something to hold over the Beldenfields' heads?"

"Such as murder?" I let my crochet-hook fly as my mind raced. "Let's not forget. Muriel lived for years under an accusation. She needed to protect Bert and lie low. I don't think she would have given Norwood any reason to kill her. No, this shows how easy it is to seize on a theory. There's a gaping hole in it."

"Which is?" My father took his seat. He'd removed his boots in the front hall and put on his slippers. I watched him as he relaxed in his armchair, his eyelids drooping. His neckcloth was askew, his exhaustion evident. My father had worked all day, then plodded through the muddy streets to Scotland Yard. I knew he still thought a great deal about Mrs. Jardain's tragic death and the malicious article in the newspaper, though he refused to discuss either one. Now he wanted to reassure his family, and I was depriving him of that satisfaction.

"Well?" he said.

"Perry Beldenfield. We've learned that Perry was not Muriel's lover. Instead, his father, Sir Percival, had vilely abused her. According to Norwood, Perry had agreed to the blackmail demand. Why would Norwood or Muriel slay the golden goose? In which case, who killed Perry and for what reason?"

"Didn't you tell Inspector Jessup about Muriel and Sir Percival?" Mama said.

Papa sighed. "Certainly I did. Jessup declines to take up the matter. He explained to me that even if it's true, rape is not often prosecuted, particularly when it comes to the nobility. What evidence could there be to find? At any rate, Muriel is dead and cannot accuse him. No, Jessup doesn't credit Christina Rook's story."

"Because it's not convenient," I said. "Will no one speak up for an injured woman in this world?"

Hurt showed on my father's face. "I did try to convince him that Perry Beldenfield's death warrants a second look. Not all men are beasts, daughter."

"I didn't mean it that way, Papa."

Bert and Fosco came into the room, so the conversation had to be shelved. Fosco took up his spot on the hearthrug, and Bert sat down nearby to lean against my mother's knees. Phoebe brought in the tea-tray, and I put down the lace collar to read aloud from Mr. Collins' *The Woman in White*, as if it were any other evening. Ordinarily, Papa would have been full of jokes about the thrilling new novels that had taken the public by storm. Women locked up in insane asylums, characters in disguise, and bigamous spouses. My father liked to say that these books were no less powerful than a dram of strong liquor in exciting the passions of silly people. Even as he hung on every word. But there were no jokes tonight. I read on, my voice sinking low, head drooping over the book, hair loosened from its pins to shield my face from my mother's too-penetrating look.

After a quarter hour, Mama stopped me. "That's enough of that, don't you think, dear? Too gloomy. Let's strive to enjoy the Christmas season despite the sadness of the Prince's death and . . . this other upheaval."

"I'm sure Bert would prefer something jollier," Papa said.

"Let's do *Les Trois Mousquetaires*." Bert's mangling of the French title made us smile. This was actually our third reading of the Dumas novel. We all loved the rollicking adventures of the musketeers, and my father had dismissed our neighbor Miss Meadows' prudish objections, stating that we could always omit the salacious bits.

As Bert brought the book to me, he made the same remark he always did. "The author got the title wrong, didn't he? There ought to be *four* musketeers. D'Artagnan is my favorite."

"Mine too, Bert." Four musketeers, I thought, just like we had four in our family. Along with dear Granny-Cook and Phoebe.

I opened the book at random to chapter four and began reading the scene in which D'Artagnan points out that Aramis has dropped a handkerchief, which is trapped under his shoe. The handkerchief belongs to one of Aramis' lady friends, and D'Artagnan has just embarrassed Aramis in front of some king's guards by calling attention to it. I was having fun with the exchange of the angry men when I suddenly broke off.

"Why'd you stop?" Bert said. "You're getting to the best part."

I addressed my mother. "The handkerchief under the shoe doesn't have a monogram but rather the device of a noble family in one corner. Do you suppose—"

"It *could* be," Mama said. "Miss Meadows?"

No doubt this remark was incomprehensible to anyone but the two of us. I knew at once what my mother meant. Putting the book down, I rushed to the door.

Bert sat up, indignant. "Where are you going?"

"I'll be right back," I said over my shoulder.

"It's bad form to leave your audience hanging, Esther," my father said.

In less than five minutes, I returned, clutching Miss Meadows' treasured volume of Burke's *Dictionary of the Peerage and Baronetage of the British Empire*. Much later, I would laugh about our neighbor's astonishment when I burst in on her in the middle of her spartan supper to request the loan. I appreciated Miss Meadows on this occasion because when she saw how much in earnest I was, she fetched the book without a quibble and without even slipping in an artful question or two about Mr. Godwin's musical reception. I knew how avidly Miss Meadows consumed the history of the great folk and had often made fun of her pretensions. Now I blessed them and kissed the old lady's soft cheek before running out the door.

Back home, I opened the book with trembling fingers. Intercepting a warning glance from my mother, I said, "It's just about a wager Mama and I made. Nothing important—the meaning of an emblem on a handkerchief we came across in a magazine."

I kept my hand over the page so Bert would not see as I turned to the Bs. Here it was: *Beldenfield, Sir Percival, baronet, of Belden-field Park in the county of Oxfordshire; town residence in Portman Square, London.* Skip, skip, skip. *Creation: 18th June 1660. Crest: a lion sejant. Motto: Nunquam Non Fidelis.* I spoke the last bit aloud.

"What does that mean?" Bert sounded suspicious, as if I'd recited a dangerous incantation.

My father answered him. "Latin, Bert. It translates to *never unfaithful.*"

"In other words, NFN." I quoted the letters of the monogram on the handkerchief found in the churchyard with Muriel Dane. The embroiderer had put the "F" for fidelity in the middle and made it larger, presumably to emphasize the key word, never mind what that did to the Latin syntax. I was right, and Inspector Jessup was wrong. Either Muriel Dane had carried a handkerchief bearing the Beldenfield device for reasons of her own, or the handkerchief had belonged to someone from the Beldenfield family who had been in the churchyard with her. Either way, the Beldenfields were connected to the crime.

"Those are ivy leaves. Ivy for fidelity," Mama murmured. Then, with a barely perceptible nod at Bert, she changed the subject.

After reading a little more from *Les Trois Mousquetaires*, my voice grew tired. I picked up my crocheting again. With my thoughts fixed on Muriel Dane, I kept forgetting to count the stitches, and my lace collar soon looked like a lopsided lump that would never lie flat in this lifetime. Hopeless.

The warmth of the fire, the rumble of Fosco's purr as Bert stroked him, the faces of my dear ones around me in our safe, quiet house—these things ought to have comforted me. But I was thinking about Muriel lying stunned and bleeding on the cold ground as night descended. Without Billings, she'd have lain there until the next morning. Someone hadn't cared a jot for her. Someone had struck her down and left her to die. My crochet-hook went faster, though I knew I was making mistakes that would have to be unpicked.

"Esther," Mama said, "you've got such a fierce expression. I don't think that collar can benefit."

Papa eyed me over his newspaper. "She looks as if she might jab someone with that hook. It's making me nervous."

Bert said, "She hates needlework. Wouldn't it be easier to buy Granny-Cook's present at a shop?"

"Maybe I will," I retorted. "No thanks to any of you."

Mama laid aside her needle and thread. "Why don't you ask Papa to escort you and Bert to Regent Street tomorrow? You can purchase some gifts. I'm sure Granny-Cook would like a commemorative photograph of Prince Albert. The one of him sitting at his desk we saw advertised?"

"By all means," I said. "Let's go Christmas shopping."

Late Saturday morning, Samuel Godwin awoke in a foul humor after one of his night walks. Even as his body had moved through the gaslit streets like an automaton, the refrain had kept time with his steps. *Can it be true? Can it, can it, can it, can it?* He'd walked mile after mile, far enough to leave the city behind if he chose. Leave London, leave England. Leave someone else to face what had to be faced.

At one point, he'd found himself outside Newgate Prison. He put his hand on the rough stone wall and let its horror seep into him. How could he be sure? He'd given himself a few days to consider the matter, and the allotted time had elapsed. No one could help him. When he found his feet moving as if by instinct toward the Hardy house in Bloomsbury, he forced himself to go another way. If young Bert or Esther were on the watch, he wouldn't want them to detect his presence. He and he alone had to decide.

Now, after only two hours of sleep, he dressed and went downstairs, relieved to discover that Lydia and Sir Percival had already breakfasted. Lydia had gone to spend the day with a sick friend, and Sir Percival was in the stables, visiting a favorite horse. The butler, aware of Godwin's habits, had left his breakfast on the sideboard. Godwin filled his plate with eggs and kippers and drank the fresh coffee the footman brought him. He ate his food mechanically, itching to get on with the business as soon as his uncle returned.

After a while, he noticed that the butler hadn't come in as he usually did. "Where's Thompkins this morning, John?" Godwin asked the footman.

"In his pantry, sir. Shall I tell him you're asking for him?"

"Don't bother. I'll have a word with him when I'm finished."

The butler's pantry adjoined the formal dining room, which was only used on grand occasions. The pantry had a pair of sinks for washing the precious crystal and china, as well as floor-to-ceiling cupboards for the household plate. This morning, Thompkins stood hunched over the counter of the long, narrow space, his eyes fastened on the pile of cutlery he was polishing.

Though Godwin cleared his throat, the butler didn't put aside his work. Thompkins' arthritic hands rubbed a spoon in a jerky fashion and set it down. He picked up a knife, lifting it to the light to check for smudges. It wasn't until Godwin cleared his throat a second time that the butler faced him.

"No letters for you, sir," Thompkins said, too quickly.

"It's not that. I have a question about the villain Scotland Yard is after. Man named Finch Norwood. It's still not clear to me why you admitted him to the house that first time. Did someone give you orders to do so?"

"No . . . no, sir. That is, not exactly."

"Explain yourself, Thompkins."

"I'm afraid I can't, sir. It was my own mistake. At the time, I didn't think—Sir Percival took me to task for allowing the man across the threshold. I . . . I regret it, sir."

Godwin frowned at this disjointed speech. "What about Dulcie? She talked to Norwood on the night of the musical reception. I'd like to speak to her, please."

"Dulcie, sir?"

"Yes, Dulcie. The under-housemaid. The youngest one. The one to whom Norwood handed his note."

"What do you want with her, sir, if you don't mind my asking?"

Godwin stared at him. The words had been flung at him, almost an accusation. "You'll find out when you bring her here," he said through gritted teeth. He controlled his impatience with an effort. "I have a question for Dulcie, Thompkins. I understand that the ruffian summoned her onto the terrace. She may recall some useful details, which I can share with Scotland Yard when I visit the police, as I intend to do."

"Inspector Jessup has already questioned Dulcie, Mr. Godwin."

"I am aware of that. But I wondered if there might be more to her story. And it seems to me, well, that something might be up with young Dulcie. I came across her crying one day not too long ago and meant to mention the incident to you. Never mind. Just fetch her for me."

The butler's gaze shifted. "I'm afraid Dulcie has left the service of the Beldenfields, sir."

Godwin's temper snapped. "For the love of God, Thompkins. Where has Dulcie gone?"

"I beg your pardon, sir. Her bed was not slept in, and she took her belongings. She must have departed in the night." Thompkins glanced back at his pile of cutlery. "I expect she's gone home to her family."

"And left without telling anyone?" Godwin broke off, stymied by the butler's palpable resistance.

"It appears so, sir."

Then Godwin saw it. The furtive, worried gleam in the man's eyes.

After an uncomfortable pause, Thompkins added, "No one knows anything, sir, and I'm afraid I haven't had an opportunity to speak to Mrs. Beldenfield about her replacement." The butler half turned to yank open a drawer. With shaking hands, he began to restore the knives, spoons, and forks to their velvet slots.

Godwin watched him. Badgering an old man left a poor taste in his mouth. What good would it do anyway? Thompkins had dedicated his life to the Beldenfields. A faithful retainer who felt pride in his employers and didn't bother with moral complexities.

Belatedly, the butler himself seemed to realize his rudeness. Still not looking at Godwin, he used his rag to wipe a stray spot off a fork. "It does seem rather surprising, Mr. Godwin. Though I suppose it's not the first time a young woman has fled this house."

The words clanged in Godwin's brain. He'd long endured evasions, half-uttered sentences, and emotions that skulked in dark corners. Ugly thoughts that crawled like scorpions across his dreams, only to be rejected as irrational when he rose from his bed. Had he lived for thirty years without understanding one salient truth about his life?

"Are you speaking of my mother?" he asked. "Or of Muriel?"

Whatever Thompkins said in response was lost on him. Godwin was in the grip of an idea that had to be proved or disproved without delay. No accounting for where it came from. It was just . . . there. Two minutes later, with no clear sense of how it happened, he'd strode away from the butler and was at the table in the library, with his penknife hovering over the locked drawer. He shoved the knife into the lock, and when his clumsy fingers couldn't force it to give way, he gouged the rosewood, feeling a savage pleasure when it splintered. Soon the drawer's secrets lay open to him.

He lifted out a bundle of letters tied up in a string. Quickly, he cut the string and flipped through the stack. Some were inscribed in his own childish hand—the letters he'd written to his father years ago when he first came to England. Others had a foreign postmark and were addressed to Godwin. The ink on some of these had faded, but one or two appeared more recent. Most of them had been opened; others had intact seals. At the very bottom of the drawer, he discovered one more letter that belonged to him and unfolded it.

It was from Muriel Dane, dated three weeks before.

CHAPTER 22

Mama chose not to accompany us on the shopping expedition, instead staying at home to supervise the new surgery assistant. Right after lunch on Saturday, Papa, Bert, and I put on our winter coats and boots and stepped out the door to find the cab driver Billings at the curb. I greeted him and let my father do the talking. Mr. Godwin had paid handsomely for the driver's time, Billings said, and the cabbie hadn't received any orders to the contrary.

Papa smiled at him. "We shall walk today. It's a pleasant morning. This boy needs to work off his high spirits."

It wasn't a pleasant morning—it was frosty and murky. And Bert didn't look the least bit high-spirited, though he wore the cheery red muffler Granny-Cook had knitted for him. Bert hadn't said much on the subject of Muriel Dane. It was as if he turned over his new knowledge in his mind, as one might lick a wound in secret.

Billings grimaced at the sky. "It won't stay like this, sir. We'll have a pea-souper before long, we will."

"Ah, our old friend, the London particular," Papa said. "Let's hope the fog holds off. Thank you anyway, my good man."

"All the same, I'll stop by later to see if Miss Hardy needs me," Billings replied, stubborn as usual.

We left the cabman to traipse through the mud and drizzle to our destination on Regent Street, where a mass of people swallowed us up. Papa kept hold of my arm, and I grasped Bert's mittened hand, disregarding his attempt to pull away.

Regent Street was one of London's main shopping districts, serving as a boundary between wealthy Mayfair to the west and the less desirable neighborhood of Soho to the east. Though Bond Street was more select and Oxford Street had emerged as a formidable rival, Regent Street had plenty of attractions, even during this time of mourning, when most of the windows were draped in black. I thought that the trappings of death mixed strangely with the glittering displays of jewelry and the confectioners' towering cakes decorated with holly and candied fruits.

My father hated crowds, deeming them cesspools of disease and crime. He looked annoyed as he shouldered his way through a trio of rowdy youths who seemed to have been imbibing spirits. Papa led us around a vendor hawking stain-removing paste and nearly bumped into a huddle of ladies laboring to keep their skirts out of the muck. "The pickpockets will be out in force. Mind your reticule, Esther," he said.

We soon discovered that the clothing warehouses and photography sellers were the busiest of all. Black-garbed "fitters" stood at the doors to cope with the onslaught of women desperate for the imported French silks and crapes suitable for mourning dress. I had intended to purchase new black gloves for my mother, but my father took one look at the line of patrons waiting to enter the warehouse, and we walked on. As for the first photography vendor we approached, customers stood ten or more deep at the windows, gawking at images of Prince Albert.

Inside the shop, the lamps had been lit to banish the gloom. Papa got the attention of one of the clerks, but the shop had sold out of the photograph of the Prince seated at his desk and had no hope of receiving more in the foreseeable future. We were about to give up when a scrubby little man in a frock coat bowed to us.

"Beg pardon, sir," the man said to Papa. "I can lay my hand on a photograph of our dearly departed Prince. Not the one you were asking about, but maybe you won't mind too much about that?" He gave an ingratiating smile.

"How much?" Papa said.

"Only four shillings, sir."

This was an exorbitant price—four shillings when the print would have cost a mere eighteen pence a week ago.

My father reached for his pocketbook. "Show it to me," he said, resigned.

Though Papa was more than ready to go home, I persuaded him to permit one more errand. After guiding my family to Mrs. Robson's establishment, I said, "I think you and Bert might feel a little out of place, Papa."

He took a peek through the glass and didn't argue. "We can browse in the bookshop. Don't be long, Esther. I should be helping your mother with Mr. Ferris."

"It'll take just a few minutes."

I was determined to make one last attempt to complete my Christmas shopping and, more importantly, secure Mrs. Robson's cooperation. I marched into the shop to find myself battling yet another throng. Ladies moved through the displays like small hurricanes, leaving hats and ribbons and feathers scattered all over the place. The chatter was deafening, and I almost gave up right then. Mrs. Robson and her clerks would be run off their feet, trying to deal with all these shoppers.

First things first. I moved to the display where I'd seen the fox fur muff and hat in the gold foil box and was just in time to snatch up the last one, earning a glare from a pushy matron. Prize in hand, I went in search of a collar and found a lovely one of Irish lace for Granny-Cook. Much better than anything I could ever produce.

I took my purchases to the front of the shop and waited in the queue. When it was my turn, I put the fox fur set and the lace collar on the counter and opened my reticule. Mrs. Robson was serving another patron, so it was the young shopgirl who accepted my money. I was turning away, disappointed, when Mrs. Robson stopped me.

"Wait, miss." The proprietress stepped into the back and returned a minute later with a piece of paper in her hand.

"I thought about what you said the other day," she said in a low voice. "You had astonished me, and I was worried the matter might reflect poorly on my business. I did recall the incident you described. Truth is, I'm not likely to forget it. Take this." As she handed me the paper, she leaned over to whisper something. I put the paper in my reticule along with my coin-purse and shook Mrs. Robson's hand with enthusiasm.

She looked anxious. "You'll make sure my name doesn't appear in the papers?"

"Yes, ma'am. I promise you."

"I must get back." She nodded at the waiting customers.

"Thank you, Mrs. Robson. I am grateful to you."

A smile lit her eyes. "Merry Christmas, miss. I do hope it helps."

Five minutes later, we were in a cab en route to Charlotte Street, laden with gifts. Besides the lace collar and the fox muff set, we had Bert's gift for his granny, a touching *carte-de-visite* photograph of the Queen and Prince Albert in their domestic bliss.

But I was even more pleased with my own present. While Bert and my father were chatting, I slid the paper out of my reticule to study it. It was a copy of the original bill for one green bonnet trimmed with two sprays of pink roses and a black plume, purchased by P. Beldenfield of Portman Square on 3 May 1850. Bill dated 8 May 1850, marked paid in full on 20 June 1850. The day before Perry Beldenfield's murder.

As my father helped me down from the cab, I noticed a coach parked a short distance away in front of Miss Meadows' house. I squinted through the increasing gloom. It wasn't Billings' cab but a plain brown coach with a coachman on the box. I wouldn't have paid it any attention had it not been for the oddity of a private vehicle in front of a lonely spinster's door. Miss Meadows had few visitors, I knew.

Papa stepped away to pay the driver while Bert and I waited in the icy rain. I started to ask the boy if he'd remembered to collect Granny-Cook's gift from the cab, but before the words were out of my mouth, the door of the brown coach opened. A man jumped down and came toward us. I saw him clearly. A young fellow with a scanty beard and a coat of chocolate-colored velveteen. His thick red lips smiled as he strode up to us, lifting his hat to show a mop of ginger hair. The gesture drew my attention to his hatband, into which he'd tucked a piece of black crape. How strange, I would think later, that such a person had chosen to honor Prince Albert, as any Englishman would do.

My father, busy with the driver, didn't notice the man bearing down, coat-tails flapping, still smiling. Even then, my brain was slow to react. I had a half-formed idea that this person wanted to speak to us. Perhaps he sought a medical consultation?

I froze as the smiling man swept Bert into his arms with one smooth motion. He tossed the boy over his shoulder like a sack of flour and moved back toward the coach. Bert drummed his heels and shouted. I could see his head bouncing up and down.

Screaming, I rushed after the kidnapper. Papa swung around, roared, "What the devil!" and threw himself after us. I managed to grab the man's coat, but he increased his pace and I lost my hold.

My father caught up to seize the young man around the shoulders. Suddenly, a second villain was on the spot. This was the coachman. I couldn't see much of his face, which was obscured by his hat and high collar, but he was shorter and stockier than the other. The coachman lumbered over to smack my father with a cudgel across the side of his head. Papa's hat flew off. I screamed again as he crumpled to the pavement. I tensed, ready to spring should the ruffian hit my father a second time. Belatedly recalling my umbrella, I jabbed my arm forward, catching the plump coachman with its point in the softest part of his belly. Grunting, he reached toward me with a growl.

Then, changing his mind, the coachman ran away to fling himself back atop his box. I cast an agonized look at my father and pursued. Too late. Bert had lost the struggle, though the boy fought valiantly, gripping the frame of the coach and kicking. The last I saw of him was the corner of his red scarf and one small mittened hand that he retracted just before the door banged shut. The driver cracked his whip, and the coach set off at a rapid clip.

I fell to my knees at my father's side, my legs turned to jelly. "Papa! Are you badly hurt? They've taken Bert!"

Miss Meadows came out onto her stoop to peer down at us in dismay. "Miss Hardy, what's happened?"

I looked up into my neighbor's frightened face. Miss Meadows started down the stairs, spectacles falling down her nose.

"Go for help, Miss Meadows," I said. "My father has been attacked, and Bert has been kidnapped."

"Kidnapped?" Miss Meadows gasped.

The new surgery assistant and I got my father inside the house and onto the examining chair-bed. Papa was too sick from the blow to help much. My mother dispatched Phoebe to summon another surgeon who operated in the neighborhood, sent Mr. Ferris with a message to Scotland Yard, and managed to comfort Granny-Cook. All the while, she was bathing Papa's injury and expertly bandaging it. She also had him out of his wet things and wrapped in blankets in a flash.

"We'll get Bert back, Granny-Cook," she kept repeating. "We'll pay the ransom demand or whatever it takes. We have a good description of one of those men."

Granny-Cook stood twisting her hands in her apron, her face gray. "How will we find the money to satisfy such wickedness, ma'am? Merciful heavens and the Lord preserve us."

"We'll find it," Mama said. "Don't forget Scotland Yard promised us that the man behind this outrage is on the verge of being arrested. The police will tell us what to do."

Perched on a stool next to my father, I gripped his hand. "I never should have involved our family in this business," I whispered. "I'll never forgive myself."

A hint of color stole back into Papa's cheeks as he sipped some brandy. "It is I who should apologize to you, Esther. I failed to protect you and Bert. I thought we could go on with our lives and let the police handle it. You were right."

I pressed his hand. "Oh, Papa."

My father glanced at Granny-Cook, who remained near the door, as if she might charge into the street to look for Bert herself. "I'll see Jessup, and the two of us will form a plan," he said.

"You've always had a hard head, Theo." Mama bent to kiss him. "But if the doctor says you're concussed, you must rest at home."

CHAPTER 23

The sound of footsteps moving through the vestibule roused Samuel Godwin from his reverie. The library door opened, and Sir Percival entered the room. His eyes fell on one of the splinters of wood Godwin had kicked aside, then on the letters from Italy strewn across the gleaming surface of the table.

Sir Percival stopped short. "What's this? Have you been prying into my private papers?"

Godwin stood with his shoulder propped against a bookshelf, Muriel's letter dangling from his fingertips. She'd broken her long silence, only for her words to be shoved into a locked drawer. He straightened and came forward. "*Your* papers, Uncle? Every one of these letters is addressed to me. As is this one from Muriel Dane."

Sir Percival gestured at the shattered drawer. "I've tried to teach you our ways, Samuel. Nothing sticks with you, does it? The taint must be in the blood. You know, you were practically a savage when you came to us. A little brown-skinned, bushy-browed scrap of humanity. Was I supposed to make matters worse by giving you letters that would unsettle you? I did it for you, my boy."

"That's rich, sir. I had my suspicions a time or two but always dismissed them. No *gentleman* would do such a thing."

Sir Percival drew a ragged breath, his jaw sagging. After a fuming silence, he said, "I preserved your father's correspondence, didn't I? Meant to give it to you when you were grown. Then Perry . . . died. I decided it was better to wait until you'd been married a few years with children of your own to spoil."

Godwin stared at him. The man's effrontery knew no bounds. "I have no intention of marrying Lydia or anyone else."

"But you must," Sir Percival said.

"Lydia once told me she didn't intend to remarry, so I have to wonder why you're both so keen on the match." Godwin paused. "Or perhaps I can hazard a guess. It's not just the money, is it, sir?"

"Come and sit down—please. Listen to me for Perry's sake."

"For Perry's sake?" Something twisted in Godwin's chest as he struggled to read his uncle's expression, looking for some sign he really was Perry's father. Perry, who had stood half a foot taller than he was. Fair and broad and ten times more handsome. Perry, who could walk into a room and make everyone in it turn toward him like the sun. He had confronted this horror and ended up dead. What did he have to do with this contemptible rogue staring at Godwin with such pathetic eagerness? Sir Percival shared nothing with his son. Blood meant nothing.

"I tried for years to fill his place in your affections, Uncle. But you kept me at arm's length. I was never good enough, was I? I came to this country as an alien and an interloper, and that's what I am to you still."

"It's not true."

"You need me because you're in a mess. Which is not the same as love or even esteem. It's not entirely your fault I didn't choose to examine our lives too closely. I didn't want to see the evil in this house."

"For Perry's sake," pleaded Sir Percival.

"The son you destroyed? When Norwood hatched his plot, he approached Perry. Muriel couldn't bring herself to name the real father of her child. Better to let Norwood extort the real culprit's heir and trust in his honor. It wasn't Perry who let her down. It wasn't Muriel who killed him either, was it?"

"It . . . it was an accident. You must believe me, Samuel."

"And Muriel's death? Another accident? I don't think so. You've been lying to me for years. Why should I believe anything you say?"

"Don't you see my hand was forced? Perhaps we could have passed Perry's death off as a robbery. But Lydia told the police some damn fool story about Muriel and a bonnet. When everyone thought Muriel had thrown herself in the river, what could I do? Perry and Muriel were both dead, or so I believed. I was left to salvage the family name."

"*Never unfaithful*. What a joke," Godwin said.

While his uncle continued to gape at him, saliva pooling at the corner of his mouth, Godwin wafted Muriel's letter. "It's all here. Not to mention my father's letters to add to the reckoning. He tells an interesting tale about why my mother ran away. By all means, let's sit down, sir. You are going to give me the truth."

Going to his uncle, Godwin hustled him into the armchair with a none-too-gentle grip.

Sir Percival was so astonished by this treatment that he didn't resist, though he spluttered a protest. "You are unfair, Samuel. You'd have died in that Italian hell-hole if I hadn't rescued you."

Godwin felt a surge of rage and knew he had to restrain it. To allow it to wash over him could be dangerous. He stepped away to pace up and down the carpet, speaking rapidly. "How did your son feel when he learned of your depravity? We do not speak of dalliance with willing women, a common enough fault among men of our class. But your foul assault on those under your care is another matter." His voice choked with disgust. "You forced them, didn't you?"

"For God's sake, nephew! It's too late. It's up to you to save the Beldenfields from ruin."

That much was accurate, Godwin thought. He stopped, his gaze traveling around a room that was masculine in essence. The marble mantel and hearth in which an over-hot fire burned, the statuary busts of Roman statesmen, the dark wainscotting on the walls, and the crimson brocade sofas and chairs. Towering shelves of books that trumpeted their owner's refinement. A place fit for a gentleman to manage his affairs, pretend to read his Virgil, and nod off over his newspaper after dinner. How stifling it was. No amount of English wealth could cloak the reek of perversion and murder.

Godwin turned back. "Just out of interest, sir, has Lydia been spared your abominable attentions?"

"Lydia is like a daughter to me. I have always protected her."

"I suppose you like them younger and more vulnerable, don't you? You and Lydia made a devil's bargain. Aid and comfort, Uncle. That's what you gave each other."

"You are unpardonably naive, Samuel." Sir Percival smirked. "Lydia is a lady. As for the others, females generally get what they ask for, don't they? Women of that sort take advantage of a gentleman's weakness. Oh, I admit I was besotted with Muriel at one time. Once her condition became obvious, I could have cast her out, and no one would have said a word. Instead, I agreed to support her and the child. I kept my promise too until she took herself to the gutter. If she was wicked enough to entangle herself with a criminal, how is that my fault? I blame Muriel for Perry's death."

"And Dulcie?"

The baronet looked baffled, as if he couldn't place the name. After a beat, he said, "Oh, you mean the maid." He sliced his hand through the air. "Are we to waste our breath discussing *her*? It's your marriage to Lydia that must be settled as soon as possible. Indeed, I think it would be best if you took her away. Marry her and you save us all."

"From *what*, Uncle? Save the Beldenfields from what?" Godwin edged closer.

Sir Percival shrank back in his chair, jutting his chin so that the wrinkles around his mouth hardened into a rictus. "You're a dreamer and a fool, nephew. Always have been."

"There's one other thing, sir. Tell me about my mother. Why did she flee this house?"

Watching the older man closely, Godwin saw the mask slip and read self-hatred in the depths of his uncle's faded blue eyes. Sir Percival broke away to cover his face with his hands. "Think, think," he said with a groan. "Your dear aunt died when Perry was only five. I never found another lady of quality to equal her. Not one I trusted to raise you boys."

"Was your wife aware of your activities?"

"Damn it, Samuel. I was lonely after she died. Hate me if you must, but I swear to you, as far as your mother goes, it was all a misunderstanding. I never . . . touched Sophia."

Godwin wanted to believe him. One of the franker letters from his father, Antonio Vincenti, had hinted as much, though clearly something had been wrong. Perhaps it was just that his mother had observed what was going on in the household. But he could not think of the letters from Italy without picturing his father waiting in vain for a response from him. Vincenti must have believed his half-British son too proud to acknowledge a humble music teacher. Another indignity heaped on them both.

Godwin wiped his damp brow and forced himself to focus. His roiling nausea was making him sweat. "That's enough, Uncle. Inspector Jessup asked you about the insignia on the handkerchief found in the churchyard, didn't he? Don't you realize that someone is bound to figure out its meaning? No doubt Miss Hardy already has. It's useless to hide anymore. I'll manage the business of Muriel's son myself."

"You're wrong, Samuel. I have matters well in hand."

Godwin almost missed the change in Sir Percival's expression, but some instinct alerted him. "What of that villain, Norwood? He's been in contact, hasn't he?"

"Leave it. It's too late. You'll kill me if you don't stop."

"Be silent," Godwin shouted.

"The fault is mine, Samuel. I confess that to you freely."

"What have you been up to with Norwood?"

"Just as you say. Making arrangements about the boy."

"Arrangements?"

Sir Percival shifted in his chair. "I couldn't stop it, Samuel. Norwood has him."

"You would do that to your son. Your only *living* son? Where's Lydia?"

The only sounds in the room were the crackling of the fire in the grate and the wheeze of his uncle's breathing. Then Sir Percival Beldenfield's words tumbled out. He spoke as someone frantic to justify himself, like a man pleading for his life in court. When Godwin finally grasped the story, he regarded him with renewed loathing. It was worse, much worse than he'd dreamed. A boy would die to make the family safe.

"No time to lose if I'm to catch them," Godwin said. "My God, I can't believe you let Lydia go alone. How did she get to Southwark?"

"She took a cab. Has a knife and my cudgel to defend herself."

The baronet heaved himself up. He made his way to the damaged table, stepping over the pieces of wood and almost losing his footing. Taking a key from his waistcoat pocket, he opened another drawer that Godwin hadn't bothered to tamper with. "You'll never be in time," Sir Percival said. "Lydia has Norwood's bribe. We couldn't have raised the funds without getting around her trustees. She told them she had gambling debts. You saw us signing the papers."

Godwin moved to the table to scribble a note. To be on the safe side, he would entrust it to the footman, not Thompkins. Sir Percival's butler would never touch his correspondence again. When he had sanded, folded, and sealed his note, he stepped around Sir Percival, brushing aside the old man's hands when they reached out to seize the lapels of his coat.

He was at the door when his uncle said, "Wait. Take this. You may need it. It's oiled and loaded."

Sir Percival held out a carved wooden box inside which nestled his favorite pistol. Godwin went back to him and stowed the pistol in his coat pocket.

"Samuel," the baronet cried, "don't go yet. I must know your intentions."

"You asked me to save the Beldenfields. Well, sir, that's what I intend to do."

CHAPTER 24

I got to Josiah Ferris first when he returned from Scotland Yard. Meeting him at the door, I snatched his coat from him and began to fire off questions. Raindrops shed from Mr. Ferris' hat as he stood there looking wet, weary, and more than a little overwhelmed. This was his first day in a new situation. Confusing or frightening him wouldn't help anyone. Unfortunately, I forgot my resolution to be calm almost immediately.

"What news?" I demanded.

"Placards advertising the crime will be posted at railway terminals, omnibus stations, and newsstands, Miss Hardy," Mr. Ferris said. "A reward has been offered for the boy's safe return. Oh, and Inspector Jessup says he'll seek intelligence from his informants and send a man to take your father's statement. He requests our patience."

"Patience? He said nothing else?" I shook the moisture from the apprentice's coat. Besides exuding the smell of damp wool, it was fraying and missing a button. I wasn't doing it any favors.

Mr. Ferris stepped closer to me in the entryway. He lifted one hand as if to lay it on my arm but withdrew it. "The business must be managed delicately. No one wants to frighten the abductors into taking any . . . er . . . desperate measures."

Mama, who'd joined us in time to hear this remark, rescued the coat from me and restored it to the rack. "Mr. Ferris is tired, dear. Let him go have a cup of tea. We can join him in a few minutes."

"Mama, there's something you should know," I said when we were alone. I explained what I'd learned at Mrs. Robson's shop. "The purchaser was a P. Beldenfield, Portman Square; accordingly, Mrs. Robson mailed her account, which included a description of the bonnet. Later, she read the story in the newspaper and was appalled that a murderess had worn her creation in the commission of a crime."

Mama put a hand to her mouth. "She never came forward."

"Mrs. Robson feared to draw unwelcome attention and didn't think her testimony mattered since everyone thought Muriel Dane was dead."

"Didn't she wonder why Sir Percival would purchase a bonnet for his son's presumed mistress?"

"She was curious about that. Not enough to stick her neck out, though."

"Lydia Beldenfield could have seen that bill," Mama said. "Perhaps she made a mistake about the name—there were *two* Percival Beldenfields."

I nodded. "The bill was paid the day before Perry's death. Which means Lydia could have learned about Muriel Dane's bonnet before the murder. Might be how she implicated a woman she probably never saw in her life."

"To protect the family? Someone killed Perry. Who was it?"

"Let's leave that for now, Mama," I murmured. "Until we get Bert back."

"How and why does our Bert come into it?" Mama's face was ashen, and a note of panic had crept into her voice. The effort to control herself had begun to tell.

"Norwood discovered that Muriel's child was alive." I slipped an arm around my mother's shoulders. "What if he traced Papa to

Bloomsbury some time ago? Recall that he followed me to Paddington Station."

"You're certain Norwood is behind the kidnapping?"

"I imagine Sir Percival would prefer that any evidence of his proclivities be kept from the public. In the hands of an unscrupulous man, Bert is a risk to the Beldenfields."

"Oh, Esther, you must be right. But what does Norwood want? If it's just money—"

I shook my head. "He was worried we might tell the Beldenfields about Bert before his own schemes could be finalized. Which is why he needed Bert in hand."

"Would any of them harm a child?" Mama cried.

What could I say? No one connected with the Beldenfields had any reason to care about Bert's welfare. Quite the opposite. They would pay to serve their own ends, but Bert's safe ransom would not be part of the agreement. How far would these people go to hide a child whose very existence was bound up with murder and scandal? Bert's abduction provided a golden opportunity to erase the past as if it had never existed, one small boy disappearing into a rookery where life was cheap.

Mama and I looked at each other. It seemed that rescuing Bert would be up to me, and my mother realized it too. Her eyes told me that as terrified as she was—for Bert, for her daughter, for our entire family—she wouldn't try to stop me.

Twenty minutes later, I was ready to leave the house. I went downstairs and into the parlor to find Mr. Ferris toasting his toes by the fire. When he saw me, he thrust his stockinged feet under the easy chair.

"Would you please make certain my mother receives this note? She'll be down soon when my father falls asleep," I said.

Mr. Ferris jumped to his feet. "Glad to, Miss Hardy." He gave an absurd bow as he stuffed his feet back into his shoes.

I tried to smile. "Tell her . . . Oh, never mind; just tell her all will be well." I set Mama's note on the table and hurried out of the room. In the hall, I snatched up my cloak and went out the front door.

Outside, the rain had turned to mizzle, but the fog had thickened. To my profound relief, I found the faithful Billings taking his ease on the high seat of his hansom, mist wreathing his still form so that he seemed like some remote deity. Over his head, he held a tasseled blue lady's umbrella that must have been left behind in the cab. His broad shoulders were relaxed, his expression serene.

The cabbie's peaceful mood vanished as soon as I explained what had happened to my father and Bert. Billings muttered a curse and twisted his whip between his hands. I handed him the singed fragment of paper the maidservant Rose had found in Muriel's rooms. Good thing I'd remembered it. It was my single clue to Bert's possible whereabouts.

"What's this?" Billings took the paper between his thumb and forefinger.

"Watch out; the edges are crumbly. Looks like part of a name. Do you recognize it?"

"Reckon that's Birdcage Alley, miss. That's in the Mint. Not someplace we cabmen care to go as a general rule."

"The rest of the inscription?"

"Likely a pub. The Silent Woman, that says."

I looked into the shrewd, weathered face and wanted to kiss him. According to Jessup, Finch Norwood was connected with various low taverns in Southwark. Did Muriel jot down information about this one, perhaps because she had met Norwood there at one time or another? And after she died, Norwood destroyed the paper as evidence of a connection between them. It had to be important, or why burn it?

"Can you take me to this pub, Billings?" I said breathlessly.

Billings directed a questioning scowl at his horse Debby. The mare's ears were turned to the side, her head down. "No, miss. Wait till Mr. Hardy feels more the thing and go with him."

"Please, Mr. Billings. I must leave without delay. My father will thank you for not allowing me to go alone."

"That bird won't fly. Sorry I am to hear about the boy, but what can a woman do?"

With an effort, I kept my voice calm. "We have a few hours until full dark. I merely intend to inquire for someone who might have heard word of the child. Besides, my mother gave her permission." True but misleading in that Mama hadn't authorized this attempt. In actual words.

Billings sucked his lower lip and regarded me with his unblinking, owlish gaze. He tugged the reins, and Debby's head came up. The horse gave a whicker, pricking her ears. Whether it was Debby's evident willingness or the seriousness of the situation that convinced him, he said, "Right, miss. No more than a quarter hour at the most, mind. If the place looks rum, we'll be on our way. Do you swear not to get the bit between your teeth?"

"I'll be good as gold. Thank you, Billings. Thank you to Debby as well." I had the coach door open and was in my seat before he could change his mind.

We covered the same route we'd taken when we last drove across the river. The cab eventually made it over the bridge and proceeded down Borough High Street, passing St. George's. Here, the fog lay heavier due to the proximity of the Thames and the fires of industry, a smoke drawn deep into the lungs of people who never got a fresh breath. I gazed at the intermittently visible church spire, which pointed like a white bone into the sky. I was remembering the clergyman Cornelius Walsh's story of a pregnant Muriel Dane walking the churchyard path, seeking her resting place.

The hansom cab turned off Borough High Street, and we

were in the maze-like streets and courts of the Mint. According to Walsh, this was a place in desperate need of hope. There were open sewers as well as broken-down lodging-houses. Women with sad-eyed children pulling at their skirts, who sometimes went home to husbands who beat them and drank to drown their despair. I was glued to the window as we passed a row of aged timber houses, then another pile of crumbling brick tenements. I watched a girl with a shawl over her head pick her way through a pile of feces and saw some boys traveling in a pack like young wolves. Someone tossed a pail of slops out an open door.

When Billings halted the cab, I stepped out to study the public house, which sat in the middle of a square. A low-slung structure, it had a porch with squat columns and latticed windows. A sign above the door depicted a woman in a red peasant gown, carrying her own severed head covered in a frilly white cap. No tavern name.

"Is this The Silent Woman?" I asked.

Billings shrugged. "That's the pub. A headless woman ain't going to do much talking, is she? One way to shut her up."

"Charming." The silence of women—I supposed it was often thus. Fear, or self-preservation, might compel a woman to maintain her silence. Or the threat of violence. As I studied the gruesome sign, an idea glimmered in my mind. An idea about why Muriel Dane had worn the ill-fated green bonnet to the churchyard to meet her death. But there was still the handkerchief with its Beldenfield device to explain. *Never unfaithful.*

Joining me on the paving, Billings looked at me curiously. "Scared, miss?"

"No, it isn't that."

He secured his horse to a post. "It'll be your doing if someone makes off with Debby."

"Stay with her, Mr. Billings. I'll be back in a few minutes."

"Reckon I'll risk it. Your father would have *my* head if I let you go alone."

I made a face at this joke, but the cabbie was busy stroking his horse's nose. After Debby was settled and I had secured the veil on my hat, we were ready. Whip in hand, Billings accompanied me through a yard heaped with rubbish. From the center of the enclosure rose a single tree, crippled with age and decaying. Lovely place.

We went through the stout oak door and down a passage. I stepped into the crowded taproom as the stench of unwashed bodies and beer washed over me. Sawdust crackled under my boots, and I felt a blaze of warmth from the fire burning in the enormous hearth. Tiny green glass panes in the windows reflected the flames, casting an eerie glow over the men and women seated at the rough wooden tables. The laughter was loud, the faces animated. I had never been anywhere like this before.

Most people ignored us, except for one grizzled man, whose eyes lingered on me as he lifted a grayish, globular cup, drinking deep and dashing the foam from his lips. The cup was in the shape of a human skull . . . *No, I must be imagining things*, I thought. The old man couldn't see through my veil but must have sensed my attention. He gave me a wink, then linked arms with his companion on either side to roar a song:

> *Britannia, alas! is lamenting*
> *And grief now is everywhere seen.*
> *Oh think, you kind daughters of Britain,*
> *The Feelings of England's Queen*
> *What trouble and care does oppress her,*
> *Her loss causes her to deplore,*
> *The spirit of him is departed,*
> *And Prince Albert, alas! is no more.*

I waited until the song was over before I went up to the bar with Billings in tow. I raised my voice to be heard over the noise. "Excuse me, landlord. I seek word of a man named Finch Norwood. Can you help me?"

The noise around us faded. The tavern-keeper put down the mug he was wiping, his cheerful expression replaced by instant hostility. "What's that?"

The change was startling. I had been reassured to see how ordinary he seemed. A solid figure in an ale-spotted apron, he exuded an effortless authority that showed in his quick movements behind the bar and commanding tones. Now the cords of his neck bulged.

"Finch Norwood," I repeated, injecting assurance into my manner. I undid my reticule as I tried to calculate how much to tip him. "I bring important information."

"Who's asking for him?"

"A . . . a friend. If he isn't here, perhaps you know where I can find him? Or may I speak to someone else about him?" I had my coins ready.

"No one here by that name." The tavern-keeper turned away.

I called him back. "Can't you at least tell me if you expect Mr. Norwood? Or permit me to leave a note? I was told to write to him at this pub, but as I chanced to be in the neighborhood—"

This wouldn't do. Showing weakness would be fatal. I pictured the headless woman on the sign outside and reached for my courage. I could not allow myself to be silenced. "Landlord, I've come about a missing child. The police will have their own questions. You had much better deal with me, don't you agree?"

The landlord leaned forward. "Folk in this place don't much like strangers. You leave your name, and I'll tell this Mr. Norwood you was wishing to speak to him. That is, if I was to encounter such a person, which I don't say I will. Take your friend and get out."

"It's no good," Billings said in my ear. "This is a right nest of vipers, miss. Let's go. Your papa—"

Before he could finish, a man who'd been leaning against the bar stepped closer. "You heard him."

Billings' expression hardened. His hand tightened around his whip. "Move away from the lady. Show some respect."

"Lady, eh?" The man grinned without humor, displaying a gap between his two front teeth. Judging by his strapping figure, I decided he might be a riverside laborer or a market porter.

A handsome fellow in a sailor's jacket and wide nankeen trousers chimed in. "We ain't got *ladies* in the house. Ladies ought to stay in their drawing rooms and leave the likes of us to ourselves." He was off his stool as he delivered this speech, and I was pressed back against the sticky wooden counter.

The crowd began to call out comments, many cheering on the men with raucous shouts, though here and there, I heard dissension.

"What you gotta do that for?" a voice bellowed. It came from the old man who'd winked at me earlier.

"She ain't done nothing," put in a woman. But these supporters were quickly shouted down.

Billings' head dropped to his chest like a bull about to charge. He addressed the sailor. "Like I said to your friend, leave her be."

I felt the change when the suspicion around us teetered into something more. My mention of the authorities had angered the spectators, and most of them were on their feet. "You're right, Mr. Billings. We'd better go," I said.

The cabman raised his left arm to block the sailor and brandished the whip in his right. "Move your carcass out of my way." This was a Billings I'd never met before with the fire of battle in his eyes, a man who'd spent years driving his cab in all weathers, in every neighborhood of the city.

The gap-toothed man took advantage of this distraction to snatch at my veil. "Whatta we got under this bit o' froth, eh?"

As I struggled to evade his hold, Billings' whip lashed out to catch his coat sleeve. Gap-tooth grinned, and his friend, the sailor, launched into action, knocking Billings flat. I watched in horror as the sailor began kicking the cabbie with obvious relish as my undaunted friend rolled around in the sawdust and spilled beer, wielding his whip in self-defense.

I swung my reticule at the sailor's head, which didn't slow him down. I'd forgotten that my veil hung askew so that one side of my face was visible. Leering, Gap-tooth yanked me hard against him. Once he had me secured, he half-lifted me, causing several of the patrons to guffaw more. How fast the atmosphere had changed. Not five minutes earlier, these men had been hollering a tribute to a dead prince.

Gap-tooth laughed. "Ain't she sweet?" he said to the sailor, who had just received a lash across his cheek that made him roar.

In response, Gap-tooth thrust his face close to mine as if he meant to embrace me. I would bite him if he tried. "Let me go," I hissed.

Rescue came from an unexpected source. "Do as she says," the landlord called. "That's enough, lads. We'll show them we're as respectable as anyone else. For the Prince's sake, eh?"

With a regretful shrug, Gap-tooth released me, and I sagged against the counter. The sailor stopped kicking Billings. He even hauled the cab driver to his feet to be thanked with a volley of curses.

"We're leaving, miss," Billings said when he finished swearing. He coughed and poked his midsection to check for damage.

"Yes, that's best." I felt defeated. What good had we done in coming here?

The customers parted to let us run the gauntlet to the exit. I felt their eyes like so many darts flung at our backs.

"Are you injured, Mr. Billings?" I said.

"Not much, miss," came the tight-lipped reply.

We gained the hall and headed for the street door. When we were almost to safety, I glanced over my shoulder toward the rear of the building. A man carrying a laden tray had just emerged from a swinging door that, if the wafting smells were anything to judge by, led to the kitchen. The man seemed focused on negotiating the door, for without looking around, he steadied his tray. He launched himself up the oaken stairwell that beckoned to the upper regions of the house.

I had recognized the ginger hair and the brown velveteen jacket. It was the young man who had kidnapped Bert.

CHAPTER 25

Godwin pulled onto a side street by St. George's church. He'd driven his curricle across the city, chafing at the usual standstill on London Bridge. His method was simple. Holding his breath, he thrust his vehicle through treacherous gaps and ignored any curses that came his way. The thickening fog played tricks on the eyes. It was a miracle his curricle had made it through without a scratch and that he arrived a few minutes past the appointed hour.

He climbed down from his perch seat to mingle with the shadowy people on the footway. A hazy glow showed in some of the windows or in passing carriage lamps—the darkness was stronger, though it was only three o'clock. Almost at once, Godwin collided with a barrow man trundling his wares and earned himself another curse, pungent and colorful. It barely registered. He tied the horse to a rail and abandoned his vehicle. The curricle would be there when he returned, or it wouldn't. He had bigger problems.

Godwin groped his way to the churchyard gate and went through, keeping to the patches of murk. On the opposite side, fog mantled the high brick wall that separated St. George's from the old Marshalsea Prison and wound its damp fingers around the gravestones. Godwin's pulse raced; he strained to see ahead. Had he missed Lydia and Norwood?

No. A figure had emerged into a clear patch of ground. A flow of drapery, a slightness of form—a woman. She would have entered from the alley off Borough High Street and now walked the path that ran along the wall. As the mist again enveloped her, he squinted, unable to tell much, except that she drifted toward the corner of the churchyard where Muriel was buried.

Godwin increased his pace, tripping on a tree root and almost falling headlong. Recovering, he pressed on. The woman waited under the archway of a large stone tomb he thought he recognized. He'd stood in that exact spot with Theodore Hardy during Muriel's funeral.

"Lydia!" He strode up to seize her wrist. She wore a bonnet with a veil, but he had no doubt of her identity. The bone structure under his hand felt solid, and he sensed her familiar presence. His exploring fingers discovered a cudgel in her gloved right hand. Godwin wrested it from her, stowing it in his overcoat pocket.

"Samuel? What are you doing here?" Her voice sounded high and thin.

For an answer, he pushed up her veil and gazed into her face. "Any sign of Norwood?"

To watch her struggle for composure was painful. This was a woman he'd known intimately, a woman he'd considered making his wife. He'd always pitied her and wanted to lighten her sorrows. He tried to read the expression in her eyes, but the uncertain light blurred her features. She wavered before him as the fog writhed around her head like ghostly hair.

"Thank God you came," she faltered. "I . . . I was so frightened."

"Don't bother," he told her. "I know everything."

She flinched as if he'd struck her and began to cry with wrenching sobs. Taking out her handkerchief, she scrubbed at her cheeks.

He backed away, bumping up against a smaller stone that hadn't been there on his last visit. The humble grave marker he'd ordered for Muriel. No matter that he couldn't read the inscription in the darkness because he knew what it said: *In Memoriam. Muriel Dane, who Departed this Life December 7th, 1861. Sleep Well.*

"Calm yourself," he said. "We'll deal with Norwood first. Then we can talk."

"That coward Sir Percival left me to deal with the consequences of his actions, and now you blame me." Lydia gripped his arm. "Or is it Miss Hardy who turned you against me?"

"Hush." He couldn't let this situation spin out of control. For the last minute or two, he'd felt the prickle of eyes watching them. Norwood would have hung back, waiting to see who showed up.

"You don't understand," she said.

Godwin ignored her. "Come out, Norwood," he called.

Gravel crunched as slow footsteps approached. "Paying your respects to the dead?" a voice said.

Godwin glimpsed the outline of a bowler hat and greatcoat. "Is that you, Norwood? I trust you've brought the boy with you?" He shook off Lydia's grasp. "Keep quiet," he hissed out of the side of his mouth.

The phlegmy voice with its curious lilt spoke a second time. "Who the devil are you? I warn you. I've got a pistol aimed at your heart."

"I'm here to help this lady conduct her business. Produce the child so we can arrange the matter to our mutual satisfaction."

"You're the nevvy, ain't you? Reckon murder's a family affair."

Godwin glanced at Lydia. "Murder? If you mean the boy, that's what I want to discuss. Where is he, Norwood?"

"I'm a fair man, sir," the blackmailer said. "You treat me right, and I'll return the favor. Hand over the blunt."

"You'll have your money when I'm satisfied." Godwin took out his own pistol. "Think before you cross me. Do as I say and you'll walk away with a fortune and no one the wiser."

He waited, wondering if he could get to Norwood and wrest the gun from him. He couldn't, not without the gun going off. The longer this went on, the worse his chances. He felt Lydia stir at his side.

"Nasty night we're in for," remarked Norwood. "Ain't healthy for folk to stand around jawing in a London particular." To illustrate his point, he offered a wet cough.

"Finch, he's got a weapon," a new voice said.

Godwin started as his heart bounded in his chest. This voice had come from behind the tree. Damn it—he hadn't realized anyone else was there. Reflexively, he pushed Lydia behind him and heard an ugly laugh.

"No need to get restive, Beldenfield," Norwood said. "Move an inch, and I'll shoot you down. You don't want to cook the lady's goose either, do you?"

"The name's Godwin," he bit out. He wanted to seize this hideous blackguard and grind him and his heckling voice into powder. "I asked you a question, Norwood."

Lydia tugged at his coat. "Give him what he wants, Samuel. He'll kill us both."

"*Where is the boy?*" Godwin said.

"Samuel," Lydia said in an urgent undertone, "that man will shoot you. Forget about the child." She fumbled at her cloak, and Godwin's ears caught the chink of gold. She meant to throw it to Norwood, he realized. And if she did, it was over.

Finch Norwood and his henchman would have heard the sound too. Leaves crunched as the fellow behind the tree shifted his position. Then from Norwood came the sound of a pistol cocking.

"Give me the money bag, Lydia," Godwin said.

"I'm sending my friend over," Norwood said. "We'll have a nice little chat when that gold is safe in my pocket."

"No, we will not." Godwin reached behind him to grab the bag, but Lydia eluded his grasp. Something thunked on the path at his feet. Before Godwin could prevent her, Lydia took to her heels and disappeared into the fog.

The ginger-haired kidnapper was halfway up the flight of stairs by the time I put my foot on the step. If he disappeared into one of the rooms, I'd never find him in this rambling warren of a place. I, Esther Hardy, had to go after him.

Billings caught up to me and spun me around. "Have you lost your wits, miss? What do you think you're doing?"

"Don't hold me back, Billings. That's one of the men who grabbed Bert," I panted.

"Bah. Even if it is, we'll summon the police like sensible folk."

"There must be multiple entrances and exits in this building, as well as numerous crannies where a child can be hidden." I cast another agonized look up the stairwell and had one last sight of the man gaining the first-floor landing.

Billings' eyes searched mine; he sighed. "Someone is bound to stick us with a knife or toss us down the cellar. Probably me." But he stayed behind me as I rushed up the stairs.

When we made it to the landing, I stopped to peer down the corridor. We were in luck. The ginger-haired man was at the door of one of the rooms. Striding after him, Billings caught up and grabbed him as he fumbled for his key while still balancing the tray. The cabbie clapped one hand over the kidnapper's mouth, hooking the other across his neck. The tray crashed onto the floorboards. Bread, cheese, and ale went flying. A short, desperate struggle ensued, but the villain was no match for a London cabman. In no time, Billings had the key to the room in his possession and had secured the kidnapper's hands with the muffler he took from his own neck.

Squeezing his prisoner's throat until his lips turned purple, Billings demanded, "How many rascals are waiting for us?"

"No one," the man gasped. "Room's empty. See for yourself."

"Think I'll do just that." Billings retrieved a large handkerchief from his pocket and stuffed it in the prisoner's mouth. "A mere puppy, miss," he observed.

The young kidnapper noticed me, his eyes popping wide.

"You're positive it were *this* fellow who nabbed the boy?" Billings said.

"He and another man." It was my turn to address the kidnapper. "Where is the child you took?" My voice was too loud.

"Quiet, miss." Billings nodded toward a door farther down the hall that had cracked ajar. To my relief, it clicked shut again.

Unaccountably, Billings seemed to be enjoying himself. He said with a fatherly air, "We'd best get out of sight, miss, afore someone comes along."

I opened the door. After a brief scrutiny of the room, Billings dragged our prisoner across the threshold. Stepping over the puddle of ale, I bent to pick up the food and tray before following the two men inside. When I shut the door behind me, I saw with dismay that Bert was not there.

We were alone with our captive in a cramped bedchamber. A high iron grate sat in the unlit hearth. The room contained a hard chair, a table on which a lamp burned, a narrow cot, and a small brazier of coals for warmth. I set the tray on the table while Billings tied the ginger-haired man to the chair with the cot's ratty counterpane.

These preparations complete, we regarded Bert's kidnapper, a somewhat pathetic specimen, though I detected a spark of triumph on his face as he registered my disappointment.

"Right," Billings said. "Let's attend to this cock of the walk. Mark me, he'll blow the gab fast enough." He stood over the man, fists clenched. The prisoner shrank back.

It turned out I was less resolute than I'd imagined I would be. "Let me talk to him first."

Billings made a skeptical sound. "As you wish, miss. Be quick about it."

I planted myself in front of the prisoner. "I promise you

money, a handsome sum, if you give me the information I require. And I'll help you get away so your friends won't punish you for peaching. If you're caught, I'll inform the authorities that you assisted us. Will you promise not to call out if my friend removes your gag?"

The man gazed back, his smooth face insolent, as the shadows thrown by the lamp flickered over him. He either didn't believe me or didn't care. Or was too afraid of Norwood to take the chance of betraying him.

Where could Bert be? And what about Finch Norwood and the second kidnapper? I told myself I was a weak woman, unaccustomed to violence. Did I have the stomach to let Billings bloody this man for Bert's sake? It seemed we would get no answers otherwise.

Billings said, "Don't fret, miss. He'll sing for me."

I hesitated. The thought of Bert—and the fear and confusion he would be feeling—appalled me. I had long accepted the boy as part of my family without thinking too much about it, even when he sometimes annoyed me by pestering me to play games or listen to his magazine stories. Actually, I'd relied on his companionship to fill the hollow place left by the loss of my baby brother. In every important sense, Bert *was* my brother. He brought the life any child brings to a home and consoled my mother in her grief. He had to be found at once.

I leaned closer to the prisoner. "Where is Bert? Where's the boy?" I said, fear thickening my voice. I looked back at Billings. *Do it*, I mouthed.

Billings approached the man with a menacing air, but as he raised his fists, I received an answer to my question. A *thump* erupted from behind the fireplace. A pause. Then came another *thump, thump, thump*, a rhythmic tattoo like the beating of a drum. Billings and I turned to the prisoner, who'd gone rigid in his chair. I could see knowledge in his gaze, which he tried and failed to hide.

I didn't wait, edging around the grate into an opening that

was deeper than it had appeared. Twitching up my dress, I dropped down to crawl through ashes and rat droppings, barely feeling my scratched knees. I could see what looked like a pile of clothing crammed into the hollow formed by the chimney column. The pile shifted; I glimpsed the whites of eyes.

In an instant, I had Bert in my arms. He was gagged and bound at his wrists. His cheeks were wet with tears, and his feet kept up their frantic thumping as dust and dirt rained around us.

"I'll get you out, my dear." I yanked the gag from his mouth, tore off my veil, and used it to mop his face. "Stop kicking. Stop kicking, my brave boy." I scooped him closer, pushing aside the loosened rope at his feet.

I was about to call Billings when the bedchamber door slammed against the wall, and the floor vibrated with the sound of heavy boots.

"No, I won't wait in the corridor. We stay together," someone said.

"Mr. Godwin!" the cab driver said.

"Is that you, Billings? Is Miss Hardy with you? I might have known."

At the sound of Samuel Godwin's voice, gladness swept over me. It was not to last.

CHAPTER 26

My arms tightened around Bert, and I laid my finger over his lips. Eyes shut, he didn't respond, as if too tired from his exertions. Or drugged. My mind teemed with questions. Had Sir Percival or Lydia Beldenfield sent Mr. Godwin? Had he come to negotiate Bert's release or to ensure no one ever learned of his existence? More to the point, *who was with him?*

Footsteps crossed the room. It was impossible to discern much through the fireplace aperture, but I espied two men, neither of whom was Godwin. One had a spindly pair of trousered legs; the other was a stocky figure with ham haunches for thighs. Dread snaked a path through my body. I was pretty sure I knew them both.

Billings stood in the center of my field of vision, his feet set wide. Guarding us. "Miss Hardy didn't tell me you were part of this business, sir. What's your game?"

Godwin's reply came from somewhere near the door. "Put down that whip and come here, Billings."

"I'll stay as I am, if it's all the same to you, sir."

Another man spoke in the hoarse voice I recognized. Finch Norwood. "Who's this, Godwin? You gammoning me?"

"He's just a cab driver I hired to watch Miss Hardy," Godwin said. "Don't worry, Norwood. The cabbie won't talk—and Miss Hardy won't either. I'll handle the problem myself."

"Sir!" Billings said.

The cabman had expressed all the doubt I was feeling. I clutched Bert tighter and held my breath. I was confident Billings wouldn't betray us, but that didn't mean we were safe. Norwood must have guessed where we were. Who else would have instructed his men to hide Bert in the fireplace? As for Godwin, he had never been more of an enigma to me than at this moment. He'd spoken as if my fate meant nothing to him. If I was a problem to be solved, how did he intend to solve it?

Godwin broke into these thoughts. "Is that trussed-up chicken in the chair your man, Norwood? Don't think he'll be of much use to you."

"Let me untie Dick. I'll teach him a lesson he won't soon forget, Finch. He's green as yet." This was a new voice—the older henchman, I decided, the one who'd struck my father down. I'd recognized those enormous calves as he moved past my hiding place.

"Later, Jiminy," Norwood said.

"Norwood and I must attend to business first," Godwin said. "Let's see the boy and Miss Hardy, too, while you're at it."

"Miss Hardy can go to the devil," Norwood snarled. "I'll send her there myself. You take a lot on yourself, don't you, Godwin? You and your family wanted that child to cut his stick. Make a hole in the river, eh? No, I don't think I can square it with my conscience to alter the bargain."

"Conscience? That's rich, Norwood. Will you force me to punish your arrogance?"

"Hand over that bag of gold. Then you and the cabman can walk out and leave the rest to me."

"Show me the boy and Miss Hardy first," Godwin countered.

All I could think was: *Run.* We needed to be ready if given a chance. I nudged Bert, and his head lolled against my shoulder. Grimly, I tackled the bonds at his wrists, ignoring the burn of coarse fibers against my palms. As I struggled, rustling noises broke out in the room. *Click.* I froze. It took me a second to understand. *Idiot, that's a gun cocking.*

Godwin spoke, sounding almost conversational. "If one of these pistols goes off in this confined space, someone may die, Norwood. Don't suppose you want it to be you or one of your men. My friend, the cabman, evens the odds in my favor."

"Don't know about that. He don't seem too agreeable."

"Oh, I'll help the gentleman knock your heads together," Billings said.

Abandoning the rope, I peered through the aperture as I considered my situation. Trapped like a rat and probably destined to be dragged from my bolt hole by the rat-catcher's ferret. Determined to protect Bert and forced to quell the instincts that shouted at me to run shrieking into Mr. Godwin's arms. For some reason, I kept thinking about the spaniel Lola and the way Bert had trusted Samuel Godwin as soon as he got a look at that sweet, noble creature. A flimsy justification if there ever was one.

More scuffling noises and footsteps pounding on the floorboards. I heard a grunt, a muffled curse, and a cacophony of voices. Not being able to see was maddening, but I surmised that Norwood's accomplice had attempted to free the man in the chair. Hands shaking, I returned to Bert's bindings. One stubborn knot resisted my clumsiness until I remembered the reticule in my cloak pocket. I untied the strings and rooted around until I found my miniature pair of scissors. The scissors weren't up to this task; however, by sawing at each strand of rope, I began to make progress.

Over the babble in the room came Mr. Godwin's clear baritone. "Compose yourself, Norwood. Stop waving that pistol around before somebody gets hurt."

"Hand over the gold. You think I'll let you finger me for that boy?"

Godwin's tone stayed even. "I take responsibility you won't be arrested. You'll have your money free and clear as soon as we are united and can leave this place together, unmolested. All of us. That includes Miss Hardy, the cabbie, the boy, and me."

In the hiding place, a smile stole across my face. Godwin had come to rescue us. How could I have imagined otherwise even for an instant? My fingers moved with more assurance as I finally managed to hack through enough of the rope to free Bert. His arms twitched as he stirred, muttering something. In the bedchamber, the argument continued.

Billings said, "He's a bad one, sir. Let me get my hands on him afore . . . hey!"

"I'll shut yer mouth," the accomplice named Jiminy croaked.

"Call him off, Norwood," Godwin said.

It was hard to follow the rapid-fire dialogue, and my chest felt as if it might explode. I huddled in the darkness, the dust tickling my throat so that the effort not to cough became painful. As more dust drifted down on us, Bert gave a tiny choke.

Norwood began again. "I says the word, and every man in this house turns against you. Here, no need for that, Godwin."

"I'm reckoned quite a good shot," he replied. "No doubt you can shoot me, if you are bent on it, though not before I put a bullet in you."

A series of thumps and grunts. Billings shouted, "Watch your back, sir," and something clattered to the ground. A soul-jarring bang as a pistol fired. I put my hands over my ears. Had Godwin or Billings been struck? I heard a stifled cry, a crash, and a clang. The chair falling over and someone kicking the iron brazier? I could see a flurry of legs moving back and forth.

"Curse you," Norwood said. "The woman will come out if you call her. Try it and see."

Godwin answered—*thank God*. "I seem to be the only one not in on the secret." He added, louder, "Esther, where are you?"

"We're behind the fireplace. Both of us."

A clinking *thwack*. "Your gold, Norwood," Godwin said. "Take it and go."

Norwood's response was muted as he moved away. "Leave them, Jiminy, and stop your moaning. You'll live. I'll look after the pair of you later." The door banged shut behind him.

"That's done it," Godwin said.

"You can come out, miss," Billings said.

I scrambled to obey, supporting a drooping Bert, who had revived a bit in the excitement. We emerged, covered in soot, into the reek of gunpowder and the light of the lamp, which had somehow survived the fracas. The ginger-haired man named Dick, still bound to the overturned chair, lay on the ground with his feet in the air. His burly friend Jiminy, older than I'd realized, kneeled next to him among the spilled coals from the brazier, which he smacked at with a fold of his coat. Jiminy's doughy face seemed stunned. He gave up on the coals to clutch his forearm, blood welling between his fingers. There was no sign of Norwood.

Billings put an arm around my shoulders, and I leaned into him with relief. The surly cab driver was long gone; he exuded a positively martial glow, like a brigand from the days of highwaymen. Billings had a vicious-looking knife shoved into his waistband, a bruise visible on one cheek, and hair springing in every direction. As for Godwin, besides the inane grin he exchanged with Billings, he too vibrated with energy, his olive skin flushed, eyes full of triumph. In one smooth motion, he swooped low to retrieve his silk topper from the floor and clap it on his head. This accomplished, he lifted Bert into his arms. I smiled at him, though the smile came out wobbly.

"Are you both all right?" Godwin said.

"We're well. Bert's a little sleepy."

"Good. We're leaving."

"You had me fooled for a minute, sir," Billings said, still grinning. "I soon caught your drift."

"You're a prince among men, Billings."

We left Jiminy, swaying on his feet from blood loss, to untie Dick and tend to his own wound. I accompanied Godwin and Bert down the stairs. Billings brought up the rear with Godwin's silver-mounted pistol in his hand.

"Drugged?" said Godwin, glancing at Bert.

I nodded. "I think so. Where did Norwood go?"

"He's the smart one of the bunch. Took the money and ran."

When we gained the entry passage, Godwin shifted Bert over his shoulder and strode toward the door to the yard. A cluster of tavern patrons had poured out of the taproom, the irate landlord among them. The landlord threw a question at Godwin, which he ignored. I feared our exit would be blocked, but Billings brandished the pistol, Godwin reached back to pull me along, and the crowd parted. I caught one last glimpse of the landlord's slit-eyed fury as we tumbled out the alehouse door.

The cold was intense. Mist smothered the sky, and the lone street lamp in the square gave off an anemic glow. Under the skeletal tree in the yard, I paused to brush the ash from my skirt and draw in a lungful of air, which I immediately regretted. Redolent of sulfurous smoke, rubbish, and dung, it was no sweeter than what I'd been inhaling in the fireplace. Still, it meant freedom. I felt giddy with my release from the anxiety of the last five hours.

"Miss Hardy, we must not linger."

"No indeed, Mr. Godwin." I hurried after my companions. My parents and Granny-Cook would be in a panic. I needed to get Bert home as soon as possible.

It was not to be. Two things happened in rapid succession and then a third that would prove decisive. A horse whinnied from some distance away. Billings thundered, "That's Debby! Some bastard stole my horse!" His footsteps pounded down the pavement, the cabman shouting as he went.

Godwin cried out, "Careful, my good fellow! Other rogues might be lurking." He added sharply, "Esther, are you coming?"

I never answered him, for as I stepped away from the tree, an arm encircled my waist and slid up the wide sleeve of my cloak. I felt a poke at the edge of my corset. Somehow, I was not surprised to have a knife threatening me for the second time in my life. At least this time, I wasn't on a train . . .

A whisper, low and urgent, said in my ear, "No one will be hurt if you stay quiet, Miss Hardy."

CHAPTER 27

I registered a pair of breasts pressed against my back. My stomach lurched as a hand encased in kid-leather and smelling faintly of violets clapped over my mouth. Hairs from a fur-lined sleeve tickled my chin.

"Samuel didn't tell you to expect me?" she said.

Turning my head to one side, I got out the words. "Mrs. . . . Beldenfield?"

"You must help me."

"Esther?" Godwin called. A moment later, he yelled, "Billings!" And again: "Esther?"

Billings' halloo floated back, muffled by the fog. He was occupied with Debby, and Godwin couldn't leave Bert alone in the hansom. As for me, I found the knife at my back oddly clarifying. I wasn't going to let Lydia Beldenfield anywhere near my boy. Instead, I had to keep my wits about me and discover why this woman had waited for me in the dark. A woman who reeked of sorrow, desperation, and rage under her perfume.

"Move," Lydia said.

I mumbled through her glove. "I won't scream."

"Esther!" Godwin shouted. He kept roaring, "*Esther, Esther,*

Esther." Nothing I could do about his distress. I hoped he wasn't alarming Bert.

Veering to the left with Lydia plastered against me, I shuffled my feet as loudly as I could. Twice I lost my balance on the slick, uneven cobblestones, and twice she hauled me up, her breath hot on my neck. I inhaled the suffocating soup that surrounded us, my eyes streaming, coughing, unable to see more than two or three paces ahead. The only thing to do was extend my arms like a blind person, as if I could clear our path with sheer effort.

When Lydia's hand released my mouth, I said, "It's no use, Mrs. Beldenfield. It's not safe. If we don't freeze to death, we'll break our necks."

She laughed. "Safe? No woman is *safe* in this world. Don't stop, Miss Hardy."

"Where are you taking me?"

"I . . . I don't know exactly."

We fumbled through one court and into the next one. Every so often, Godwin's muted shouting reached us on the wind. Each time, Lydia pricked me with the knife tip, and once I felt a droplet of blood under my dress.

I shifted away from her. "What can you hope to gain from this, Mrs. Beldenfield?"

She tightened her grip so that my corset dug into my ribs. "Don't play the fool. Samuel confides in you. He'll have told you I was in the graveyard with Norwood."

"There's been no time for him to tell me anything. Why didn't you accompany Mr. Godwin to the tavern?"

"I ran away, though not far. I followed him to the public house. When you emerged, I saw my chance to speak to you alone."

"At knifepoint? So we have you to thank for the horse's disappearance?"

"I led the beast a little way down the street," she said. "No matter. The cabman will recover it."

As the blanket of fog loosened, I glimpsed the upper stories of a building that loomed above our heads. Other human beings, thousands of them, lived in this district, people dreaming their private dreams and huddling together for warmth. The thought steadied me. Then I barked my shin on an obstacle and almost tripped over a bucket, which I kicked aside with a clatter. A well. Suddenly, I'd had enough of this groping around in a morass. I trod hard on Lydia's foot and tried to wrench myself away. The knife punctured my skin a second time. I cried out.

"Don't be stupid, Miss Hardy. I just want to talk to you."

"Let's find somewhere warm and discuss this together."

A window creaked open above our heads. A baby wailed; a woman shushed her child. If I called out, would this person come to my aid? I doubted it. The fog seemed to have settled into every corner of this congested area, a deadening weight that oppressed the spirit as much as the body. No one would wade through the noxious stuff for the sake of a stranger.

"Who's there?" It was a woman's voice.

"We won't bother you," Lydia said. The window slammed shut.

"Go ahead, Mrs. Beldenfield. Talk," I said.

"Not yet."

With Lydia Beldenfield wrapped around me, I inched across the court. Then, out of nowhere, a light appeared to float in mid-air a few yards away. Someone had entered the court from the opposite side. The light drew gradually nearer, a bright thing in this endless murk. I felt a surge of hope. A voice whistled a jaunty tune as the torch swung back and forth. Lydia muscled us to the left to avoid the whistler, but I dug in my heels. *Squish.* I was ankle-deep in foul-smelling muck. What did that matter? Another human being was near—a link-boy, I guessed. Link-boys had evil reputations, especially during fogs when they were suspected of stealing from the customers they guided through the streets. I would take my chances with this one.

"Will you light our way, boy?" I said.

"Where are you?" a voice replied. Gruff and young with the edge of suspicion.

"Go away," said Lydia. "My sister has made a mistake."

"No, I haven't. Over here." Taking advantage of the distraction, I threw myself to one side. I looked back over my shoulder and saw Lydia's face in the torchlight. She'd thrown her veil over the crown of her bonnet, presumably to help her see better. Tiny circles of fire sparked in her eyes. Her face was set, almost inhuman in its determination.

"What've we got?" the link-boy said. "Two pretty pigeons ripe for the plucking?"

I managed to stumble on a few more steps while a struggle broke out behind me. I heard a grunt, a howl, and a hiss—the torch falling to the ground and being extinguished.

"You crazy bitch," the link-boy said. "You pinked me."

Lydia's voice was cold. "Get away from us, or I'll do it again."

I squelched through another puddle, the hem of my gown sucking at my legs. The link-boy cursed, and footsteps retreated. He was gone.

I opened my mouth to shout for Billings and Godwin. But to my horror, I felt my foot come down on emptiness. I screamed as I landed with a splash, one ankle twisted the wrong way under me. The shock and pain were so intense I fainted.

I had stepped through a gap in the pavement, left open as a hazard to any passer-by. When I came to a minute later, water sloshed around me, and I was soaked to the waist. A caustic odor assailed my nostrils. My ankle throbbed; my hair hung in hanks around my face. But I wasn't alone because my papa's voice whispered inside me. *Wake up, Esther. You wanted to be a lady detective.*

Thrusting my hair away, I sat up, knowing the voice would

never relent. Papa would never abandon me, no matter what I did. Such was my new life. Already tonight, I'd traced a stolen child to a villains' lair, brawled with drunkards, and hidden in a fireplace while blackmailing kidnappers debated my fate. At this point, why not add a tête-à-tête with a knife-wielding murderess and a bath in a wet hole to the night's itinerary? In my mind, my father heaved a sigh of exasperation.

By extending my arms, I discovered that my hole was not large, perhaps five feet wide, and not as deep. Wriggling, I drew up my knees to check my ankle. The fact that I could move it, albeit with a wrench of agony, encouraged me. But my sodden skirts clung to my body, and dank walls surrounded me. When I looked up, I could see nothing.

An unpleasant thought jolted me. Did I share this space with skittering creatures? As though I'd summoned them, I felt a touch graze the top of my head and gave a yelp.

"There you are," Lydia Beldenfield said. "Give me your hand. I'll pull you out."

"I'll remain as I am, thank you."

"You've fallen into a coal-hole or some such. Are you hurt?"

"Nothing to speak of."

"You're well paid for your interference, aren't you?" She gave a humorless chuckle.

I fought off waves of panic. What should I do? Lydia had spoken with a hint of impatience, as a lady might speak to an inferior. As if her behavior were entirely reasonable. I decided it was better to keep away from the knife since running away was no longer an option.

"What do you want?" I said.

"Without you, Samuel and I would have married and gone away. I could have put this ordeal behind me."

Contempt stiffened my spine. "Put two murders behind you? You killed your husband and Muriel too."

"Perry? I've never forgiven myself for that. Now Sir Percival has made Samuel despise me. Who will take a woman's part? Have you no pity, Miss Hardy?"

I spoke between chattering teeth. "I'm devastated by your loss, Mrs. Beldenfield, as I told you the first day we met." The sarcasm might have been unwise. I didn't care.

"We'd been so happy in those first few months," she said, her tone earnest. "But everything went wrong. One day, Perry received a letter. He went white and stormed out of the breakfast parlor. I learned later that Norwood had found Muriel in the gutter."

"Norwood threatened a scandal?"

"Muriel was an innocent when she came to Beldenfield House. She fell pregnant, and Sir Percival sent her away. That was before my marriage—it's not my fault."

Dear God. Lydia's mistrust of Perry Beldenfield had killed him as surely as that fireplace poker.

"Didn't you ask your husband to explain?"

"He refused. I'd overheard Perry and Sir Percival arguing. They kept repeating her name: *Muriel Dane*. I was the poor, deluded bride, treated like a child. My grandfather may have been a cloth merchant. Still, with Perry at my side and my rightful position in society, I could hold my head high. That was the bargain. As it was, I had to endure the servants' insolent glances. I knew Perry had married me for my money. But he'd been so good to me. I thought—"

Craning my neck, I could just make out the pale moon of Lydia's face as she bent over the hole. "You thought he could love you?"

"*She* destroyed our marriage. When I confronted Perry, he denied everything. I . . . I didn't believe him."

A tear fell onto my upturned face, or it might have been the mist. Had Perry deemed it too early in his marriage to burden his wife with the ugly story about his father? Not so surprising, perhaps. He'd behaved like many gentlemen of his class. Lydia's duty was to look the other way, pretend she saw and heard nothing. A natural duty, many would say. A cruel one, it seemed to me. "What happened, Mrs. Beldenfield?"

Lydia groaned, and her hand descended to brush my head. I ducked, spitting as I inhaled a mouthful of foul liquid. If it rained in earnest, would the water level in this hole rise? *Banish the thought*, Papa scolded. I focused on Lydia.

"A few days after Perry received the letter, he came home late," she said. "I pretended to be asleep. Something else had happened that upset me."

"You found a bill for a bonnet."

A pause. When Lydia spoke again, I heard a rueful acknowledgment in her voice. "Well, you've been a clever girl, haven't you? Yes, I found the unpaid milliner's bill on the library table. It was just a piece of frippery a man had purchased for his mistress. And yet, if Perry could be so brazen, what future did we have?"

"You should have given him the benefit of the doubt." Even as I said this, I knew why she hadn't. Marrying above her station, she'd been out of her depth, driven mad with wounded pride.

"How would you react?" she cried. "The next day, I was in the library when Perry came in. When I showed him the milliner's account, he insisted he knew nothing about any bonnet. That made me . . . angrier. He informed me he had to go away on 'business,' and I was certain he meant to take Muriel with him. I accused him of intending to leave me. He would disgrace his family and turn me into a laughingstock."

"You hit him with the poker? How many times?"

"I . . . I can't remember. He shook me off and turned to go. Somehow, I had the poker in my hand." Lydia's sobs were harsh in my ears, and I hugged my knees.

"When I realized how bad it was," she continued, "I fetched my flower basket and pruning shears from the hall table. I . . . I escaped into the garden. In the meantime, Sir Percival came home. He found Perry and called to me from the window."

"Did you confess your crime, Mrs. Beldenfield?"

"I could barely utter a coherent sentence. Sir Percival sent me upstairs and summoned the authorities. Think what I've endured, Miss Hardy. I could have been carrying Perry's heir. I acted for the child I believed we would have."

"By blaming Muriel Dane for Perry's death."

"What was to be gained from exposing our shame? We were told she was dead in the river."

"Whose idea was it to claim Muriel had been in Portman Square?"

"Mine. It seemed . . . fitting."

How was I to respond to that? By now, the pain in my ankle had faded into the background. The only useful thing to do was to store up every word the murderess uttered and bear witness. If I ever made it out of this hole.

What Lydia had told me made a hideous kind of sense. The perpetual mourning had been her punishment and safety. A living death. Who could suspect a widow who mourned so tenaciously? In a way, the mask had created a partial truth. She *had* mourned. She'd been stuck playing a role she hated, and in the end, the mask had fit her well. Too well.

"Muriel Dane returned to punish me," she said, echoing my thoughts. "When Norwood called in Portman Square a few weeks ago, I demanded proof she was still alive. We agreed to meet in the churchyard. I borrowed Sir Percival's cudgel for protection and took a cab to Southwark."

"Where was Norwood?"

"Nearby, watching us. He had no evidence to use against me. But he had witnesses to swear Muriel had been elsewhere at the time of Perry's death, and he would have taken her story to the papers. I meant to give them the money until . . . I saw that bonnet on Muriel's head and lost my temper."

"It was a message to remind you of your lie. Your lie had turned her into a fugitive and separated her from her child. Though she couldn't speak out with Norwood controlling her, she wanted you to feel what you'd done to harm a defenseless woman. Did she also show you a handkerchief?"

Lydia fell silent. Then she said, "How could you know that?"

"Muriel must've worn the bonnet for a good reason. Why not also carry the embroidered handkerchief? It didn't seem accidental. At first, I thought the device was someone's initials. It's the Beldenfield motto, isn't it?"

"Yes," Lydia said, and I trembled at her desolation. "Perry once had several handkerchiefs very like Muriel's. Maybe he gave her that one years ago. She held it out to me. Her eyes, I'll never forget them."

"*Never unfaithful.* You struck her down despite the fact Norwood would know what you'd done?"

"She tried to run away, and I wanted her dead . . . I heard a man calling her and fled."

"The cab driver."

"Are you coming out of that hole, Miss Hardy?"

"No," I said. "Sir Percival was the real culprit, Mrs. Beldenfield. Sir Percival raped Muriel and fathered her child. She was telling you that your husband had been loyal. You didn't need to murder anyone."

"How absurd this is." Lydia laughed through her tears. She laughed and went on laughing. It was a sound that would remain with me for a long time, powerful enough to haunt my dreams. The laugh of the permanent exile, of the human being ousted from the fellowship of her kind with the mark of damnation on her.

"I'm not that big of a fool, Esther Hardy," she said. "Sir Percival told me the truth about Muriel soon after Perry died. Why should I care about another woman's suffering?"

"What of her son? Because of you, Norwood took him from his home. He meant to kill the boy once he got his gold."

Lydia took time to weigh her words. When she spoke at last, that terrifyingly sincere note had returned. "The fruit of an old man's perversion? That child was a mistake, who became *my* mistake once Perry was dead. While either the boy or his mother breathed, I would never be safe from men like Norwood. Without

Muriel and her baseborn brat to parade before the world, what mischief could he do? Not to mention that Samuel had shown far too much interest in the boy. Far better the boy should die."

"You're wicked," I said.

Her sigh floated down to me. "No, Miss Hardy. I regretted the necessity. But I simply couldn't afford the risk."

CHAPTER 28

W hen Esther disappeared into the fog and Billings took off in pursuit of Debby, Godwin was flummoxed. The first thing he did was open the cab door and deposit Bert on the seat.

"Stay there," he said.

"What's happened? Where's Esther?" Whatever drug had been given to the boy to keep him quiet had not worn off. He fought to prop his eyes open.

"I'll get her," promised Godwin. "Go to sleep, Bert."

Anxiety pulsed through Godwin's veins. What could've happened to Esther? He would never forgive himself if she was hurt, but leaving the child alone was not an option. With no idea what to do, he stood at the carriage door, bellowing. In between, he listened. He thought he'd caught the sound of footsteps along the side of the tavern. Had Esther gone that way, and with whom? His first idea was that Norwood had seized her to extort an additional ransom. Not likely—though the man was a weasel, he'd been hellbent on escaping with his ill-gotten gains, and his men were otherwise occupied. Someone else?

My God. Had Lydia followed him to the pub? Godwin pounded his fist on his thigh. Taking out his pocket watch, he watched the minute hand go around while he drummed his fingers and writhed in his helplessness. When he started to think he might burst out of his skin, he heard the cabman returning.

"It's me," Billings said. "Looks like a prank. Debby were tied to a post down the way."

"Hurry, Billings."

Billings and the horse emerged from the murk. "Debby's all right, sir. Needs a good feed and a rub is all. She let me know where she was, all right. She—"

"Esther's gone. Stay with the boy. I need to look for her."

"What the devil!"

"Stay with Bert," Godwin said.

No time for explanations. If Esther was with Lydia, they couldn't be far away. He retraced his steps to the pub door. Esther had been right behind him when they came out. He recalled that a passage lay between the pub and the next building, a few feet from the door. This alley offered one escape route. Yes, it was there. After fumbling his way down the passage, he stepped into the adjoining court and paused to listen. Nothing. He had to go on.

Then, from somewhere nearby, a woman screamed.

Godwin ran toward the sound. He suffered through another frustrating interval of stumbling around in the murk until he blundered into an even narrower corridor between two tenements. His relief was profound when he heard the voices, and he tiptoed forward. The fog stifled sound, but he was close enough to catch most of the conversation.

"I knew Perry had married me for my money. But he'd been so good to me. I thought—"

"You thought he could love you?" Esther said.

Godwin sagged. Esther sounded fine. Where were they? He took a few more steps before common sense reasserted itself. Better not to advertise his presence until he understood more.

For the next few minutes, he listened, all the time remembering his big, kind-hearted cousin Perry. Though Sir Percival had revealed the facts earlier that day, hearing the story from Lydia's lips was different. She might have acted on impulse, desiring ever since to make amends. That wasn't what had happened. He felt aghast, furious, sad beyond measure. And awed by Esther's cleverness.

Lydia was laughing.

"You're wicked," Esther said, and Lydia responded with something Godwin didn't hear.

Time to put a stop to this. "Lydia." Godwin walked forward as he spoke. He saw her turn in his direction. "It's over, Lydia," he said. "Esther, where are you?"

"Samuel? I'm in the coal-hole. I've hurt my ankle. She's got a knife."

"She won't attack me." Godwin kept going, praying he was right.

Silence enveloped them. Then Lydia said in a small, defeated voice, "Goodbye, Samuel."

"No, wait!"

She was gone, and he had a decision to make. Rescue Esther or pursue Lydia? No choice at all. Esther and Bert had to come first. It didn't take Godwin long to locate her leaning on the edge of the coal-hole, her hands extended to him. With some difficulty, Godwin hoisted her into his arms. "Can you walk?"

"I don't think so."

"I'll carry you. If you don't mind a bit of huffing and puffing."

Her laugh was shaky. "Aren't we going to look for Mrs. Beldenfield?"

"No, I'm taking you and Bert home. Lydia must fend for herself."

For one moment Godwin's heart swelled with pity at the notion of any woman wandering the Mint with no refuge. Until he remembered Perry, Muriel, and the child. Suddenly, he was thankful that in his boyhood, he'd been brave enough to offer Muriel Dane his honest love. She'd deserved that and so much more.

~

Godwin and I heard quarreling voices as we approached the cab. "Damn you," Billings was saying. "Scotland Yard knows all about it. The boy in my cab was abducted. Now we've gone and lost a gentleman and a lady."

"Stop kicking up a fuss, or I'll teach you your mistake," a stern voice replied.

A police constable confronted Billings, a truncheon dangling from one hand. I gathered that the constable was expressing himself reluctant to traipse around in the fog, looking for missing persons, without some stronger incentive.

I lifted my head from Godwin's shoulder. "We're here, Billings."

The greeting I got did not surprise me. "You promised you wouldn't do summat stupid, Miss Esther," the cabman said.

"I couldn't help it, Mr. Billings. We'll explain later."

Opening the cab door, Godwin plumped me onto the seat next to Bert, careful not to jostle my ankle. "There's work to be done," he said to the constable.

"Yes, sir. At once, sir," the man said, clearly impressed by the unexpected appearance of a gentleman.

"Take that, you pigheaded fool," Billings jeered.

"Inspector Jessup at Scotland Yard," Godwin said. "Tell him the boy is safe. The police will find Norwood's men in the pub, one of whom is wounded. I have Norwood's pistol in my pocket, but no doubt you'll uncover a cache of other weapons in that den of rogues. You won't find the chief villain himself. I expect he's long gone."

"Very good, sir."

"Most urgently," Godwin went on, "a gentlewoman must be located at once. A Mrs. Percival Beldenfield, last seen near this establishment. She's in distress and capable of hurting herself and others. Be aware she carries a knife. Tell Jessup I'll come to Scotland Yard to make my explanations after I escort Miss Hardy and the child home. Oh, and one more thing, constable. Send someone to fetch the curricle and horse parked on the side street by St. George's church and drive the vehicle back to Beldenfield House in Portman Square. If it's still there."

"Another lady lost?" Billings said. "I don't want nothing to do with that, sir."

Godwin sounded grim. "Don't worry, Billings. Your part in the night's affair is over except to convey us home." Addressing the policeman, he added, "Be off, if you please."

"Yes, sir."

On the way back to the cab, Godwin had apologized to me for the lack of his greatcoat, which he'd given to Bert. Now I spread a corner of this garment over myself and gratefully absorbed the boy's warmth. I was sodden, bedraggled, and exhausted, though at least my ankle had subsided to a dull ache.

"Mind how you go in the fog, Billings," Godwin said as he joined me.

Bert's head bobbed up. "Did I hear you talking to the police, Mr. Godwin? I want those bad men clapped in irons."

"Never fear. They will be." Godwin gave the signal to depart.

"Esther, you smell bad, and you're getting me all wet," Bert complained as the cab lurched off.

Godwin smiled down at him. "You must take her as she is, my boy. She's had her own adventure."

As he leaned back against the cushion, I eyed his haggard face. When the cab was rattling over the bridge, I murmured, "Don't think I'm not grateful to you, sir. But it goes against the grain that you gave Norwood what must have been a king's ransom."

"Perhaps the money will be recovered. It wasn't mine, anyway."

"Indeed?" I cast a wary glance at Bert, who was fighting a renewed battle against sleep.

"Esther," the boy said, "can you guess what trick I played on those villains? I read about it in the penny bloods. I braced my ankles when they were binding my legs to leave a gap. And I rubbed against the stone until I got my feet loose. Hurt like the deuce, though. Made it easier to kick up a racket when I heard your voice."

"Well done, Bert," Godwin said.

The child's head dropped on my shoulder. He began to emit light snores.

Godwin looked at me. "How's your ankle?"

"Sore but not broken. My father will fix it." After a beat, I asked, "How did you organize the meeting with Norwood?"

"Lydia had withdrawn a large sum from her bank and was to deliver the funds. I persuaded my uncle to share the plan with me." His tone was matter-of-fact.

"Tell me the rest. How did you end up at The Silent Woman?"

Godwin related his tale. Following Lydia to St. George's churchyard. The meeting with Norwood and the older kidnapper named Jiminy. Their eventual agreement to free Bert in exchange for the gold. "Norwood saw I was determined to fight. He didn't want to cause a stir."

I cleared my throat. "We were fortunate he is more greedy than vicious, at least marginally so. I won't soon forget the way you burst into the room while I cowered in the fireplace. Who fired the pistol?"

"Billings objected when Jiminy started to untie his young co-conspirator. Jiminy's next idea was to stick his knife in me. Billings knocked the knife out of his hand with his whip and saved my life. At almost the same instant, Norwood fired his pistol. Missed me, managed to wound Jiminy. Just a flesh wound, I'm sorry to say. The rogue can nurse it in prison. I kicked Norwood's gun out of his hand and clouted him with my cudgel, whereupon the fight went out of them."

"It could've been so much worse, Samuel," I whispered. "Norwood didn't intend to let Bert go."

"We were lucky." His breath was warm in my ear.

"My father will say you had the matter well in hand and I

ought to have remained at home." I told him about my papa's injury and watched his expression darken further.

"My relatives have a great deal to answer for."

"Not so loud," I cautioned him with a sidelong glance at Bert, whose eyelids had flickered. I hesitated, uncertain how much to say. "Your uncle—" I broke off, embarrassed.

He raised a hand. "Sir Percival has confessed all, Esther."

"All?"

"Yes." The bald syllable held a wealth of revulsion. So Godwin knew about his uncle and Muriel. Compassion stirred as I recalled that he had once been in love with Muriel himself. He'd paid a high price. Would he lose the only family he had, along with any future in England, because of this day's work? I admired his willingness to put a child's welfare first.

"It's worse than you realize," he said. "Other women were affected, mostly our female staff. And my own mother, though not to a criminal degree in that instance. One of our housemaids ran away from Portman Square this morning."

"The girl with scared eyes?"

"Yes, Dulcie. On top of everything else, I'll have to go in search of her. Lydia knew and did nothing to help."

"Poor little thing," I said. "Lydia was more concerned about saving herself."

He nodded. "After Norwood came to Portman Square a few weeks ago, Lydia told our butler she would handle any dealings in regard to Muriel Dane. Later, when I found out about Norwood's visit, she lied to me, claiming she'd rejected his blackmail attempt. Actually, she'd demanded proof Muriel was alive and arranged to meet her in the churchyard."

"I wish you could have done something to stop it."

"Muriel wrote to warn me," he said in a low voice. "I never got the letter."

"Wrote to you?" That explained the letter Rose had posted for Muriel, as well as Muriel's eagerness for a reply. She'd sought another means of escaping Norwood.

"Unfortunately, my uncle had instructed his butler to intercept my correspondence. Letters from Italy too." Godwin shook his head in bewilderment. "For years, Esther."

I groaned at the cruelty of it all, the stupid waste. "What did Muriel's letter say?"

"She stated her belief that Lydia had murdered Perry in error. Muriel knew my uncle well. Depraved and weak but not a killer, certainly not capable of murdering his son and heir. In a sense, Muriel blamed herself because she'd extracted a promise from Perry not to tell his wife the truth. He planned to settle Muriel and her child somewhere Sir Percival would never find them."

"And after Perry's murder, Norwood told the police she'd committed suicide because he still hoped to blackmail the Beldenfields when the uproar died down. But she eluded him for years."

"That's about the sum of it," Godwin said. "Her letter mentioned how he found her. One day, as she left your father's house, she looked back and saw one of his men in the street."

"Did Norwood know Muriel's real story?"

"I doubt it. As far as Norwood was concerned, Perry was responsible for Muriel's ruin, and Perry's wife had killed him in a fit of jealousy. More than enough dirt."

"It's horrible." I hesitated as Bert gave another little snore. My voice barely a thread, I added, "Did you ever tell Muriel you loved her, Samuel?"

"I asked her to marry me. Of course, she rejected me, though she tried to be kind. By then, she must have been with child. She had her own problems, and I was making matters worse. I sometimes wonder if I was as bad as my uncle."

"It's not the same thing. You gave her a choice." Anger braced me, filling me with strength. I would have liked to be that Greek sorceress who lured bestial men like Sir Percival and transformed them into swine.

"I hate him," I said. "I hate him for Muriel's sake. For Perry, Bert, and for you too, Samuel. I hate him as much as I hate Lydia.

Murdering Perry had been a disaster. She didn't need to make matters worse by killing Muriel and plotting against a child."

Godwin leaned closer. "The situation will take careful handling."

"Bert thinks Perry was his father."

"Better than the alternative, isn't it? One saving grace of this disaster is that my cousin has been restored to me in his true light. I would see him vindicated in the eyes of the world and Muriel too. But matters are . . . complicated. If Lydia is brought to trial, we cannot prevent—"

"I see what you mean," I whispered back.

"Awaiting you at home, you'll find a note explaining my plans for Bert's rescue. I owe you an apology for letting you think I could wink at murder. That day in the cab, I recognized your description of the handkerchief but needed time to consider. A man does not readily admit the worst suspicions of his kin."

"I always wanted to trust you."

His lips quirked. "It was you who kept me on the trail when I might have faltered. Today, you brought Billings whose presence tipped the balance in our favor."

"Thank you." I hated my stiffness.

He reached out to brush my hair with his fingers, a feather touch. "You don't seem convinced. Shall I tell you what I see when I look at you, Esther Hardy?"

I studied the mist-shrouded window. The hansom clip-clopped at a steady pace, Billings calling out to alert other drivers and climbing down every so often to lead the horse a short distance. Hazy carriage lamps sailed in and out of view, and I heard the rumbling of wheels mixed with disembodied voices. I had a feeling of unreality in this time-suspended moment, as Godwin and I spoke to each other with the sleeping child between us. My acquaintance with this man had been something new in my experience, and I felt that the old rules did not apply, not with him.

"If you wish," I said at last.

"I see a woman who requires a wider scope for her talents. Stubborn and pure of intent. My dear Esther, it is our great misfortune to live in a society that lacks imagination when it comes to women. Women who are half the human race and so much more than our cherished mothers, wives, and daughters. I cannot tell you why we persist in confining the lot of you to airless rooms and china-doll lives. Or, worse, to lives of drudgery in servitude to undeserving louts. Which is why, despite the tragedy of these crimes, *you* may pride yourself on using your God-given wits to some purpose."

He hadn't touched me again. It was as if he wanted what he said to stand on its own merits. I had not believed it possible to find a man who saw beyond the chains of the mind, no less powerful than prison walls. A failure of my imagination too? I met his gaze. We exchanged a glance that held promise, as well as melancholy. Samuel Godwin was a rootless man whose heritage had been ripped from him when he was too young to protest. Later, he lost the only family member who'd ever been good to him, along with the woman he'd wanted to wed. He had no reason to remain in England. I wouldn't in his shoes.

When I had command of myself, I answered him. "A woman's wits are no guarantee of success or even survival, Samuel. When Norwood came back into Muriel's life, she couldn't fight him on her terms. Still, she did everything she could to protect Bert. Perhaps part of her relished the opportunity to make the Beldenfields pay for what she'd suffered. Why shouldn't she chart her own course despite the risk of . . . shipwreck?"

"One might say the same of you. And with the chance of a happier outcome because you have friends to back you. Look, Esther. It's likely I'll be busy for a while. You know how much I must remedy before I can be free. I also have other obligations abroad. But I will return. When I do, it may be that I'll have a proposal to make."

My breath caught. "A proposal?"

One of his sudden grins lit his features. "A business proposal. I don't want to say too much now."

"Does this proposal of yours involve further mayhem, Mr. Godwin?"

He lifted my hand and kissed it. "Would you have it any other way?"

I smiled at him. "Just tell me our work won't end with Norwood's arrest. Evil as he is, he didn't kill your cousin or Muriel Dane. I'm very much afraid no solid evidence exists to make sure the real culprit is punished."

Samuel Godwin's reply was terse. "We have to catch her first."

CHAPTER 29

In Charlotte Street, the entire household swarmed into the hall to greet our bedraggled procession, Bert in Billings' arms, I in Godwin's. Tears of joy were on my mother's cheeks. Before we went to bed that night, she would repeat to me what Papa had said upon waking groggily from his nap and discovering my absence.

"How could you let her go? Or are you telling me she went without your knowledge?"

"No, dear. I knew exactly what Esther meant to do. If you'll only reflect, you'll understand why it was right and proper. Remember that she has Mr. Billings with her. We must trust her. You do see, don't you?"

"Absolute insanity." But he'd stopped scolding.

Now a hubbub prevailed for some minutes. Mama pushed past the others to rush to my side. Papa scanned Bert, then joined her. He gave an audible sniff when he caught a whiff of my damp skirts, prodded my ankle, and frowned at my wince.

"We opened your note from Mr. Godwin, Esther," my mother said. "We hoped you would find each other in the Mint."

"We're fine. Bert is unharmed, just sleepy. We're all fine," I kept saying.

It was true, despite the fact that my brother and I looked like chimney sweeps. Under ordinary circumstances, Granny-Cook would have felt shy in front of a "prime gentleman" like Samuel Godwin. Tonight, she sobbed unabashedly over Bert. Swathed in Godwin's greatcoat, the boy was cross and rumpled.

"Put me down," he said to Billings. "Nothing wrong with my legs." The cab driver complied, and Bert marched over to greet Phoebe. "Won't you stare when you hear about my kidnappers, Phoebe?" Despite these fighting words, I could see that his eyes were dimmed, and he soon retreated to Granny-Cook's sheltering arm. "I've got your Christmas present in my pocket, Granny," he said. "Only a little creased. The bad men didn't take it."

Granny-Cook squeezed him harder. "That's a blessing, love."

My father fired off more questions for Bert while Mama produced a chair for me. When Papa was satisfied with the boy's condition, he turned to me. "Do you have any idea what you've put us through? Foolish question, I know."

"I won't hear a word against Miss Esther," Granny-Cook interrupted. "Not today, sir. Not ever. She brought our boy back." As she spoke, she was peeling Godwin's greatcoat off Bert and planting smacking kisses on his cheeks while he squirmed.

Papa hugged me. "I can't argue with that logic."

Neither could I.

After breakfast the next morning, we received Inspector Jessup in the parlor. The December wind had made his cheeks glow, and the look of gratitude he threw Mama when she offered him a fresh plate of scones would have melted a tyrant's heart.

"Too kind, ma'am." He sank into a seat by the fire.

"We've been anxious for news, Jessup," Papa said from his easy chair.

"Let the inspector finish eating first," my mother said.

Jessup took a few more bites, then lifted his napkin to pat his beard, which was shiny from the butter. "I'm quite ready to satisfy your curiosity, ma'am. First, the good news. We've arrested Norwood's men at the tavern in the Mint and have hopes of persuading them to turn queen's evidence against him once he's charged with kidnapping, extortion, and perjury."

Papa took a scone. "No sign of Norwood himself?"

"Not yet." I caught a fleeting compassion on the policeman's face. "I'm afraid there's more," he said. "A mudlark discovered Mrs. Beldenfield's body in the Thames early this morning. The man was scavenging near Southwark Bridge and caught sight of her in the water." The inspector's good-natured expression hardened. "Her cloak was spread wide, her crinoline bearing her up. He saw her unearthly white face with a bit of river weed draped across it and knew she was dead. Mr. Godwin has identified the corpse."

"Dreadful," my mother said, and I think we were all a little surprised by the bluff policeman's touch of poetry.

Papa and I looked at each other. How ironic that Lydia Beldenfield had ended her life in the Thames, the fate once attributed to Muriel Dane.

"Lydia wanted to spare herself the shame of arrest and trial," I said.

Jessup's eyes were keen. "We may not have had sufficient evidence to convict her, so perhaps it's better this way, Miss Hardy. As it is, the coroner's verdict on her death will probably be suicide while the balance of her mind was disturbed. I imagine that additional details of the case will emerge when Muriel Dane's inquest resumes."

"The story of Mrs. Beldenfield's crimes will leak out, and the press will descend on us." My father sounded gloomy. A good night's sleep had brought his color back, and he insisted his headache was gone. But his worries about protecting his family and his livelihood lingered.

"A scandal is inevitable." Mama rose to refill my father's coffee. "Everyone's absorbed in the preparations for the Prince's funeral tomorrow. Once that's over, this will be a sensation to rival one of Mr. Collins' novels."

From my seat on the sofa, I said, "Sir Percival will figure as an object of sympathy. However, if we correct the record about Bert's parentage, he'll suffer."

"My superiors are in agreement it's best not to publicize that bit, miss," Jessup said. "As for Sir Percival, he had an apoplectic fit when Mr. Godwin returned alone to Portman Square last night. Godwin will make arrangements for his uncle's care. A sanatorium in a remote Belgian town with doctors and nurses to supervise him. He'll trouble no one again."

The surgery was closed for the holiday. After Inspector Jessup departed, Fosco and I spent the rest of that Sunday cuddled on the sofa while Bert decorated the parlor with evergreens, my parents hovering over us like a pair of elves. Downstairs in the kitchen, Granny-Cook and Phoebe threw themselves into the preparations for the Christmas feast, including the vital business of the plum pudding, which had been wrapped and boiled and left to simmer in its juices on the pantry shelf. There was also the Christmas goose to attend to. Everyone agreed that it needed to be the tastiest, juiciest bird ever to make an appearance on a Hardy platter. Samuel Godwin and Billings had been invited to share the festivities.

"While we're at it, we'll have Billings' wife and children too," Mama said. "Even if he has half a dozen of them. Though where we are to put them all is anyone's guess."

On Monday, 23 December—the day of Prince Albert's funeral—we awoke to more bad weather and tolling bells. The Billings family and Godwin had accepted their invitations. With his reply, Godwin sent over what he called not a gift but rather a debt owed to my mother. This was a gold chain with a single luminous pearl to replace the one Finch Norwood had torn from my neck.

"How's the ankle?" Papa said when I hobbled downstairs for breakfast.

"Much better, Papa." My father's treatment had reduced the swelling; nonetheless, he'd commanded me to get around on crutches for a few days.

After much discussion, I persuaded my father to push me to church for Prince Albert's memorial service, using the wheeled invalid chair he kept for his patients. I hopped down the stairs on my good leg, sat down in the chair, and accepted the crutches to lay across my lap. Mama and I wore our blacks. We had scrounged for suitable gloves since recent events had left us no time to increase our stock.

On our way out the door, my mother noticed my cuffs. "You've got a smudge on your sleeve. Do you want to go up and change, dear?"

I brushed at the material, but the smudge remained. "It's ash, Mama. It must have happened when I toasted Muriel Dane's bonnet over the kitchen fire. Oh well, I don't want to be late."

"You destroyed the bonnet?" Papa said. "I thought I smelled something burning."

"I had to get rid of the horrid thing. Muriel would be pleased."

In church, I had the dubious pleasure of listening to Benedict Caxton droning on about death stalking the palaces and stealing God's representative of virtue on earth. And so on. It was a good thing I was feeling mumpish myself. Otherwise, I might have broken into a nervous giggle at the way my father flinched every time Benedict spat his words through a clenched jaw. For all the clergyman's heroics, the congregation's grief was genuine. Grown men sobbed as they listened to the sermon, while their wives wept into their handkerchiefs. The service over, we came out into the church porch, where we'd left the wheeled chair, which had gotten a little dinged in its bumping over uneven pavements and curbs.

Our ears rattled to the sound of guns from St. James's Park—the signal that Albert's ceremony had begun twenty-five miles away in Windsor. The papers had described the hearse, drawn by plumed horses and accompanied by fifteen mourning coaches. Victoria and Albert's eldest son, Bertie, and his eleven-year-old brother, Prince Arthur, would lead the procession, their mother having retreated to the Isle of Wight. How would Victoria cope? To her, Albert had been a paragon, capable of no human frailty. It struck me that such an attitude was dangerous and unhealthy. I had only to recall Lydia Beldenfield and her honeymoon bliss turned to violence . . .

Benedict Caxton waited to speak to us. He was a tall man with a cool, assessing gaze, Grecian-coin features, and sculpted brown hair. "Mr. Hardy. Mrs. Hardy. Esther." He shook hands all around.

"A rousing sermon, Benedict," Papa said. "You had your audience in the palm of your hand."

He bowed. "Thank you, sir. Your words are a comfort on this most lamentable occasion. I hope I brought a measure of fortitude to my flock." Benedict addressed me. "How did you hurt yourself?"

I waved an airy hand from my chair. "A foolish accident. I tripped over Fosco. My cat."

"I never understood why you let a filthy stray run tame in your house. The kitchen is the place for a feline." Benedict stared at my soiled sleeve, clearly suspecting the fastidious Fosco of being the source of my dirt.

Trust him to notice my soot marks. What had I ever seen in him? It felt as if our betrothal had occurred in another lifetime. I gave him a teeth-baring smile and motioned to my father to proceed so Benedict could greet the next parishioner.

Having given Prince Albert his due, we went home. My pensiveness returned as my papa pushed me down the street past boarded-up shops and pedestrians hurrying along the pavement, faces averted. I thought of Perry Beldenfield, cut off in the flower of his youth as he tried to salvage his family's reputation and help an unfortunate woman. Muriel, who'd been separated from her child to live in secrecy and fear. Bert, who would never know his mother, nor be told about his father until he was grown. Samuel Godwin, who had promised to be my friend and possibly something more. But most of all, I thought of Lydia Beldenfield, who had chosen to live a nightmare instead of fighting her way back to the light.

Despite the darkness of these musings, I rode like a queen in my wheeled chair, clutching the hand of my mama, whose touch gave me far more fortitude than any sermon of Benedict Caxton's ever could. I would need every ounce of this strength in my future career as a lady detective.

Dear Reader:

Reviews are very important to authors. If you enjoyed this novel, please take a moment to leave me a short review on the site where you purchased it. Your kindness would be much appreciated!

Would you like an opportunity to be notified of further Esther adventures and also receive a FREE SHORT STORY?

Subscribe at skrizzolo.com/newsletter-sign-up.

Acknowledgments

I would like to thank Sue Trowbridge of Interbridge web design services for updating my website and formatting this book. Since this is my first independently published novel, her patience and expertise made a huge difference. Thanks are also due to Rolf Busch, my talented cover artist, who created a compelling design that presents my new series in the best possible light. What a beautiful book they have produced for me!

I am also grateful to my dear friend Kathy Ouimette for her willingness to read and comment on the manuscript. She has been unfailingly supportive of me and my writing career over the many years we've known each other. And many thanks to Sally Archer, who kindly took the time to read a draft. Sally is the sort of appreciative reader every writer dreams of finding.

Most of all, this book could not have been written without the loving support of my writers' group: Sheree Wood, Mary Hawley, and Mary McDonough. Our meetings never fail to inspire me, and you have each offered immensely valuable contributions to my story. In particular, Mary McDonough, your fingerprints are on every page. Thank you for all you've done, dear Witches!

Finally, as always, I thank my wonderful family: my husband, Michael; my new son-in-law, Rob; and especially my daughter, Miranda, who contributed her insightful editing skills and ongoing encouragement.

Historical Note

In an 1864 sermon, the Archbishop of York railed against the modern mania for sensation fiction that was taking Britain by storm, calling the trend an "overwrought interest" and claiming that these pernicious books "want to persuade people that in almost every one of the well-ordered houses of their neighbours there [is] a skeleton shut up in some cupboard" (qtd. in Patrick Brantlinger, *The Reading Lesson: The Threat of Mass Literacy in Nineteenth-Century British Fiction*). In keeping with the gender norms of the era, sensation stories were thought to be a particular moral hazard for women readers, deemed easily excitable and led astray. Other famous examples of the genre include *East Lynne* by Ellen Wood and *Lady Audley's Secret* by Mary Elizabeth Braddon —both "guaranteed to make the flesh creep and the hair stand on end" (*Punch* magazine, qtd. in Winifred Hughes, *The Maniac in the Cellar: Sensation Novels of the 1860s*).

Given this backdrop, I had fun playing around with some of the typical sensation elements in my traditional mystery. In this case, we have murder (of course!); suspected adultery and seduction that aren't what they seem; mistaken identity; blackmail; illegitimacy; persecuted innocence—and even a cat named after the villain from the novel that started the sensation craze when first serialized in 1859–60, Wilkie Collins' *The Woman in White*. Collins' story inspired a host of new products: Woman in White perfumes, bonnets, and even waltzes.

More seriously, the popularity of the new fiction was bound up with the Victorian debate about the role of women in society. This was an era that saw the stirrings of feminist activism and brought much-needed revisions to the laws for divorce and women's property rights. The "redundant" woman question was a very real concern for some Victorian commentators. After the 1851 census, which asked for marital status, these commentators pontificated about the "surplus" single women—hundreds of thousands of them—who contributed nothing to society and therefore weakened Britain's imperial might and prosperity. Unbelievably, the social scientists really did want to ship all the excess women off to the colonies! I suppose that such views are unsurprising in a milieu in which single women were a threat to the established patriarchal order, especially when they dared to hunger for fulfilling lives outside the home.

And yet it is also true that the patriarchal order was never as absolute as we sometimes imagine when we trot out our assumptions about stuffy old Victorian England. The system was, in fact, contested and evolving. In "On the Trail of the First Female Detectives in British Fiction," Dagni A. Bredesen highlights the careers of two hitherto obscure, fictional female detectives of the 1860s: "G" and Mrs. Paschal, who appeared in the pulp fiction sold as "yellowbacks"—cheap, eye-catching books with bright yellow covers sold at railway stalls. "G" and Mrs. Paschal pursue varied cases, such as theft and fraud, and their femininity makes it easier for them to infiltrate private homes. What's even more intriguing, however, is that Bredesen has uncovered examples of real-life working women or "police officers in petticoats": "While women were not accepted into the official ranks of the Metropolitan Police until the twentieth century, mid-nineteenth century newspapers and court records indicate that there were actual women who identified themselves or were designated by others as female detectives." How could any historical novelist resist the temptation to create her own pioneering female sleuth?

With due acknowledgment to Richard Broad's essay "Water and the Fallen Woman in Victorian Literature and Art," I'll add a word about the fascinating relationship between water and fallen women, those unfortunate females who commit sexual transgressions and descend to disgrace and tragic death. Broad's essay tells us that the Victorians often situate the corrupted fallen woman near a water source, sometimes the highly polluted Thames. One example occurs in Dickens' *Oliver Twist* when the fallen woman Nancy leads the virtuous Rose and her protector Mr. Brownlow to the riverside: "Look before you, lady. Look at that dark water. How many times do you read of such as I who spring into the tide, and leave no living thing, to care for, or bewail them. It may be years hence, or it may be only months, but I shall come to that at last." In *Safe in Death*, by contrast, Muriel Dane isn't "fallen" at all but is instead a victim of hideous brutality, and my murderer is a seemingly respectable lady who ends up in the river.

Finally, many of the rich historical details about the sudden death of Prince Albert come from Helen Rappaport's *Magnificent Obsession: Victoria, Albert and the Death That Changed the Monarchy*. I enjoyed weaving these details into my narrative and found it fruitful to consider some parallels between my fictional widow, Mrs. Beldenfield, and the newly bereaved Queen Victoria. Victoria's extravagant, ceaseless mourning was only getting started in December 1861, but it would cause increasing dismay and controversy among her subjects in the remainder of the decade.

July 13, 2024

ABOUT THE AUTHOR

S.K. Rizzolo earned an M.A. in literature before becoming a high school English teacher and author. A lifelong history enthusiast, she loves writing about crime-solving in 19th-century England. Rizzolo has published four Regency mysteries with the highly regarded Poisoned Pen Press. *Safe in Death* is the first book in a Victorian series introducing a bored spinster who finds her purpose in life as a detective.

9 7 9 8 9 9 9 1 4 7 8 5 0 2